Best Bet in Beantown

A Will Beaman Baseball Mystery

G. S. Rowe

Pocol Press
Clifton, VA

POCOL PRESS

Published in the United States of America
by Pocol Press
6023 Pocol Drive
Clifton, VA 20124
www.pocolpress.com

Publisher's Cataloguing-in-Publication

Rowe, G. S. (Gail Stuart), 1936-
  Best bet in Beantown : a Will Beaman baseball mystery
  / by G.S. Rowe.
    p.cm.
    ISBN 1-929763-14-X

    1. Baseball—Fiction. 2. Baseball teams—Fiction.
3. Boston (Mass.)—Fiction. 4. Baseball stories.
5. Detective and mystery stories. 6. Historical fiction.
I. Title.

PS3618.O874B47 2003   813'.6
                    QBI33-900

Cover art © 2002 by Todd Mueller.

Disclaimers

Although many of the events and personalities depicted in this story are taken from history, this is a work of fiction. Names, characters, places, incidents, and dialogue either are the product of the author's imagination, or are used fictitiously. License has also been taken with chronology and with conversations by historical figures for purposes of plot.

Base ball is spelled here as it was in the late 19th century.

Acknowledgments

Though an often lonely and solitary act, writing is in the end more often than not a collaborative effort. I accumulated many debts in the process of writing this book. I owe particular thanks to members of Alpha Group, an affiliate of the Rocky Mountain Fiction Writers, who suffered through the early draft and many revisions, and who provided thoughtful suggestions and boundless encouragement. They include Margaret Bailey, Jim Cole, Karen Duvall, Shannon Dyer, Vicki Kaufman, Janet Lane, Michael Phillips, Bonnie Smith, and Linda Sparks. John Loftis, whose opinions I greatly value, has been a long-time friend, colleague, and savvy critic of my work. Sarah Dougherty gave the manuscript a careful reading and offered suggestions. No one has been more supportive or helpful in shaping my writing than Mary Borg whose sensitive reading of my efforts, unwavering friendship, enthusiasm and encouragement, and insightful criticisms and suggestions can never be repaid by me. Thanks, too, to my wife, Mary, who has graciously endured my obsessions with baseball and earlier times, and has offered helpful suggestions to improve my work. Finally, I'm grateful to all those who have written on 19th century baseball, especially the many members of SABR from whom I have learned so much.

Prologue: Game Day

He stands there, naked, holding his brown, leather-tough hands out before him, palms down, examining his fingers, a craftsman critically assessing the tools of his trade. League records list him as 5' 9" and 160 pounds. If he is, it is only when he is wearing his kangaroo leather playing shoes with their steel plates at toe and heel, and at the beginning of the season. Now, early in June, in the third month of the National League schedule, his weight is closer to 150. And, naked here, he looks like he'd have to rock up on his toes to reach 5' 8". His skin where the sun has not roasted him nut-brown is doughy-white and his hair, which he wears short, is fair. His broad face, more open and accepting than handsome, sports a half dozen thin, pale scars, reminders of fielding errors or quirkily-bouncing balls. There is something about his compact and muscular physique and his quick, fluid motions, that proclaim him an athlete. His eyes, faded blue, almost gray, but alert and confident, convey the same message. And why not? Hell, he is an athlete. A very good one. And, he's proud of that.

He lets his eyes drift to the heavy wool uniform hanging in his cubicle. He's worn the white blouse with its gothic scarlet B of the National League's Boston Beaneaters for seven years now. And the Boston nine has been pennant winners in three of those seasons. They're in contention again this year. To play professional base ball in 1897 is a remarkable accomplishment; to play shortstop as he does on a championship caliber National League squad is, well, even more remarkable, he thinks. People in Boston know Herman Long. Cheer him. Cranks around the League roast him, but concede he is a formidable opponent, sure-handed in the field, swift on the base paths, surprisingly powerful at bat. Not bad for a son of struggling German immigrants. Few of his chums from his old neighborhood have come as far.

He examines his uniform. Unlaundered for several games, it is more dirt-brown and sweat-gray than white. The shirt collar, so useful in keeping the sun from his neck, is rimmed black with sweat and grime. Yet, he knows that once he pulls it on later that afternoon and trots onto the grass of the South End Grounds under sunny skies, it will seem to him as brilliantly white as the first time he'd worn it. It is a thrill he experiences each game.

Herman Long—mates and opponents alike call him "Germany"—returns to his study of his fingers. They are battered and crooked, two nails swollen dark blue and purple and clotted with blood. He turns his left hand over, his glove hand, and examines the puffy yellow-purple knuckles. He probes the knuckle of his index finger and winces at the soreness there. He works his left thumb, discovering again what he already knows: he can't flex

7

the joint. Quickly losing interest in his thumb—hell, he hasn't been able to bend the little finger on this throwing hand either for four years now; it hasn't stopped him—he continues his medical inventory. He studies his pins. The oil-colored bruises covering his ankles and shins don't bother him any more than the large contusion on his thigh where recently he was hit by a pitch. Of greater concern is the angry cut below his right knee that hasn't fully healed. He was spiked during a double play attempt more than two weeks ago and the wound hasn't closed completely. Fifteen stitches and it still leaks puss. And pains him. He'll have to watch that rascal, watch that the redness doesn't spread in thin lines up his leg. But of even greater importance to him at the moment is his right ankle that has ballooned. He rolled it badly the previous day and knows that without treatment he'll have trouble playing today.

And playing today is critical. The team is finally doing better, largely because of his play, and that of his infield chums. In past weeks they've thrown up a stone wall against opposing batters. His absence from the lineup could kill the team's momentum. He pushes at the swollen ankle and feels the dull ache there creep up and meld with the sharper pain from his knee wound. He realizes he's clenching his teeth hard enough to make his jaw throb.

Five minutes later, he completes his tally of wounds and afflictions, and sighs deeply. Just another day in the life of a professional base baller. He pulls a tub holding a block of ice noisily across the planked floor, and begins to stab at the ice with a pick, shattering the block into hundreds of glistening shards. Satisfied that the tub is ready for his ankle, he puts down the pick and wipes his hands on a towel. He is an efficient man, on and off the field. Concluding that it will be a waste of time doing nothing but nursing a bad wheel, he hobbles toward a shelf holding a half dozen books that provide escape for players.

He's barely pulled a well-thumbed copy from the shelf and turned toward the tub when he senses movement behind him. He twists to see who's joined him for pre-game medical treatment. Before he can greet—or even focus on— the newcomer—what feels to him like a sledge hammer crashes into the side of his skull, bringing with it searing pain and the rush of muddied colors: dirty-yellows, varigated blues, purple-oranges. It is as if all of his bruises have become one and have sucked him in, enveloping him in pain. Then, blissfully, there is nothing but blackness for Germany Long of the Bostons, jewel of League short stops.

1

Herman "Germany" Long was deader than my love life. The best short stop in base ball. Dead At least, I thought he was. For heaven's sake, it was my first day as a base ball executive, although a very minor one; I'm no coroner. Anyway, it was a damned unnerving sight to stumble upon during my first minutes in the major leagues. And I had enough problems without adding Germany Long to them.

Germany Long was my hero. Had been for years. A crackerjack short stop, the linchpin of the 1896 Boston infield that included such snappy gloves as Billy Nash and Bobby Lowe. Top shelf, all of them. This year's infield appears even stronger. And Long's the guy who holds it all together. Any crank'll tell you that. Obviously, I never imagined that the first time I'd meet Long he'd be soaked in his own blood and keeping company with a dead rat.

I suppose all this would make more sense if I started at the beginning. I awoke that morning fatigued from my long train ride and fuzzy-headed from a recurring nightmare. In the dream, my father, who has never so much as picked up a bat or stood on a base ball diamond, was hitting ground balls to me. I was in position as short stop on a field otherwise unoccupied. My mother, thirteen years dead, sat in the stands, the lone spectator. My father hit daisy cutters to me, an expectant expression on his earnest face. I caught none of them. They sailed over or under or beyond or off my glove. They scooted between my legs, caromed off my chest, left bruises and welts on my arms and neck. Try as I might, I could not catch the bouncers he hit. To his credit, he slavishly hit to me, masking his disappointment at my futility. Throughout it all, my mother sat pale and grave, her thoughts her own. As always, I awakened exhausted and depressed.

Knowing how critical the day was to my future, I struggled to brush aside the cobwebs of images and emotions lingering from the dream. I forced myself to concentrate on my two goals for the day—and Germany Long had nothing to do with either. To be honest, I'd sunk lower than Robert Peary's thermometer. I needed to impress my new employers, the owners of the Boston National League Base Ball team, and do it quickly. Living on borrowed money and already embarrassingly low on funds, I had but a brief time to prove my value to the team. My hiring had been contingent on an interview with the owners and a more formal look at my references. I was told that even if I were hired my employment would be probationary.

Old man Conant—William Conant—Deacon Bill behind his back—hired me conditionally as an assistant treasurer and promoter. He persuaded his partner, Arthur Soden, that the Boston Beaneaters needed to improve revenues. They gave me sixty days. That was Soden's idea. Sixty days!

So it was that I began that morning with a simple agenda. The first item on it was to impress my new bosses. And that meant getting to the ball park early to meet Anna Anspach, Conant's stenographer, in order to get acquainted with the team's operations. I imagined that if I could squeeze her for some quick information, I could persuade my new employers that I was alert and eager to please. And if I could succeed in that, I might pull off my second goal: to keep them from probing into my often morally indefensible activities of the past several years.

To ensure an early start to my first day in Boston since my graduation from Harvard four years before, I'd stayed at the American Hotel across Walpole Avenue from the field. The American was an ancient and faded edifice with the glamour and appeal of a superannuated streetwalker. Its weather-beaten bunting sagged liked the bags under a chippy's eyes, its exterior was as uneven and discolored as makeup hastily applied under a street lamp. I have often enjoyed better accomodations. If the truth be known, however, in recent months I have found harbor in much poorer quarters.

Upon arriving from Minneapolis, I found a message waiting for me from Anna Anspach telling me that Conant and Soden would not get to The Grounds before 10:00 a.m. She said she'd see me at 9:00, if that were convenient.

Eager beaver that I wanted to be—and without so much as a fleeting thought about Germany Long—I shaved and pulled on my stiff, boiled shirt and newly-purchased wardrobe. It was an outfit that had precariously lightened my purse, but one that I hoped would help me recoup my fortune soon enough. I gulped down a room-service breakfast laden with grease, brushed my teeth, and splashed on a generous dose of Bay Rum.

I'd already pulled on my greatcoat when it struck me that my walk was to be brief and the weather probably mild. To confirm conditions outside, I paused before the window and drew back the heavy drapes. I was startled instead to see my own image staring back at me. Taken aback momentarily, I studied my reflection, noting the broad chest and large hands of generations of my father's Welsh forebears who mined the damp valleys of South Glamorgan. I saw, too, the height and coloring of my mother's Norwegian ancestors. I'm taller than most men, blond, fair skin with wide pale blue eyes and straight nose. *Species Scandinavian Stereotypicus.*

Lately, appraising my reflection has become an obsession with me. What draws me to mirrors and reflections is not hubris. On the contrary, it's as if I can't believe that I see what others do. I see all my warts. To me, my eyes and the set of my mouth hint of bad judgment, impulsive behavior, lack of resolve. Maybe I hope to see more, to see the positives others see in me. I flexed my shoulders, further contemplating myself and my spiffy new duds.

"Well, you've got the surface look of an honest and successful man, Mr. Will Beaman," I spoke aloud, fishing in my pocket, and extracting my remaining coin. A half-eagle and two quarters. "And fortunately for you, neither reflections nor the human eye can detect how empty a man's pockets are, or how pathetic his character."

By 8:45 a.m., without my greatcoat—and still without so much as a thought of Germany Long— I was pounding on the bright green gate of Boston's South End Grounds. I could hardly hear the noise I made with my fist over the sharp clacking of horses' hooves, the rattle and hum of electric streetcars, and the shrill whistle of trains on the New York, New Haven, & Hartford Railroad tracks a block away. Adding to the cacophony were yelping dogs and yapping peddlers, including the ubiquitous oystermen working Columbus Avenue.

A medium-sized, but muscular man with a full mustache cracked the gate an inch and squinted out. He'd shed his coat in the morning heat in favor of an open-necked shirt and vest. His strawboater was the worse-for-wear and badly discolored by perspiration. Chin stubble suggested he hadn't shaved this morning. He welcomed me with the same enthusiasm that cows save for icy-handed farmers on winter mornings.

I recognized the ol' boy immediately. During my Harvard days his picture frequently blessed the pages of the *Herald* and the *Globe*. He was John Haggerty, grounds keeper, famous throughout base ball circles for his ability to put a ball field into playing shape. "Here now," he grunted, "And what's all this banging about, lad?"

I pushed gently against the gate, trying to extend my other hand to him as I did so. "Sir, I'm—"

His substantial brogan kept the gate from budging. He made hacking sounds, like a cat spitting up a hair ball, all the time squinting at me with sharp brown eyes. "There'll be none of thet, me boy. The gate won't be open fer another hour er so."

I shook my head in protest. "Sir, I have an appointment with—"

"Come back after tin, m'boy. No one gits in 'ere afore tin."

I drew upon my most authoritarian demeanor. "My good man!" I replied, "I am employed by Director Conant!" I thought my more

11

aggressive manner and Conant's name might make him pause, and one of them did.

His squint deepened and he canted his large head to look at me out of the corners of his eyes. "You don't work for Mr. Conant."

The residue of gloom from last night's dreams left me with little patience with Haggerty's intransigence. Without the meeting with Anna Anspach I would lose my edge with Conant and, later, with Soden. Without this job, I was going to slip deeper into an already staggering debt. If nothing else, my Harvard career had taught me the art of groveling. There, I had learned to grovel effectively enough to move even the most impervious and supercilious of the Crimson faculty, and this rube was no Harvard academic. So now I groveled.

"Mr. Haggerty, I have an appointment with Miss Anspach. Pullleeeze," I told him, adding what I considered just the right amount of whine. "She's expecting me."

For the first time he looked at me with real interest and permitted the door to open another inch or two. "Miss Anspach tol' me to peel an eye fer you. Yer Mr.Will Beaman, then?" He pronounced it Beh-amon. "I was expecting an old codger, like me self."

"Sorry. And it's pronounced Beaman," I corrected him. "Will Beaman. Like seaman. Hard e."

He nodded and vaguely extended a huge, knobby hand. Had knuckles on him like Gentleman Jim Corbett, and the crooked fingers of most ball players and former players.

"John Haggerty here. Well, Mr. Will Beaman"—he drew it out into an exaggerated Beeeeman—"If Miss Anspach sez ye can come in, ye can come in, man." He flung open the gate. Seizing my arm, he pulled me in and directed me toward the Grandstands with its single-decked pavilion. "There's no one around at the moment so far as I know other'n workers 'n one or two players. Miss Anspach is to yer left," he said. Without another word he moved off toward the field, leaving me standing there.

I glanced anxiously at my pocket watch. 8:48 a.m. So far so good. I had barely looked up from my timepiece when I spotted Miss Anspach moving toward a short flight of stairs. She was a pale, slim, strawberry blond. And clearly agitated. My God, did everyone get up this morning out of sorts? Again, I peeked at my watch. Surely she was not upset with me. I was a full five minutes early for one of the few times in my life. Still, she was unmistakenly disturbed. Hesitantly, I stepped forward, hoping my suit remained unwrinkled. Glancing down at my recently purchased shoes, I was dismayed to see that each wore a thin coat of dust. After first checking to see if she'd seen me, I quickly wiped off each shoe on the back of my calves. That done, I waved at her. "Miss Anspach, I presume?"

She stopped abruptly, swung her head toward me, and nodded and blinking rapidly, but did not speak.

I stepped forward and extended a hand. "I'm—"

"Yes, yes, I know," she said, nodding vigorously. Her voice was high and thin. She ignored my proffered hand.

The fact that I had not been allowed to complete most of my sentences since entering the South End Grounds was beginning to gall me. But knowing that first impressions were important, especially for me under the circumstances, I stifled my irritation. "Do you have a few minutes for me, Miss Anspach? Please?" Even as I asked her I knew from the look of her that she didn't want to talk to me—or anyone, for that matter.

She frowned and looked about as if expecting someone else. She then moved a few feet away, chewing nervously on her unpainted lips and shuffling her feet as if the pavement were too hot to stand on. "Actually, I don't, Mr. Beaman," she mumbled. She pronounced it Bay-man. "I'm sorry, but I must postpone our meeting. Something unforeseeable has come up. I really must attend to it."

"It's Beeman, ma'am. Hard e. Perhaps I could visit the office? Maybe look at attendance records?"

"No!" She barked it as if the thought of my presence in the office horrified her. She shook her head and fluttered her hands in apology, much like a discomposed Old Maid. "I'm sorry. Perhaps tomorrow. Really, I must go."

She seemed on the verge of hysteria. Without waiting for my response, she strode rapidly away, her dark-blue full-length skirt billowing behind her, her hair bobbing like a buoy in a choppy sea. An odd keening trailed her, the sound of an alley rat being crushed under the wheels of a freight wagon.

Hardly an auspicious beginning. I looked around, bewildered by my predicament. Haggerty was hovering around second base with several workers. The distraught Miss Anspach had disappeared up the stairs. Denied access to her and the office, I figured I might as well do the next best thing: refamiliarize myself with The Grounds. I'd last been here in 1893 when I frequently skipped classes in Cambridge to watch the Beaneaters and their National League foes. The park had burned down since then and been rebuilt in diminished dimensions. No upper deck pavilion with twin spires now. To size up changes in The Grounds, I drifted through the stands and spent twenty minutes or so in the left field bleachers. The fence enclosing the outfield was plastered with advertisements for Schlitz Milwaukee Beer, Dr.

Sage's Catarrh Remedy; and other of life's necessities. Puffs of steam from passing trains drifted above the fence. The clank of railroad cars hitching and unhitching provided a hypnotic metallic rhythm as they approached and departed the roundhouses and repair sheds. The grass on the field was yellow and sparse and large patches of earth dotted the sprawling outfield. One glance at its dimensions made clear the necessity of having a centerfielder that could cover ground. The infield was virtually bare. Haggerty's reputation as the National League's best groundskeeper aside, I'd seen better fields.

Contemplating the infield did little more for me than conjure up the dark implications of last night's dreams. I moved on. Eventually meandering under the main pavilion where I'd never been before, I came across the public pump, the ground around it dark and muddy. Next to it was a shed built over a drainage ditch. Obviously a dressing room, though as in other ball grounds, it was primitive. Visiting players still dressed in their hotel rooms.

Recalling Haggerty's remark about one or two players being around, I decided there was no time like the present to meet them. After all, how many times does one get an opportunity to exchange pleasantries with players such as Hugh Duffy and Kid Nichols? Or with cherry pie young players like Jimmy Collins? And, of course, there was my hero, Germany Long. Standing there under the stands was the first time I'd consciously thought of Long.

A single badly-stained window permitted me to peer inside. There I saw a wood-planked room divided by clotheslines from which uniforms hung. A bench ran in front of crude cubicles which served as players' closets. I assumed that the side out of my vision had additional cubicles. From my angle I could see one end of a large bath tub in the far corner. If there were any players in the tub—or the room, for that matter—they were beyond my sight. I moved around to the door and knocked. When no one responded, I eased my way in. After all, I told myself, I was part of the club now and soon to be a familiar figure around The Grounds.

Inside, I paused between tall cabinets on each side of the entrance. The door of the one to my right was ajar and I pressed it shut to allow passage. Both doors sprung suddenly open and a man slammed into me, driving me toward my left. The sound of base balls bouncing and of bats tumbling on the planked floor filled the room. I braced myself against a locker and whirled to face my assailant just as he struck me with a weak looping right hand. Instinctively, I ducked inside the punch and drove a hard right to his chest. As I did so, my right foot stepped on something round, which skidded away. With my feet thrown out from under me I landed awkwardly on my bum, padded only by my left hand that I managed to get under me. My attacker crashed against the open cabinet from the impact of my punch, then toppled past me. Bouncing against the closets, he spun limply to the floor, landing face up, mouth open.

I scrambled awkwardly to my feet in the narrow passage, angry and breath rasping, wincing at the pain in my ankle. Why 'n thunder would someone attack me for entering the dresssing room? Equally confusing, how had I managed to stop him with one punch, and that to the chest? I stared down at my adversary.

And, jeezus, there he was. In the bright shaft of light from the opened door, Germany Long was sprawled amidst scattered bats and balls. Nothing graceful and dignified about this crackerjack ballplayer at the moment. His head rested in an expanding crimson pool near an ice-filled tub. His eyes were bruised and swollen. His left arm was flung away from his body and his hand was oddly bent. Someone had pounded on it—and Germany—well before I hit him. By heavens, he'd been unconscious—dead, perhaps— long before he fell into me. I could tell that much even without medical training.

At his feet, as if dozing, was a large dead rat.

Now, you may well mutter, 'We know what's coming, Will Beaman. Surely you'll not insult us with a story so trite and singularly unbelieveable.'

But for all its triteness, I must relate it. You see, to my mortification, it's the way it occurred, and I am a man now striving to put aside my penchant for exaggeration and obfuscation in favor of a more honest and truthful nature. If the beginning of this tale is trite, believe me, its unfolding was anything but.

So, sure enough, as you have doubtless anticipated, while I was leaning over Long, eyes bulging and mouth agape, Mr. Soden and Mr. Conant appeared suddenly behind me.

"Good Lord, man," cried Soden, peering over my shoulder, "what in God's name have you done!"

2

The chair on which I sat in Deacon Bill Conant's sweltering chambers was small and uncomfortable. I'd been sitting there for forty-five minutes. My bum hurt. So did my ankle. But my head throbbed worse than either. The collapse of my plan to impress Conant and Soden had given me a fierce headache. The question now was could I cut my losses? Could I convince my new bosses that I had nothing to do with the assault upon Long? Could I persuade them to keep me on?

To my left, John Haggerty shifted uncomfortably in his chair for the dozenth time, like a man with a mouse in his pants. Hooking his thumbs in his braces, he tugged them away from his sweat-soaked shirt and let them snap noisily back into place. His thick-soled brogans tapped an impatient rhythm on the carpeted floor. "Jayzus, Mary, and Joseph," he muttered, half in boredom, half in exasperation.

On the other side of Haggerty, a slim, hatchet-faced man, unknown to me, tipped his chair so that its back rested against the wall and its front two legs were off the floor. With his head against the wall, his bowler tilted low over his eyes, resting it seemed, on his thin, blade-like nose. His feet were hooked on the chair's rungs and his hands were crammed deep into his jacket pockets. "Cheap bastards won't even buy comfortable chairs for their own offices," he groused.

I made a face to show my own discomfort. The three of us were waiting to be questioned further on our whereabouts during the assault on Germany Long. The office was stark. Its four windows were closed and the room throbbed with heat. Except for its expensive looking Persian carpet, the room looked like it had been furnished by mendicants. Three of the four walls were bare. A small photograph of the South End Grounds prior to the 1894 fire broke the monotony of the fourth wall. Conant's desk and chair were modest.

We'd been sitting in stony silence until just recently, eyeing each other warily. From the muffled sounds and voices that at times penetrated the walls, we knew Conant and Soden were interrogating Anna Anspach, and had been for some time. Twice we'd heard her sobbing.

Despite my initial impression that Long was dead, he'd survived. He'd been hustled off to the hospital, still unconscious. The rodent hadn't fared as well.

To give some momentum to the remarks by Haggerty and the man in the tipped chair, I indicated the plain desk and chair across the room from us.

"It doesn't look like Mr. Conant's own chair's much more comfortable than the ones we're sitting on."

The mystery man snorted. "Anything to squeeze six pennies from a nickel."

"Skinflints." mumbled Haggerty. "You couldn't force a dime up their arses."

The man in the tipped chair spoke directly to me for the first time. "Didja know it was Soden hisself who brung up the idea of writing a reserve clause into each ball player's contract? Back in the late '70s, it was. Bound players to their nines."

Haggerty lurched forward, suddenly animated. He removed an unlit cigar stub from his mouth and spat out a piece of tobacco with small pneumatic sounds, apparently unmindful of whether he spotted Conant's carpet. "That reserve clause has been keeping profits up for the owners ever since. An' players' salaries down. It's slavery, is what it is, " he snarled.

The second man bared his teeth and pointed a slim, almost feminine finger at me.

"Soden has a certain, eh, manic frugality. In the '80s he convinced owners to charge players for board on road trips and for their own uniforms and equipment."

"Hell, the miserly bastard made even bigger cuts by giving up sleeping cars and the better hotels," Haggerty added. "He'll piss in a bucket 'n tell you it's cream."

Our laughter at Haggerty's observation was cut short when the doorknob rattled and twisted slightly. The three of us stared at the door in expectant silence, waiting for it to open, and for one of us to be beckoned. The door remained closed.

The slim man drew from his pocket a handful of coins. "Fifty cents says it'll be the kid first," he said, glancing at Haggerty.

Haggerty shot me a look, then turned back to the stranger. "You're on."

"Want part of it?" the man asked me.

Without contemplating how few coins I had, I told him I did.

Haggerty pointed at the second man and arched his eyebrows. "You know Billy 'ere, then?"

The man touched the brim of his bowler with a finger. "Billy Ewing. Utility infielder."

"Will Beaman here," I said, nodding to acknowledge him. "It looks like you'll get some playing time, what with Long injured now."

He shrugged and fluttered surprisingly pale and delicate hands.

17

"'Sweet Billy,'" they call him," Haggerty said, jerking a thumb at Billy Ewing and chuckling.

Billy smirked and jauntily tipped his hat.

"What's the 'sweet' for, your bat or your glove?" I asked.

Before Billy could answer, Haggerty laughed—a short, loud snort. "The *ladies* is his game."

"That, too." Billy chuckled wickedly.

I ignored the good-humored banter and tried to drag them back to the topic of the Boston ownership. "Surely, the Boston owners aren't as close-fisted as you say?"

"Worse," spat Billy Ewing, letting his chair settle back on the floor and leaning toward me. "Conant and Soden pinch pennies at every turn, especially Soden. Jesus, he makes the press and players' wives buy their own tick—"

He never finished. The door swung open and Soden stuck his head in, giving us a look that would clabber sweetmilk. "Billy, would you join us now?"

Billy stood, stretched in an exaggerated way. He groped in his pockets and extracted two coins, flipping one to each of us. He then pasted an unconvincing smile on his puss and followed Soden like a lad on his way to the principal's office, his bravado suddenly diminished. The door clicked shut behind them.

"He'll tell 'em nothin'," Haggerty sniffed.

"He knows something?"

"Don't matter."

Haggerty had no more to say about Sweet Billy Ewing and we lapsed again into silence, except for an occasional muttered profanity directed at the stifling heat. Even with the distraction of the sweltering room, I couldn't get the men's observations about Conant's and Soden's parsimony out of my mind. Working for skinflints was no way to recoup one's luck. I brooded about my ill fortune in silence for several minutes. "I thought the Bostons were high flyers," I finally mumbled.

Haggerty looked at me like I was still in knickers. "Ah, me boy. They lay out a dollar here and squeeze out two somewhere else, usually at the players' expense. Jayzus, Mary, and Joseph," he groaned and shook his head, "Soden still keeps *sheep* on the grounds rather than pay a mower."

"And I'm one of them," I sighed, "Or hope to be."

Haggerty waggled a sausage-like finger at me. "Nah, boyo, you ain't one of 'em. You might work in their office, but you won't never be one of the bosses. No sir. There's labor 'n there's management. You're labor, sure. Like me." He spat another fleck of tobacco across the room and then stared after it as if judging the distance of its flight. "The bosses'll teach you *that* soon enough."

I stood by my chair and stretched, bouncing on the balls of my feet to increase the circulation in my legs and to test my ankle. Fumbling in my pockets, I again counted the coins there. Billy's fifty-cent piece was a welcome addition to my pitifully small hoard.

Haggerty watched me examining my coins. "Fifty cents says you're next."

This was easy. "Done."

I'd already stripped off my coat and it lay limp across the back of the chair. I tugged my wet shirt away from my body and swiped the perspiration from my brow. "Any idea what happened to Long?" I asked. "Someone beat him and stuffed him in that closet before I got there. The only reason he fell out against me was I bumped the doors."

Haggerty blew air noisily through his nose and smiled enigmatically. "Some one tried to pound on him a week ago. Outside The Grounds. Long got away."

"Have other players been attacked?"

He waved me off with a huge paw. "Nah."

"Why Long?"

"Like Billy, what I know and what I tell are two different matters."

"You *know* who beat Long?"

He made a strange sound in his throat—that hair ball thing again—and jerked a thumb toward the other room. "I'm tellin' them I don't know a damn thing."

What in Libby's knickers did that mean, I thought? Did he know something, or didn't he? And if he did know something, why not tell Conant and Soden? Surely, he'd want to help Long. "Telling the bosses what you know is one thing. Telling the truth is quite another," I pointed out, struggling to get him to open up.

He grinned at me, then, the conspiratorial grin of a companion. He removed a speck of tobacco from the tip of his tongue with two fingers, peered at it, and then flicked it carelessly across the room. "You've lied to the bosses, have you, lad?"

"No, no," I protested. "But I don't always tell the *whole* truth to my superiors." I smiled at him, one chum to another. "It's a fine line I've learned to skirt."

He barked and slapped his knees with his hands. "A man after me own heart." He removed the cigar stub from his mouth and inspected it intently. "So why'd Conant and Soden hire you?" He looked at me, eyebrows raised in anticipation. "The truth now, lad."

19

"Conant persuaded Soden that they needed to improve revenues."

"Why you?" he asked, continuing to fiddle with the unlit cigar butt.

"Well, I have a Harvard degree—Class of '93, and I'm familiar with Boston. And they knew that I'd helped my father at his Minneapolis detective agency. I also spent four years in the lower levels of professional base ball."

He nodded his head as he sucked theatrically at his dead smoke. "So you had the experience they wanted, and a baseball background?"

I made sure the door was tightly closed. In for a penny of candor, in for a pound. "Maybe, but I didn't exactly excel in any of those roles."

"And why do I think women were involved?"

I looked at him with renewed respect. The man wasn't stupid. "Women *were* my downfall," I confessed. "I've lost more jobs over women than Tom Edison has patents."

"My guess is you could give Sweet Billy a lesson or two. So, how did you get this chance?"

"Conant and my father are long-time friends. They became pals as Union soldiers during the '62 Peninsula Campaign."

Haggerty's eyes widened. "Ah."

"My father called in IOUs to get me this job," I told him. For reasons not clear to me I felt relieved to have confessed even a minuscule portion of my failings to Mr. Haggerty.

Haggerty bared tobacco-stained teeth as he chewed on his unlit stogie. "The bosses don't need to know everythin'," he snorted. "An' they won't hear nothin' from me." He pointed a thick finger at me and closed one eye. "Forget them sweet words and fine gestures of theirs. It's them agin us. Always has been. Always will be."

We lapsed into silence for the next half hour. The room got hotter and my chair harder. If Haggerty wanted to believe I was labor, fine. I needed all the friends I could muster, but I hoped eventually to make management money with the Bostons, and that meant keeping Conant and Soden happy, too. I was like a fish between two cats. The perspiration, having soaked my shirt and waist, trickled into my trousers.

Without warning the door swung open, and Soden's head appeared. He crooked a finger at me.

I stood and swallowed hard. Quickly extracting the few coins from my pocket, I tossed my recently won fifty-cent piece to Haggerty. I then stepped through the door, following in Soden's wake, trying to appear more confident than Billy had. But I knew my future would be largely determined in the next few minutes.

3

I was wrong. Ninety minutes later I sat nervously at a table at J.J.
Cosgrove's Base Ball Exchange on Tremont, a block from the South End
Grounds, eating lunch with the Bostons' braintrust, still unsure of my status.
The restaurant swarmed with businessmen and clerks in vested suits,
celluloid collars, and bowler hats. Workingmen occupied the tables away
from the front windows. Against the far wall, a half dozen leather-aproned
butchers were celebrating someone's birthday. Ceiling fans moved
soundlessly, their noise overwhelmed by the clacking of dishes, the rattling
of silverware, and sudden bursts of raw laughter.

Everyone inside The Grounds had by then been rounded up by Soden
and Conant and grilled. And not always civilly, if I can judge from the
treatment I received. Soden especially spent more than an hour pressing me
on where I had been and what I had done after Miss Anspach left me. He
was not a pleasant man. As cold and cynical a man as you'll ever meet.

Though I suggested it repeatedly, so far as I could tell, no one had
alerted the police.

Now, an irritable group of team owners and directors was gathered
solemnly for lunch, and for further discussion of the morning's events. This
was a management affair. John Haggerty was not there. Nor was Miss
Anspach. I could not tell if Miss Anspach's absence was the result of her
sex, her lowly station within the club's hierarchy, or the fragile mental
condition I had glimpsed. Perhaps she was still too agitated to join us. I
decided not to ask.

Having apparently convinced themselves that I was neither a possible
murderer nor an abettor of assault, Conant and Soden had included me in the
lunch. I sat there fidgeting, sipping a beer, my ankle sore and swollen, trying
not to be too distracted by the steady parade of winsome young ladies past
Cosgrove's windows.

You may well ask, 'but why still be unsettled? After all, your new
employers exonerated you in any complicity in the assault upon Long. The
road ahead is clear and smooth.'

Alas, not so. My trial was just beginning, for I had much to hide
from those weighing my hire. Not dark and desperate criminal things, mind
you, but a train of unworthy behavior, certainly enough to concern pending
employers. Heavens, my own father had fired me after reaching his limits
with my antics! Being included in this meeting, I reasoned, did not guarantee
my continuation with the team. Not if there was full disclosure of my past. I

hoped I was still employed when the lunch was over—indeed, that my hiring would be established at this meal. For the past several hours no one seemed interested in confirming I was really with the organization. My goal, then, was to be as honest with them as possible, but not so frank as to undermine my position.

As I was fretting about the precariousness of my position, a gent in a derby and black greatcoat sauntered to our table and shook hands with Conant. Though it was an innocuous act, it immediately put everyone on edge. I leaned toward Frank Selee, the team's manager, briefly introduced myself, and asked who the gentleman in the derby was.

"T. H. Murnane of the *Globe*," Selee said. "Tim follows the team for the *Globe* and *The Sporting News*. He's the last man the bosses want snooping around today."

Apparently Murnane had entered Cosgrove's for a lunch engagement with Conant. I looked him over. Now in his mid-forties I would guess, he sported a shock of gray-white hair and extra pounds around his girth. He had once been a fine first basemen with the Bostons. Like Haggerty, he displayed the distorted fingers of a ball player. "Ah, so that's the famous Tim Murnane," I said, more to myself than to anyone in particular.

Murnane glanced over Conant's shoulder and caught my eye. Disengaging from Conant, he sidled over, smiling broadly and taking my hand. It was like gripping a bag of peanuts. "And who's this handsome young stranger?" he asked. He didn't wait for an answer. "I hear Mr. Beaman will be working in the office." He pronounced it Beh-eh-man.

"It's under discussion, Tim," Conant told him. He said it too non-committally for my taste.

"What'll the darlin' lad be doing?" pressed Murnane, still clutching my hand and pumping it.

Conant scowled and dabbed at his mouth with his napkin. "Tim, we have some business to transact here. Will you excuse us? You and I'll have lunch some other time. Perhaps tomorrow?"

Murnane released me. He thought about Conant's question for a moment, rubbing his forehead vigorously. "Of course," he finally said. "Sure 'n I understand, Bill."

"I apologize for the inconvenience, Tim," Conant said. "I do. Tomorrow, then?"

"Certainly." Murnane said. "Perhaps Mr. Beaman could join us?" He winked at me, doffed his lid, and departed.

"Judas Priest!" Conant grumbled as Murnane moved away from us. Not until Murnane stepped into the busy street did Conant turn to me. "Stay away from him. He's got a long nose, Tim has." And then, as if he had dismissed me, he turned gruffly to Soden who had just returned from the hospital. "Germany know who attacked him?" he asked.

Soden was a burly man with thinning hair and a perpetual stony expression on his face. He also had the coldest eyes of any man I've met. Conant's question seemed to deepen his already foul mood. Soden's thin, bloodless lips moved briefly but he said nothing.

"Does he have any idea why someone would try to kill him?" Conant pressed him.

Soden took a draught of dark lager and sighed. "Germany's conscious, but not talking yet. He's got a lump on his head, a bad gash at his hairline, and a fracture in his hand. Glove hand."

"Nothing from other players?" Conant wanted to know.

"Nobody knows nothin'," Soden growled. He added half under his breath, "By damn, someone knows *something*." He looked at me with pale, frozen eyes.

"We'll have to question Miss Anspach again tomorrow," Conant said, shaking his head sorrowfully. "She fainted when she heard about Germany. She's still very upset."

"Poor distraught lass," murmured Frank Selee. Selee was beginning his eighth year as manager of the Boston nine. With his dark hair, receding hairline, bristling mustache, and piercing black eyes, he appeared larger and more fierce than he was. He was, all in all, a gentle man and a gentleman. His teams eschewed the rowdyism and dirty ball that characterized the play of the Orioles in Baltimore and the Spiders in Cleveland. He was once described to me as being as sober as a salesman for a mirror firm. In the seven years that he had managed the team, he won three pennants. I could see by his intensity the basis of his success. I may not demonstrate much character at times but I recognize it in others.

"Lowe and Ewing showed up early for some doctoring," Selee said, sweeping the table with his piercing eyes. "But they had no idea what's going on. I called Captain Duffy to tell him about Germany." He looked around the table as if asking for questions. When there was none, he tossed his napkin down on his plate. "Billy Ewing'll start in place of Germany today. We'll get by."

"When he regains his wits Germany'll tell us what this's all about," Conant assured us, "He'll probably be fine tomorrow. He's all wool and a yard wide."

Soden raised a thin eyebrow. "Maybe," he said coldly and unconvincingly, "But perhaps in the meantime we ought to hear from—and about—young Will Beaman here." There it was again: Bay-man.

23

"It's Beaman, sir. As in seaman." I was starting to feel like a second banana in a third-rate vaudeville act.

Conant launched into a brief description of my expected duties with the club, then turned to me. "Tell us about yourself, Mr. Beaman." He pronounced it Bay-man, as Soden had, saying it slowly and deliberately, like a challenge.

Whether he did it to mock Soden or to warn me to toe the line, I couldn't tell. I did know it was a prickly welcome mat he'd tossed down before me.

4

Everything now depended on the clock. I surreptitiously checked my timepiece. It virtually screamed out my strategy for survival. The game would start at 3:30 p.m. and the owners had to be at The Grounds well before then. There was time to impress my new bosses. And yet, if I talked fast and long enough—kept the floor, so to speak—there'd be no time for embarrassing questions.

I wasted no time describing my Harvard years or my time in the lower levels of base ball. Even my talent for hyperbole couldn't make those careers appear sterling. I talked instead about my time with my father's detective agency. I knew that that episode in my life would also stretch my talents for verbal misdirection, but fortunately, Frank Selee came to my rescue.

"Did you catch any killers while working for your father?" he wanted to know.

For the next twenty minutes I embellished the facts from a few cases I knew about with a generous ladle of fancy. These weren't malicious lies, mind you, but rather what I would term harmless additions. Icing on the cake, as it were. My audience gulped down the concocted details, faces aglow. All except Soden, who watched me with the expression of a man who'd discovered a turd on his plate. Still, he remained silent, and I thought I was home free.

Until Conant broke in. Whether he did so to help me out or to turn the screws, I don't know. "You were responsible for increasing your father's staff and income?" he asked. "According to your letters of reference, you doubled your father's workforce and increased income. The letters were quite explicit about this."

I swallowed hard. This was not going to be easy.

"Uh, yes, that's so," I managed to mutter, hoping that my hesitancy would be interpreted as modesty rather than confusion. Apparently my father had laid it on in my interests and had bludgeoned friends to do the same. There was no doubt in my mind that his support stemmed more from a desire to rid himself of a wayward and parasitic son, rather than from any pride in or appreciation of my worth. I chose not to confess that two additional hires were employed to tail me. Or that, as I discovered later, on two occasions I was the subject of investigations carried out by new operatives at the instigation of suspicious husbands. Added staff is added staff.

But readers will protest, 'You told us earlier that you were striving for a habit of greater candor and truthfulness, a reformation in your personal conduct and standards.' And for fair, readers, I did tell you that. But here I was emphasizing truth in the parts rather than the sum.

I knew my father's letter omitted details about how I had embroiled myself with several young ladies in the office that accounted for some of the employee turnover and the hiring of fresh secretarial help. In the same spirit of my father's and his friends' calculated amnesia, my summary of my past twelve months was severely edited. Summoning up my most convincing demeanor, I assured those around the table that my return to Boston was prompted by a desire to see if I could succeed away from any connection with my father.

Soden suffered a coughing fit at this point, but quickly recovered. I pushed on. If a man chooses to smoke inferior cigars, he must suffer the consequences. When at last he'd brought his cough under control, he interrupted, "And you think you can turn our revenues around? Boost attendance?"

"I do," I replied. I had learned the art of bluff—assertiveness, I prefer to call it—in the halls of Harvard. Indeed, I would be remiss if I didn't concede my entire academic career had been a testimony to bluster. But bluff and confidence are two pods of the same plant, and to confess one is to admit to the other.

"Can you boost revenues quickly?" pressed Soden, doubt radiating from his question. "Our attendance has been mediocre. If it continues to decline we'll have to put fractions on the turnstiles."

I ignored his attempt at humor, if that's what it was. "I believe I can do it quickly, yes sir."

"Hmmmph." He sounded as if someone had just told him the world was flat. But, then, Soden delivered most of his observations with the warmth of a mortician. Certainly, he was not entirely taken by me nor my record. The good news was that neither he nor anyone else had asked questions that unearthed my less than admirable record. For that I was relieved and thankful.

Soden employed a frown and a curt head gesture to order me to stay put when the luncheon broke up. The other participants, heavy with chowder, oysters, and sausage, and lubricated with ample amounts of butter, grease, and alcohol, moved out the big twin doors and toward the ball grounds. A sudden thunderstorm had chased away the sunshine and streets were now slick and puddled. Small clusters of people joined members of our lunch group drifting toward The South End Grounds, picking their way among trolley cars, hacks, carriages, and steaming horse droppings in the rain-splattered street.

26

I glanced at Soden. Here it comes, I thought. He's seen through my glibness.

But we sat there in silence until the last of our mates was gone. A faint whump of thunder could occasionally be heard and the dark gray sky brightened periodically as lightning darted about. Haggerty would have his work cut out for him to get the game played today.

Soden stared frostily at me. "You know why I asked you to stay?"

"No sir."

"In part, it has to do with your experiences in Minneapolis."

"Oh." Bill Conant might do my father a favor by overlooking my failings, but Soden the Unfeeling wasn't about to.

"You've worked for your father long enough to get a feel for things like this." He spoke slowly, deliberately. "What do you really think of the Long thing?" His dead blue eyes locked mine.

I let my breath out and spoke the obvious. "A serious crime has been committed. It should have been reported to the police."

He acknowledging the validity of what I'd said with a shrug. "I don't want to call in the police. And neither does Bill." Meaning Conant, I assumed. As if to say he wasn't about to explain their reluctance to notify the proper authorities, Soden suddenly asked, "What do you make of the rat? Odd that, eh?"

I shrugged. For heaven's sake, this wasn't like explaining electricity. "Whoever attacked Long brought the rat with him. Thinks it's a message of some kind. I don't think Germany was supposed to be killed, simply put out of play and left with a message for him or someone else—or both." I paused dramatically, a habit I had picked up from my father and other pompous men, including a number of my Harvard professors. "Perhaps for *you*, Mr. Soden, sir."

He ignored my last observation—and my dramatics. "What kind of message? Who leaves rats as messages?" He reached into his vest and withdrew two huge cigars. "Cigar?" he asked. He pronounced it "seeger."

I waved him off. "I haven't the faintest idea," I told him truthfully.

He hunched forward, dropped his arms on the table and leaned toward me. Conspiratorially. "Potentially we have a great club," he said, "but we have problems, I know that. There's tension on the team." He held up his hand and counted on his fingers as he talked. "Tucker is afraid he's going to lose his first base job. Tenny isn't happy about not having a set position. Collins is new to third. Ewing is pressing Long for playing time. Stahl thinks he should be playing every day." He waved his hands as if to say it goes on and on.

He took a deep drag on his cigar, tipped his head up, and blew a long stream of blue cigar smoke toward the ceiling fan. "I'm not about to share news of the assault on Long with the police or the newspapers," he told me," "I've already talked with Haggerty about warning his work crew that if I find out they've talked to anyone outside the club about Germany, it'll cost them their jobs. Selee will speak to the players. I'll take care of Germany."

He pointed a finger at me. "You stay away from Tim Murnane. I don't want to lose my shirt because of violence in the grounds, and I don't want to lose attendance because people are afraid to come to the park. There's enough concern about crime in Boston already."

"You're just going to ignore this attack?" I asked in disbelief. "What'll Long and the players think?"

"Great Lucifer," he hissed. "I didn't say I was putting anything behind me. I'm going to talk to Germany the first thing in the morning." He jabbed his cigar at me much as one might hold a pistol. "But if Germany doesn't talk—and he ain't the talkative type—or if he doesn't know who's responsible, that's where you come in."

What the hell? "Where I come in, sir?"

"Yessir. That's what you're going to do, lad. You're going to get to the bottom of this."

"But I never worked as an operative for my father," I sputtered in a burst of candor. "I don't know the first thing about field work. For God's sake, hire a Pinkerton or a private investigator. There are dozens in Boston."

Soden leaned toward me, fixed me with his ice-cold eyes. "No, sir. This stays within our organization. I sense in you a large measure of cynicism and larceny. And I suspect those are the very qualities essential for discovering the people involved in this nonsense."

"Yes, sir," I muttered, abashed at how quickly he'd read me.

"Cheer up, Mr. Beaman," he smirked, still pronouncing it Bay-man. "We may eventually have something positive to tell your father, after all."

5

It was twenty-five minutes after three when I slipped into a seat next to J. B. Billings, the third of the Boston owners. He was sitting directly behind the catcher and half way up the still-damp stands. Less than a thousand spectators were scattered throughout The Grounds. The rain had tapered off, but the weather remained overcast and humid. Though John Haggerty and his workers had applied generous amounts of sawdust, players were already busy fussing with mud-clogged spikes.

Without so much as a farewell, Soden, who had walked to the game with me, drifted away. By then he and I had worked out the details of my clandestine assignment. If Germany Long could not—or would not—clarify what led to the attack upon him, and who was responsible for it, I was to find out. While ostensibly carrying out my official duties for Conant, I was to make discreet inquiries into Long's activities, and those of his team mates, to determine who might want to hurt him. Soden was convinced my duties with the team would facilitate access to players and hangers-on.

My repeated suggestion that I be given remuneration for my additional duties was met with a silent glower.

As I settled next to Billings on the wooden planking, the Boston nine was already on the field and their twirler, a lefthander, was tossing warm-up pitches. Rooters were shouting unpleasantries at the visitors waiting to take the field. A young gent in a yellow suit, who seemed to know everyone, was glad-handing his way through the sparse gathering in the third base stands.

Billings and I had exchanged civilities at lunch. He was a tall chap with the look of someone both terribly unhappy and about to fall asleep. In a black light wool three-piece suit with a pearl gray fedora shading his hooded eyes, he appeared more Presbyterian minister than the shoe manufacturer and baseball owner he was. His perpetual grimace suggested a clergyman who'd discovered that hell offered cold lager and loose women. He was busily filling out his scorecard, biting his lower lip in concentration.

I flashed him a smile. Similar smiles had melted many a Minneapolis maiden's heart. Billings, however, studiously ignored my overture, continuing to mark his card in a small, precise script.

Unabashed, I turned my attention to The Grounds and the players. Three years earlier, during a riot between Boston and Baltimore players, a fire had started in rubbish under the stands and razed the entire double-decker structure. The fire swept nearly twelve acres. Besides destroying much of the ballpark, it incinerated more than one hundred structures along the railroad tracks and a nearby neighborhood, including—it was said—two very busy brothels. It was estimated that some seventy-five thousand dollars in damage had been done to The Grounds alone. So far as I can tell, the replacement costs of the whorehouses were not divulged.

Watching the Bostons on the field, I began to fill out my own scorecard. I closely observed each player as I completed the card. Charlie Ganzel was behind the plate, playing in the stead of Marty Bergen. Fred Tenny was at first, a fact that clearly did not sit well with Tommy Tucker who strolled up and down in front of the bench pouting. Bobby Lowe was at second, the mercurial Jimmy Collins at third and my new acquaintance, "Sweet Billy" Ewing, played in place of Long at short. Captain Hugh Duffy patrolled left field, Billy Hamilton center, and Happy Jack Stivetts right field. Even in practice, the speed and quickness of the nine astonished me. Infielders caught everything and got rid of the ball as quick as any group of daisy sweepers I'd seen. The outfield was pure candy, swift in their pursuit of fly balls. Soden hadn't exaggerated their potential. He could win the pennant with this lot. *If* the club got decent pitching. A big if. It's the key to each team's fortune every year. Always has been. Always will be.

The tasks of completing my scorecard and assessing the skills of the players did not block from my mind the personal predicament facing me. I was in trouble and I knew it. I had no real familiarity with investigative field work. To this point my life had involved trying to confuse the bloodhounds, not locate the scent. I'd be lucky to hang around long enough for a second paycheck. A sense of desperation began to crawl up my spine. But, as you have doubtless gathered from my earlier comments, desperation and failure were no strangers to me. In truth, they'd become intimate companions of late. Besides, If I'd let a little failure and rejection deter me I'd have missed out on many a steamy night with some of Minneapolis's fairest.

And so, despite his obvious indifference toward me, Billings became the object of my first interrogation. Observing that he was no longer marking his scorecard, and trying to be as nonchalant as possible, I turned to him and pointed to the lefthander finishing his warm ups. "Klobedanz looks in fine fettle. He's swift."

"When Kloby is at his best his tosses look like onion seeds," Billings acknowledged.

The icebreaker behind me, I plunged on. "Who brings spirit to this team? Tucker seems to have fire."

"Tucker is quick to erupt," he said, his words crisp, his thoughts precise. "So is Bergen, and he can blow higher than Killian's kite." He pointed to the southpaw working in front of us. "Now, Klobedanz there harbors grudges and sulks, but he's not fiery." Obviously warming up,

Billings turned toward me. "The pussy cats are Collins, Lowe, Nichols, and Duffy. They seldom get steamed, although Duffy has ginger."

He scowled at me, no small feat for a man whose face expressed constant displeasure. "You don't think any of them beat Germany Long?" He didn't wait for my answer. "That *is* why you're inquiring, isn't it? To find out about Germany?"

I struggled to hide my shock, and to radiate a combination of hurt feelings and exasperation. "Now, why would you think *that*?"

His small black eyes bore into mine. "Because I know Art Soden, son, that's why. And I know that before that frugal bastard would pay for professional help, he'd hire a kid who hung around his daddy's detective agency. He'd opt for the cheap hire."

What was I supposed to say to that? Unable to come up with anything clever, or even intelligent, I settled back, embarrassed and silent, to watch the game. The gent in the yellow suit was now behind third base in deep conversation with a handsome older man wearing a silk topper.

The game moved through the early innings as I sat in humbled silence. Despite Klobedanz's wildness, it didn't appear the Philadelphias had the snap to take advantage of it. Except for maybe Lajoie and the big Delahanty kid in left. As the sky darkened and lowered, Boston took a two-run lead in the third and began to coast.

Neglecting my scorekeeping, I mulled over my exchange with Billings. Clearly Soden had saddled me with an impossible assignment: asking a stranger to finagle personal information from close-knit players and cranky owners did not make sense to me. Even a gifted stranger would be hard pressed to elicit information from them, and I had no experience or skills as a detective. Still, trying to be optimistic and bent on being successful—and wanting to prove my father wrong about me—I was determined to turn up information.

Not from the irascible and all too perceptive J. B. Billings, however. As the bottom of the sixth inning began, I excused myself and joined the team, taking a seat between Manager Selee, dressed in streetclothes and gray bowler, and catcher Marty Bergen who cradled a heavily-bandaged hand. Bergen had had his thumb lanced. He wore the sour look of a man who'd made a long trip on a bad road. Only Selee sat close to him.

I nodded to both men and raised a finger to my hat.

Selee greeted me cordially. Bergen ignored me. He said not a word to me for a full fifteen minutes. Just watched the game, worrying the wad of tobacco in his mouth and spitting furiously, occasionally very near my new shoes. I decided to test how incommunicative he truly was, and when Selee moved several seats down from us to converse with the still-pouting Tucker,

31

I tendered Bergen my hand. "I'm Will Beaman," I told him. "Mr. Conant's assistant. You're Martin Bergen?"

He pumped my hand once, firmly, with his good right hand. "Marty'll do."

"Hell of a thing that happened to Long," I ventured.

He jerked his head toward me, eyes wide, as if I'd just spat on *his* shoe. He eyed me with the intensity of a botanist with a rare orchid. After what seemed an eternity, he nodded almost imperceptibly and lobbed a wad of blackish goo into the dust an inch from my shiny new footwear.

"Surely it was no one connected with the team," I hastened to add.

He frowned and again snapped around to look at me, as if I might launch an attack on him at any minute. "Why're you askin' these fool questions? The boys put you up to it, did they?"

"No, I just thought—"

"Get away from me," he snarled, glancing around as if to find something or someone. "Go sit by Nichols. Hell, he's nice to everyone. I've got enough problems without adding your piss to my pot."

My hairline was suddenly moist and I felt heat on my face. "Now see here," I flared, and stood to emphasize my advantage in height and weight over him. "I was merely expressing concern for a teammate of yours and, I assume, a friend. You have no cause to be abusive." Hell, ball players were rough characters. I knew that. But Bergen seemed unnecessarily offensive.

I failed to intimidate him. He barely shot me a glance. Several others on the bench, including Selee, reacted to the irascible catcher by looking away, suddenly very interested in events on the field. My gut told me that they were accustomed to Bergen's flareups and wanted no part of them.

Bergen indicated the end of the bench with his good hand. "Go pester Nichols. Go on, now, or I'll smash you, sure."

I glanced toward Nichols. John Haggerty, who sat on the far side of Nichols, leaned back and caught my eye. He beckoned me.

"I'm not afraid of you," I told Bergen, "In a different place—"

Without even deigning to look at me, he growled, "An' if warts were precious, banks'd hoard 'em."

My face aflame, I walked away from Bergen and sat next to Nichols. I could hear the low murmuring of the players as I moved away from them. I wasn't afraid of mixing it up with Bergen—I can handle myself pretty good and I had him by four inches and thirty-five pounds—but to what end? Now certainly wasn't the time and, in any case, slugging Bergen wouldn't encourage his chums to confide in me.

I turned my attention to Nichols. His uniform was freshly laundered. His cap, glove, and tobacco plug, wedged into his back pocket, caused him to sit slightly lopsided. A wispy mustache partially obscured his upper lip. My last year at Harvard I had watched him pitch the Beaneaters to the pennant. He was still a premier tosser.

Haggerty leaned forward and spoke to Nichols. "Kid, this young 'un is Will Beaman. Deacon Bill's new assistant." He straightened up, reached around Nichols, and patted me on the back. "'Tis his first day on the job 'n he's green as early corn."

Nichols smiled and bobbed his head in greeting. He made no effort, however, to start a conversation, preferring to study the game.

I sat in silence, soaking up the game and thinking of my father. Obviously, he'd been no more forthcoming in detailing my career in Minneapolis to the Beaneater owners than I had been at lunch. And in my father's lies of commission and omission I realized his desperation to rid himself of me. My resolve to reform and to change my father's opinion of me did wonders for my courage. I turned to Nichols. He couldn't be as sour as Bergen and Billings, I thought. And I knew I had an ally in Haggerty. "Klobedanz isn't puzzling the Philadelphians like he did earlier," I observed.

"He's tiring," Nichols conceded. For several minutes we talked about the game and our mutual admiration for the crisp play of Delahanty and Napoleon Lajoie of the Quakers—or the Phillies, as some called them.

"Sorry about Long," I finally said. "Who could do such a thing?" I tried my best to make the question sound innocent enough, the type asked by any caring person.

Nichols answered me politely and seriously. He was a serious man. "Who could do it? Well, Tucker and Bergen are hard chaps and rough enough to whip Germany," he said, "but neither would. Germany's well-liked."

"No enemies?"

Nichols shook his head. He seemed to trust Haggerty to keep quiet about his observations. "Bergen and Long have had a few fiery exchanges," he chuckled, " but, then, almost everyone on the team has had shouting bouts with Marty. He's convinced everyone is conspiring against him. Marty's, ah, unpredictable. Understand, he's probably the best catcher in base ball right now. Great range. Quick. Strong arm. Graceful. Cagey. But you never know what will set him off. Most give him a wide berth."

Haggerty was bobbing his head in agreement.

Doubtless realizing he'd been too candid with an outsider, Nichols added quickly, "Marty wouldn't hurt a mate. Besides, he's got that bad thumb."

Well, well, I thought. Several toughs capable of roughing up a teammate. But how likely was that? And why do it at The South End

33

Grounds? Ballplayers frequently settled their differences with fists, but they didn't decorate their victims with dead rats.

"Who, then?" I asked. "From what I understand, Germany is solid. A married man. Respected citizen. And you tell me he's a gem of a team mate."

Nichols compressed his lips. "He'll tell us when he regains conciousness."

Haggerty said nothing, seemingly content to watch the game unfold before him.

Nichols' eyes scanned the sparsely occupied stands, eventually coming to rest on several flashily dressed men huddled together behind third base. "Gamblers are thick around here," he said, gesturing with his head toward the men. "Like flies on road apples."

My eyes followed his. Several of the men were exchanging bills, often peeling off several at a time. The young man in the yellow suit was in their midst. Who's the swell with the sandy hair?" I asked. "The flashy gent in the yellow suit?"

"Mikey Mul. Small time grifter."

"You see Mikey at all the sporting events," chimed in Haggerty. "Showed up about a year ago. Now he's a permanent fixture."

"Seems like he's raking it in today."

Nichols shrugged.

"They regularly bet on the games?" I wanted to know.

"Oh, yeah. On the games and on individual player's performances. On balls and strikes. On anything. The league and ownership have tried to discourage gaming, but nothing has worked," Nichols told me.

"Them touts'll bet on which mutt is gonna piss first," Haggerty said.

I couldn't help but recall our earlier bets on who Conant and Soden were going to interrogate first. I leaned back, stared harder at the men behind the Quakers' bench. Well, now, gamblers, is it? I rubbed my face with the palms of my hands. Huh. Besides recognizing my own inadequacy for Soden's task, so far I'd learned at least three things. Despite Germany Long being well liked, there were players with temperaments to assault him. Art Soden was not a beloved man, not even among his co-owners. Finally, I'd learned that gamblers stood to gain from the slick-fielding Long's absence from the Beaneaters' lineup.

I winced. Three facts. Three is an unlucky number in base ball. Three strikes and you're out. I suddenly felt like a turtle crossing a wide, busy road.

6

The Quakers chipped away at Klobedanz for single runs in the seventh and eighth and then, following Sweet Billy Ewing's errant throw in the ninth, put the game away to the dismay of Boston partisans. I joined disgruntled rooters filing from the South End Grounds. The game had taken two hours and five minutes.

I hoped to get a light supper and then use the remaining daylight to find lodging. I couldn't afford to remain at The American which charged a dollar a day. A couple more days there and I'd be broke. I was determined to find something more suitable, but first I was going to get a light meal to tide me over during the evening's hunt. And I was hoping to eat alone, to collect my thoughts and to consider my next moves.

It occurred to me to try Tommy McCarthy's which served inexpensive fare. McCarthy, a former Boston player, had been retired a year now. His restaurant and bowling alley on Washington was a popular hangout for players, bachelors, and hangers- on in the sporting community. I'd heard players hung out there before games but preferred pubs closer to The Grounds following games. I had just grasped the rail to swing up onto an open electric car when I heard my name shouted.

"Mr. Beaman?"

I turned to see T.H. Murnane running toward me, his coat tails waving in the now cool wind, his bowler pushed low on his head and held there with his huge, lumpy paw. He still moved well for a man who twenty years ago had stolen the first base in National League history.

Running at his heels like a mongrel pup was a muscular young red-headed man in a cheap light blue suit, clutching a large drawing pad under one arm and a pencil in his fist. He was a real carrot-top.

"Mr. Beaman?" Murnane called again, still pronouncing it Beh-eh-man. I stepped away from the trolley and he extended a gnarled hand. "I'm Murnane of the *Globe*," he puffed. "Remember? Tim Murnane." He indicated the carrot-top. "This is my co-worker and crack cyclist, Sean Dennison. He does illustrations and caricatures for my column—when he's not racing bikes."

We shook hands all around. "My name is Beaman. As in seaman. Hard e."

"Sorry," he said, but didn't appear contrite. "Would you join us for a light meal?" Murnane asked. "We thought we'd try McGreevey's. I'd like to hear your views on your new duties with the club." He smiled and winked broadly. "My treat, of course."

The last thing I wanted to do was dine with Murnane and his friend. And answer questions about my new duties—or my past. After all, Soden had specifically warned me against associating with Murnane. "McGreevey's?" I asked, dragging it out to give me time to think of a way out. "I'm sorry, Mr. Murnane," I finally told him, "I have to find more permanent accommodations. I'm going to use the next few hours to do so. Perhaps some other time, sir?"

He put a strong arm on my back and urged me toward McGreevey's, three blocks down on Columbus. "Oh, hell, m'boy," he said, "Sean here knows every room to let within five miles of The Grounds. After our meal, he'll share his information with you, save you lots of time." He smiled broadly. "Come on now, lad, on to McGreevey's."

"'Nough said," chortled Sean Dennison, wedging his pencil behind his ear and swinging in beside us.

Murnane chuckled and nodded in agreement. "'Nough said."

It was a common joke in Boston. Michael T. (Nuff Ced) McGreevey was the best known of the team's fans, the leader of the "royal rooters" who attended games and shouted—or sung—their support of the local players, and their disapproval of Beaneater opponents. McGreevey's saloon, The Third Base, on the corner of Tremont and Columbus, was a popular meeting place for cranks, players, local sports celebrities, and gamblers. When arguments there became shrill or threatened to become violent, McGreevey would quiet the place by pounding on the bar and booming, "'Nough said!"

Dark, warm, and smelling of spilt beer, old peanuts, sweat, and grease, the saloon was already crowded when we arrived. The floors creaked and peanut shells crackled to the tune of scores of patrons. Photographs of base ball players adorned the walls behind the long oaken bar. Dozens of bats and balls lined the shelves. Polished spittoons were placed at intervals under the brass foot rail that ran the impressive length of the bar. We took a seat at one of the few tables in the place. The Irish prefer to drink standing up. For as long as they can, that is.

I had barely settled in when someone behind me spoke. "Yer a new 'un."

I looked up to locate the owner of the lilting voice. Standing at my shoulder, poised to take our order, her eyes riveted on me, was a voluptuous, blue-eyed young lady with hair the color of wheat and the most mischievous smile to bless me in many a day. Perspiration glistened on her face and ran in rivulets down her neck and between her ample breasts. Oh, my, she was candy.

"Are you addressing me?" I asked, flashing her my most practiced, innocent look. I relish this part of the game between men and women.

"I am," she replied brazenly. "These two gentlemen" —she indicated Murnane and Dennison— "are old news. 'Sides, one's married 'n the other's a mere child."

Though Murnane and Dennison guffawed and pounded the table, I sensed that they'd heard that remark, or similar ones, from the young lady many times.

"My stars, Molly," Murnane managed to gasp, "You're absolutely shameless."

"What you think cheeky," she said sassily, "I call curiosity." She looked boldly at me for what seemed a long time. "Name's Molly. Molly Muldine. I work here. Anyone wants to find me, kin find me here."

She left no doubt with her demeanor and saucy tone that any interest I had in her would be reciprocated.

Molly Muldine, was it? Well, well. I returned her bold look as I told her my name. She took our orders and brought them swiftly. As she set our drinks and meals before us, she stood so her soft thigh pressed against mine.

When she finally left us, Sean Dennison shook his head and whispered, "By the blessed skirts of Mary, she's one wild rose, she is."

I watched her move toward the back of saloon. "You don't see many women working saloons."

Murnane confirmed my observation with a nod. "Molly can take care of herself."

"McGreevey hired her on last summer and lunch crowds increased two-fold," Sean added.

The beer was luke-warm and the fare barely passable. Still, as I occasionally caught sight of Miss Muldine scurrying to tend customers, and listened to her laughter above the din, McGreevey's appeared more and more attractive. I wondered how many of the customers around me frequented McGreevey's so they could gawk at Molly.

Talk during the meal was general. Base ball, of course. Professor Horton's new pitching machine. Deepening problems in Cuba. The gold strike in the Yukon. Jim Corbett's upcoming bout with Jim Jeffries. John L. Sullivan's rumored comeback. The current cycling craze.

Young Dennison (I judged him to be a year or two younger than me) besides being a sketch artist, was a cyclist of growing prominence, it seems. A real scorcher. Good enough to compete for the rapidly-growing purses offered in city and commonwealth races. Murnane assured me of this several times over the protests of the blushing redhead. When Murnane finally turned to business Dennison seemed relieved to have the spotlight off him. Clearly "business" was the purpose behind Murnane's eagerness to pick up my supper tab. Lighting a cigar, exhaling loudly and pushing back in his seat, he smiled at me. "And what is it you do for the Bostons, lad?"

"Tim's a reporter," Sean Dennison explained unnecessarily, "He's a lovely way with words and a wondrous supply of them."

I nodded that I understood. "The usual administrative duties; nothing very exciting, I'm afraid," I told Murnane. I couldn't tell him much more if I wanted to. I didn't know what my full duties were.

"The usual, is it now, darlin?" Murnane smiled more broadly at me. "Routine work, eh?"

I shrugged. "Helping Mr. Conant raise money for the club." I rolled my shoulders to accentuate my disinterest. "And being whatever help I can."

His eyes, serious now, never left me. "What was all the commotion before the game today, eh? Haggerty wouldn't let me in The Grounds. Blathered something about an inventory."

I wanted no part of his questioning. I could sense my job hanging in the balance. I held up my hands like a crossing guard halting traffic. "I don't know. This was my first day," I told him in a bored tone.

"You weren't there, then?"

Eager to change the subject, I turned to Sean Dennison who had been sipping his beer, content to listen while making small sketches in his drawing pad. "If you have some suggestions for accommodations for me, I'd appreciate hearing them. It's getting late. And, frankly, it's been a long day for me." .

"Yer dodging me, lad." Murnane said lightly, jabbing at my arm with a stiff index finger. "Something's funny going on at The Grounds, 'n you know what it is."

"No."

He leaned closer to me. "Why didn't Germany Long play today?" His white eyebrows went up a notch. "He wasn't even at the field."

I shrugged my shoulders.

Murnane looked knowingly at Sean Dennison. "The darlin' lad *is* dodging me!" he exclaimed in mock horror.

The man was tough to read. He capacity for shifting from amusement to being dead serious made me uncomfortable. "No," I assured him again, "but I must find accommodations—and quickly. It's been a very long and hectic day for me."

Dennison's freckled face broke into a huge grin. He looked up as Molly Muldine whisked past our table lugging a loaded tray. His eyes followed her swaying buttocks as she swept through the crowd.

My eyes swung to her, too. I caught her thrusting a provocative hip and pointing a teasing finger at one of the gents at the bar. When I turned to Sean he was watching me.

He took the pencil from his ear and tapped it on the table. There was an enigmatic smile on his face when he spoke. "Oh, it'd better be Claire Denihur's for you, Will; for a certain, it'd better be Claire Denihur's for you."

Tim Murnane roared with laughter.

7

The storm returned and deepened as Sean and I made our way to Dorchester by way of the Washington and Dudley street lines. By the time we stepped off the royal purple streetcar at Magnolia the claps of thunder and flashes of lightning were virtually simultaneous. A torrent of black rain assaulted us. Sean removed the pencil from behind his ear and stuffed it into his pocket. He tucked his sketch pad under his arm inside his coat, snapped open his umbrella and pointed to the south.

"Take heart, Mr. Beaman," he shouted above the pounding of the rain, "It's a short distance only."

We sloshed past a row of fashionable homes, not always bothering to dodge the puddles that plagued our progress. Our shoes, stockings and trouser legs were quickly soaked, so what did it matter? My ankle, still tender from stepping on the bat, held up well despite our rapid pace.

Sean was no pup following Murnane now. He stayed ahead of me, suddenly the competitor. As a result, I not only got soaked from the water my own feet launched, but I was drenched by water thrown up in Sean's wake. Clearly, he'd learned a lesson or two about positioning and drafting from bike racing.

"Why is it so important to you that I stay at Miss Denihur's?" I hollered above the sound of the wind and rain, and of our feet pounding puddles.

"She needs the business," he shouted back. "It's not easy for a young woman in business for herself, especially one as particular as Claire Denihur."

"And what's your interest in her welfare," I panted. "A love interest, is she?"

"No, no. My interest is her sis, Caitlin," he said, laughing and leaping over a small black lake.

"And you stay there to be near Caitlin?"

"And because they need help. Their father's death left them with the house and a mountain of debt. Claire opened it to boarders and is trying to make a go of it." Sean seemed unaffected by our sprint along the wet street and through the blossoming puddles.

My breath, by contrast, was now coming in ragged gasps. "You see me . . . as additional coin . . . for the Denihur coffers?"

His shouted reply was almost lost in the wind. "Oh, no. It's more than that. You and Claire are destined for each other."

Could you imagine a more Irish observation than that? Claire and I were destined for each other. This red-headed son of the *auld saud* barely knew me, and he was arranging my marriage! Destined for each other, my Aunt Maggie! I didn't give a fig about Sean's chimerical visions. I needed a cheap room near trolley lines to the South End Grounds. That's all I cared about.

"Here," shouted Sean above the roar of the rain, and urged me up a walkway to a large gray home with dark green shutters. A two-story affair with multiple windows jutting from the mansard roof. We huddled, drenched and breathing hard at the front entrance which was protected by a small columned portico. A neatly printed sign by the door declared, "Room Available."

The neighborhood—what I could see of it with the help of the street lights—reminded me of sections of Minneapolis, no longer new but desperately trying to maintain its original grandeur. Like their Minneapolis counterparts, homeowners here had grafted mansard roofs on their stone and shingle classical-style homes for additional living space. Some had converted their buildings into duplexes; still others, like the Denihurs, had turned their private residences, including the low-ceilinged attics, into rooms for boarders.

Sean seized the knocker and rapped several times. "Some prudence and restraint is in order here, me friend," he told me, as he wrestled to shake his umbrella free of water and close it.

"What?"

He leaned toward me, spoke confidentially. "Look m' boyo, this is a prime situation. Good accommodations, excellent food, reasonable rates, nice location, but it's no sure thing. You can't just bust in, wave money, and get a room from Claire Denihur. No, sir."

I was more than a little put off by his assumption that I was some clumsy oaf. "I think I can pretend to be civilized long enough to secure a room," I huffed. "Trust me."

He waggled his head as if I'd misunderstood him. "No, I mean don't mention—"

The door opened just as the darkness turned white from a lightning bolt. The thunderclap, instantaneous with the strike, rattled the home. Sean and I ducked involuntarily.

The young woman didn't flinch. She stood in the lighted doorway, slim and tall with dark tresses and the milky skin of the Black Irish. She looked expectantly at me with the most luminous eyes I'd ever seen. "Yes?"

But her eyes shifted almost instantly to Sean. "Sean?" she said softly.

41

Sean eased past me, sweeping off his soaked bowler. "Yessum. This is Mr. Will Beaman, Miss Denihur, ma'am. Claire. He wishes to let a room."

She took a hard look at me before stepping back. "Please. Come in."

As we wiped our feet and brushed water from our clothing, I glanced around. The vestibule was cozily warm and tastefully decorated. Beyond, was an equally pleasant parlor. The easy chairs and stacks of magazines established it as a meeting place for boarders, although at the moment it was empty. Through the parlor I could see a dining room, dominated by a long, gleaming table.

Claire Denihur led us into the parlor, but did not ask us to sit. She looked at me with unfeigned interest. "I'm Claire Denihur. You're visiting our fair city?"

She was beautiful. My God, Boston was teeming with attractive women. In two days, I'd encountered three lovelies. First, at the ball park, the agitated but still tempting Anna Anspach, then at McGreevey's, Molly the Abundant. Now Claire. I knew nothing about Anna beyond that she had wonderful eyes and a mouth that begged to be kissed. Molly was voluptuous, and impudent in a vulgar but alluring way. Claire Denihur was stunningly beautiful. Hers was a classic, untouched, perhaps untouchable beauty. She was enough to make any chap dizzy with desire.

If Sean's truncated warning had put me on alert, her mesmerizing eyes short-circuited my alarm system. I gave her my most engaging smile and tried to ignore the fact that I was still dripping on her highly polished floors. "If I were merely traveling through, under the circumstances, I would certainly reconsider," I told her in my most seductive voice. Out of the corner of my eye, I saw Sean wince.

"And why is that, Mr. Beaman?" she asked cooly, her eyebrows inching upward.

My impeccable antennae told me retreat was in order. I shifted into my most unctuous manner. "I meant only that your city *is* a fair place, fairer than most, and I look forward to seeing more of it."

"I see. And for this you need a room?" The corners of her mouth moved almost imperceptibly upward.

"I do."

"And where are you employed, Mr. Beaman?"

"I'm with the Boston nine."

Sean, standing slightly behind Miss Denihur and facing me, grimaced, showing his teeth, and took a step backward. He shook his head frantically.

Miss Denihur leaned toward me as if she hadn't quite heard what I'd said. "Base ball!? You are a base-ballist?"

I couldn't read her. Clearly she was excited, but I couldn't judge if she were outraged by my comment, or terribly impressed. I opted for impressed. "I've spent several years in professional ball, yes ma'am."

Wrong choice. Sean's head was swiveling more vigorously now and he continued to ease back as if he feared Miss Denihur was going to become suddenly violent.

For her part, she was grim, her mouth now a thin line. "There'll be no base ball players staying in this house," she announced adamantly. "No, sir."

As a player on the field and with the females off the field, I prided myself on my swift moves. I moved quickly here. "No, No," I protested. "I'm not a *player* with the Bostons. I'm an *executive*. I work in the office— with the *owners*."

She mulled that over for several seconds as Sean and I held our breaths. "Well," she said tentatively.

Sean stepped toward me. "Last year I, ah, suggested a bachelor from the Beaneaters as a boarder. He, ah, imbibed more than he should have." He glanced at Claire Denihur and shrugged. "He . . . had to be . . . restrained."

"He had to be arrested and incarcerated," she corrected in a steely voice.

Sean lamely waved off her clarification.

She held up a long, white delicate finger, in the manner of a minister. "There'll be no players. That lout wrecked my home and nearly ruined my reputation. Nothing but a drunkard and ruffian," she said emphatically. "A hooligan," she scolded. She turned to Sean, hitching her eyebrows. "You should be ashamed of yourself for bringing that man here. You're through with that nonsense, I hope."

"Absolutely. By all that's holy, I swear—"

"You're not up to another of your schemes?" she asked suspiciously, in a low voice.

"Absolutely not," he mumbled.

I wasn't sure I was following this exchange. Apparently it involved more than Sean's introduction of an inebriated Beaneater into the Denihur boardinghouse last year but just what, I couldn't figure. Nor could I tell whether Claire Denihur was truly miffed with Sean, or whether she was scolding him with her tongue-in-cheek. The depth of Sean's guilt—and of his remorse—also escaped me.

Claire Denihur interrupted my rumination, smiling pleasantly and telling me, "Decent folks won't board where there are base-ballists staying."

I held my hands out as if to calm her down. "Things are much changed with the Bostons," I assured her. "Most current players are married, with families. Tenny, Duffy, Lowe, Stahl, and Lewis are all college men.

43

Much the same is true of those of us who supervise the team." I paused to allow her to absorb what I'd said; then, always more comfortable on the offensive, I added, "I'm a university man myself. Harvard."

"Oh, you are, are you?" she smiled. "My neighbors, the Doughertys, invited me to join them in watching the Baltimores against the Bostons last year. On Ladies Day, it was. Against my better judgment, I accepted. I saw Mr. McGraw and Mr. Jennings." She paused dramatically. "Both college men, I believe."

Ouch. This beautiful lady with the whitest and smoothest skin I'd ever seen, was nobody's fool. The Baltimore Orioles in general and their third base-shortstop combination of John McGraw and Hughie Jennings in particular were among the very rowdiest and profane in the National League. When you played the Orioles you'd better pull your cap on tight. And if you were sensitive to foul language, plug your ears.

I tried to put the best face on my situation. "The Beaneaters are known for their skill and civility every bit as much as the Baltimores are infamous for their rowdy and detestible antics," I assured her unctuously, much as a father might calm a small child. "As an *executive* of the ball club, I plan to do my best to enhance our reputation for gentlemanly play even further."

I held my lid before me, like some supplicant, rolling its brim in my fingers. "I assure you, Miss Denihur, my conduct is, and will remain, above reproach."

"There'll be no drinking or swearing in this house," she said.

"Of course not."

"And no young ladies in the rooms."

"Never," I sniffed. "The young ladies I meet would never enter a man's room unchaperoned," I assured her, piously.

Again, the movement at the corner of her mouth, the slight arching of the eyebrows. "Perhaps we could agree on a trial period of two weeks," she said. "Will you be staying that long?"

"Yes, ma'am. And that would be quite acceptable. What's the rate?"

"It's—" Her voice was lost in the sound of pounding on the front door. The sound was repeated, more urgent still.

We moved toward the entrance, and Claire Denihur opened the door. Hopping from foot to foot, clearly agitated, was a young lad, his clothes dark from the rain, his hair plastered against his skull.

Sean looked at me aghast. "Why, it's Mr. Murnane's cub from the *Globe*."

The boy shuffled nervously and peered at Claire Denihur. "'S'cuse m' ma'am. Is Sean 'ere?"

Sean moved up behind her. "What is it, boy?"

44

"Tim says tuh come quickly, Sean, some 'uns. . . ." The crack of thunder drowned out his sentence and the brilliant explosion of light that accompanied it made us all flinch—this time even the cool Miss Denihur.

Sean recovered first. "What's that, lad?"

"Some 'uns dead in Mr. Conant's office," the ragmuffin squeaked.

8

Ten minutes later I was on a Washington line trolley with Sean and Tim Murnane's towhead heading to The Grounds. At the boardinghouse the lad had responded to Sean's question about who'd died by hopping from foot to foot as if in the middle of an aquatic version of children's hop scotch, and mumbling " I dunno." He did say Murnane wanted Sean and his sketch pad at The Grounds quickly.

Sean pressed me to remain at the boardinghouse, arguing I should get acquainted with Miss Denihur and catch up on my sleep.

Undeniably, the thought of spending time with Claire Denihur was appealing. So was the idea of getting some rest. However, my blood was pumping and my imagination was racing regarding the death in Conant's office. For heaven's sake, my job might be over before it began! I promised Claire I would complete our transaction in the morning and followed Sean and the lad out into the rain.

The storm was abating as we hopped on the streetcar at Dudley. By the time we switched to the Washington line the clouds had broken and the moon shone through. Truthfully, I was eager to know more about the cryptic exchange between Claire and Sean regarding what she called his 'schemes.' She seemed inordinately suspicious of his motives and I wondered where— or if—I played any part in his *scheme*. However, the presence of Tim Murnane's cub, as Sean dubbed him, prevented me from broaching the subject.

Sean pointed his pencil at me. "Two bits it ain't Conant."

I waved him off, the short stay of Billy Ewing's coin in my pocket flashing in my mind. For the first time, I really looked at Sean. He was maybe 5'8" and stocky. His suit was worn, a tad too tight, and its pantlegs and sleeves a mite short. It revealed skin covered with freckles. His hair was bright red and parted on one side. For all his blockiness, his hands were slim, almost feminine.

"You bet on everything?" I asked.

"Everyone in my neighborhood does."

"Where's that, South End?"

"You got it. Before he died, my da' worked in a press shop on Atlantic. My ma'am took in laundry. Both died afore I was six. Turned into quite the hellion, I did. They put me in the Guardian Angel Home for Boys. John Haggerty used to treat us to a half-dozen games at The Grounds each year. He'd buy us peanuts and lemonade, make a day of it, don't you know? I got to know him pretty good. He saw me drawing players one game and liked what he saw. I was seventeen by then and he introduced me to Tim. When Tim found out that I could leave the Home if I was employed, he took me on as an apprentice. Then he convinced the *Globe* to hire me. Been with Tim four years, I have."

He regaled me with adventures, both good and bad, from his orphanage days. Though he grinned and chortled at his accounts of life in the Home and its personnel, his eyes betrayed him. His eleven years in the home clearly weren't as full of good times as he let on. He was in the midst of a tale involving the theft of chocolate from the kitchen one night when our arrival at The Grounds interrupted him.

We found a crowd in Conant's chambers. A policeman attempted to block our way, but was waved aside by Deacon Bill himself. So, Sean had been right: it wasn't Conant who'd died. He was very much alive, red-faced and sweating. The question remained: who was dead, then? Arthur Soden? J. B. Billings?

Nope. Neither. Soden and a very pale Billings were milling about with several uniformed bulls, a chicken-necked jasper who apparently was a medical examiner, a young man who appeared to be a plain-clothed detective, and Tim Murnane. The only missing person, so far as I could tell, was the corpse.

Glancing around, I saw no one who was not very much alive—and very agitated. No one seemed in a hurry to reveal the cause of the general milling. I caught Soden's eye and raised my eyebrows. "Who—?"

He didn't wait for me to finish, jerking his thumb toward a small room off the main office where the company safe was housed, and where the team's ledgers were shelved. "In there," he growled.

I peeked around the corner. There on the floor before an open safe was Anna Anspach, her strawberry-blond hair still occasionally stirred by the gusting wind from an open window. My stomach roiled and I found myself swallowing loudly as I took a few halting steps toward her.

"Don't touch nuttin'," one of the bulls bellowed.

He could have saved his breath. I wasn't about to touch her. She looked like she'd curled up to sleep, her arms still folded beneath her. Her hair was splayed around her head, largely obscuring her face. I could see no sign of violence, and no blood. Coins and currency were spread randomly around her and a money tray was partially hidden by a pale leg.

"How did she die?" I asked Soden who'd moved up behind me, white as milled flour, his steepled hands pressed to his mouth.

"Lightning strike. J.B. saw the strike from his window, heard the thunderclap, then the sound of something or someone falling. He rushed in, found poor Anna lying there. Checked her pulse. She was dead. A terrible

47

thing. Just terrible." He chewed at his thin, blue lower lip and his eye twitched nervously.

"She was putting money in the safe," the young detective added, sidling up beside Soden and flicking his finger toward the open window. "May even have been touching the steel safe when the bolt came through the window. Two others have been killed by lightning tonight. A window washer on Tremont, 'n an elderly woman in Franklin Park. There may be others. That's why the ambulance's slow getting here."

Sean squeezed in between Soden and the detective and began to make rapid sketches of the death scene.

"Has anyone done anything?" I asked, nodding toward the medical examiner and the policemen.

"We'll wrap this up quickly as soon as Dennis gets here," the detective told me.

"Dennis?"

"Dennis O'Dwyer. Lead detective. Handles suspicious deaths."

Soden filled his lungs as if he were about to hop off a pier. Then his words poured out in a rush. "He'll have nothing to do here. There's nothing suspicious. As soon as the ambulance arrives and removes the body, I'll contact her parents. They live in the Mission Hill district. Her father works at a brewery in the South End, I believe."

Mulling over what Soden had told me, I wandered over to Murnane who was leaning against the wall in the larger office, talking in low tones. He had sent the cub packing. Sean completed his sketches and joined us.

"How'd you find out about this?" I asked Murnane.

He expelled his breath noisily and wiped the inside of his derby brim with a finger. "I was coming to talk to Billings when I heard him screaming like a banshee. I ran to see what he was shouting about. Thought perhaps Soden or Conant had keeled over, sure. Big story." He shrugged dismissively, as if to say it's not going to be a big story now. "I sent for Sean in case I needed sketches." He paused and eyed me quizzically. "Of course, it does seem to be a small epidemic."

I froze at his allusion, knowing exactly where he was going with it. Nonetheless, I chose not to admit that I knew what he was alluding to. "Epidemic of what?" I asked, purposely furrowing my brow.

"I know that a player was taken to the hospital this morning. Bleeding badly and unconscious."

I glanced at Sean whose face remained blank, then met Murnane's gaze. "Really?"

"Could it've been Long? He didn't play."

I rolled my shoulders, then drew in Sean as a diversion. "You heard anything?"

"No," he muttered, "but, saints preserve us, *if* it's true and this *is* the second piece of bad news, the players ain't going to like it."

I snorted and again tried to move attention away from the attack on Long. "Obviously the players will be upset. Many of them knew and liked Anna." I didn't know if that was literally true, but it is the sort of thing one says on such occurrences, and at the moment I was treading water.

"No, no," protested Sean, "what I meant was that with all this bad luck—Germany's beating and Anna's death—the players'll think the team's jinxed. This is worse than running into someone who's cross-eyed or humped-back."

I noticed that he'd jumped to the conclusion that the earlier victim *had* been Long. I scoffed as best I could, muttering "Oh, for heaven's sake, Sean!"

"Superstitions shouldn't be ridiculed darlin', no sir," huffed Murnane. "We had a pickaninny mascot when I played in Philadelphia. Everyone rubbed his head before batting. By Christ, we never lost a game when that little rascal was at the park."

I was in no mood to discuss player superstitions. "Well, I don't think we ought to read too much into an act of nature," I told them. "Miss Anspach's death was pure fate."

At that moment, two white-clad ambulance men pushed in, one clutching a collapsible stretcher under his arm. "Dr. Yancey?" he called.

The medical examiner separated from the crowd and moved toward them. "I'm Dr. Yancey." He pointed to the room where Anna lay. "The body's in there."

I joined the parade following Yancey and the stretcher bearers into the annex. "Is she ready to be moved?" one of the ambulance men asked Yancey. "All the pictures taken and sketches made?"

"No. No. All that's unnecessary, Yancey said. "We have an accidental death here. Lightning strike. Just put her on the stretcher until Dennis gets here."

The young man nodded and gestured for his fellow ambulance man to unfold the stretcher and put it next to Anna. They hoisted her off the floor.

I froze. "Hold it," I shouted, and pointed.

There was a collective gasp. Lying on the floor was a small pistol, .22 caliber.

"Here now, what's this?" the portly doctor grumbled, frantically motioning for the bearers to return Miss Anspach's body to the floor. "Let's take a look here."

As they returned Anna to the floor, the stretcher bearers inadvertently turned her on the opposite side. Her hair fell away from her face.

Soden sucked in his breath. "Look there," he cried, reaching down and pushing aside her red tresses. There was a small black hole in Anna's right temple. That it was a bullet hole was clear, but bleeding was almost non-existent. "Great Lucifer," he murmured.

"Judas Priest!" Conant cried, his eyes bulging.

"No one comes in or goes out," the older policeman shouted, moving toward the door. "We're starting this investigation over from scratch." Taking his cue from his chum, the younger copper quickly ushered us back into Conant's office.

"What's this all mean?" Conant pleaded in a bewildered tone.

"It means," I told him, "The question now is, did she kill herself or did someone do it for her."

"It means," whispered one of the stretcher bearers to the other, "that ole Yancey's as useless as a scarecrow's pecker." He rolled his eyes. "Wouldn't know a well from a turd pit."

If Murnane heard the bearer's remark, he ignored it. He turned to the ashened-faced Soden. "You've hit a run of bad luck sure, Art. First a player, now this."

Soden pierced him with a look that would kill. "I don't know nothing about *a player*—'n neither do *you*."

At that point, an elongated man with a pipe screwed into the side of his mouth as if it were there permanently, burst into the room. He was wearing a nearly floor-length rain slicker and a rain-darkened derby. "What the hell's going on here?" he barked, taking in the room in a glance.

The stretcher bearer whispered to his associate, "Dennis O'Dwyer is here and I know a medical examiner, two bulls, and a young detective who have their tits in a ringer."

Later that night, having moved what few possessions I had to Claire Denihur's boardinghouse and settled into my new quarters, I brooded over the day's occurrences and my growing predicament. Tim Murnane was persistent, intent on sniffing out anything newsworthy. I wasn't sure I could escape his perseverence. On top of that, I'd already recognized that identifying Germany Long's assailant would stretch my skills as an amateur detective. If Anna Anspach's death wasn't a suicide, and was somehow connected to Long's beating, I had about as much chance as Coxey's Army had had in 1894 convincing Congress to provide poor relief. I was out of my depth. As the stretcher bearer had indelicately put it, useless as a scarecrow's pecker.

9

The following day the lunch crowd filled McGreevey's to over-flowing. Late patrons milled outside in the heat and drank their noon meal. Kids running the growler pushed past the doors, bumped through the crowd, and raced into the streets, the beer sloshing in pails thirstily anticipated by the boys' fathers and men friends. The going rate for pushing cans was a penny a growler. Enterprising lads used poles to carry a half dozen at once. The lads extended few courtesies to those hindering their progress.

Cranky and ill at ease, I was among those cramped on the sun-baked sidewalk. I had awakened despondant from another dream about my parents. In this one, my father stalked off the diamond after each miscue on my part. He'd stand at home plate and hit hot grounders to me. Manning my position as shortstop on a field otherwise unoccupied, I would lunge at the ball only to have it carom off my chest, my arms, my glove, my face. My father, scowling, would stride toward the sidelines, flipping the bat in disgust. Only the most abject, obsequious pleadings on my part would convince him to return and repeat our sequence. Sitting in otherwise vacant stands, my mother never changed expressions. So far as I could judge—and I struggled mightily to read her-she was neither dismayed by the antics of her spouse and offspring, nor entertained by them. At each miscue on my part she would fade, her image seeming to retreat and dissolve. Only to reappear solid and real as my father once more tossed the ball into the air and prepared to hit it.

The hot sun outside McGreevey's did nothing for my disposition. Or my attire. Perspiration had already soaked my hatband and wilted my starched collar by the time Tim Murnane and Sean Dennison found me and insisted that I join them inside. As a steady patron and famous personage Murnane was guaranteed one of the few tables in the saloon.

Still tired from my long day yesterday and grouchy from last night's familiar dream, I was thankful for the invitation to join them inside. Even before being discomfited by the dream where I endured the prolonged humiliation of failing my father and the pain of not being able to read my mother's expression, I'd been tired. I hadn't stopped by the American Hotel to collect my belongings until nearly 9:30 p.m. the previous night. And it had been past 10 when Sean and I finally reached Denihurs' and I was shown to my new quarters. Sean hung around for another hour, talking, while I put away my clothes and a few personal things. It took me another half hour to bathe. I finally got to bed just before midnight, thoroughly spent.

Molly Muldine shouldered her way through the crowd toward our table, looking very much like she'd gotten plenty of rest. All full of ginger, she was. Her fair skin shone with perspiration and her eyes sparkled. Wisps of her wheat-blond hair lay damp on her forehead. After nodding at Sean and Murnane, she turned to me. "It's Mr Beaman, ain't it?" She used the hard e.

Pleased that this handsome lass had remembered my name, I had to smile. "It is. And you're Miss Molly Muldine?"

"I am." She mimicked my tone and brevity.

After flirting with us briefly, she took our orders. She brought our beer quickly and assured us that our cheese, pickles, and hard-boiled eggs would follow in a wink.

Murnane swept his lid from his head and plopped it down beside him. He wiped perspiration from his forehead with the palm of his left hand and then ran his battered fingers through his thick, damp hair. With his right hand he jerked loose his cravat and loosened the top three buttons of his vest. "It's an oven in here, sure," he groused.

"I'll drink to that," Sean chuckled, and saluted us with his overflowing stein.

We drank thirstily, plunking down the steins in unison and wiping the foam theatrically from our lips. Three trained bears in a vaudeville act.

Murnane cupped his stein in both hands and moved it in small circles, smearing the water rings formed under it. "Heard anything regarding poor Anna Anspach?"

The casual manner of his question didn't fool me. By now I knew he was a serious man for all his surface humor and conviviality. I told him I didn't know any more about her death than I knew the previous night.

He assumed a look of exaggerated disbelief. "Isn't that your job, me darlin', to find out?"

I struggled to keep my face expressionless. I wasn't comfortable stone-walling Murnane and Sean. Both were gregarious types, men I enjoyed spending time with. Moreover, I was already in debt to Sean for finding me quarters at Denihurs' boarding house, and for introducing me to Claire. But could I trust them to keep my secrets? I wasn't sure yet, and until I was, I preferred to deflect their questions, to mislead them if necessary. "I'm Deacon Bill's flunkie," I told him. "Nothing more." I tried to sound bored with having to repeat my job responsibilities.

He nodded, but his facial expression made it clear he didn't believe me. "Billings mentioned that your father is a detective."

I shook my head vigorously, increasingly uncomfortable with Murnane's prying.

"My father is *not* a detective. He *runs* a detective agency. There's a difference. I haven't talked to him in more than a year and I never worked for him as an investigator. I don't know the first thing about sleuthing. Conant hired me to boom attendance. He took me on as a favor to my father who was an army chum of his." I hoisted my stein again and gulped from it.

Murnane and Sean contemplated my heated sililoquy in silence. Neither looked convinced, but each held up his hands in front of himself, as if to say, 'Okay, I'll buy that for now.' Murnane reached into the inside pocket of his jacket and removed a small notebook, rapidly flipping through its pages until he settled on one that he studied with the concentration of a biblical scholar. "Well, word is that the police have ruled Anna's death as 'inconclusive,'" he finally said. "Everyone down at City Hall seems to know about it. I just came from there."

Molly arrived with our food. "And will you be needing anythin' else?" she asked above the din.

We shook our heads. She put her hand on my shoulder in familiar fashion. "And would you like—?" Apparently sensing that we were preoccupied she made no further effort at banter.

When she'd sashshayed away and the three of us had managed to pry our eyes off her bum, I said, "If Conant and Soden have heard about the coroner's ruling, they didn't say anything to me this morning."

Murnane took another deep draught of his beer, flipped a few pages of his notebook. "According to the medical report Anna died of a single gunshot wound to the temple by person or persons unknown. She wasn't pregnant or, apparently, ill. Ownership of the gun is unknown, as is how the death weapon came to be in the room." Murnane's brogue tended to wax and wane with the circumstances. The more serious he was, the less accent he exhibited.

"No one was seen in the office but persons suppose to be there," I told him. "Conant. Billings. Soden. And Anna herself. What do your sources make of that?"

Before Murnane could answer me, Sean broke in, stabbing at the table with the blunt end of his pencil. "Have the bulls talked to Anna's parents? They may know something."

Murnane checked his notebook again. "City Hall gossip has it that the police interviewed the Anspachs, but learned nothing useful."

Sean smirked. "Parents are the last to know their childrens' shenanigans."

"Maybe," conceded Murnane, "but the Anspachs are adamant their daughter had no reason to take her own life. No romantic troubles. No personal problems." He paused. "And I trust my sources, darlin'."

We fell silent then, each tending to his plate. The three of us sat chewing, eyes vacant, like the cows I used to watch at the feed troughs on my grandfather's Minnesota farm. Good thing that the beer was cold and our waitress pretty and perky.

It was only after I'd swallowed the last of my meal that I picked up the conversation about Anna's death. Curious to know how much Murnane knew, I was confident I could couch my questions in an innocent manner, much like an unlucky witness to an unpleasant act. "Well, if someone shot her, robbery obviously wasn't the motive," I pointed out. "The money she'd been putting in the safe was still on the floor beside her. None was missing. I heard Conant tell Soden."

It didn't work. Murnane winked at me. "But you're going to get to the bottom of this, eh, darlin'?"

I drained my glass to give me time to judge the seriousness of his question, and to prepare a reply. Over the top of my glass I could see Sean leaning forward, grinning expectantly. I couldn't tell whether this was all personal curiosity on their part, or what they perceived to be Murnane's job as a reporter. "I thought we'd agreed I was no detective," I eventually replied, trying hard to appear puzzled. "And I'm the last one in the office to be told anything. Or consulted."

Murnane shook his head, smiling mischievously. "You're a tad too modest, b'hoy. The fact is, Billings told me you have *unusual* duties with the club."

I exploded, more for effect than from real outrage. "He didn't!"

Murnane held his hands out and made patting motions, as if to say, calm down, now. "Well, he hinted that your duties were a bit of a surprise to him," he said, retreating slightly.

I snorted to convey a sense of disbelief. "Libby's knickers! You're a reporter, Mr. Murnane. You're supposed to report facts, not make them up, or twist them for your amusement."

He winked at Sean who was busily sketching me, then turned to me. "You're telling us—serious now—that you have no other duties than to be Deacon Bill's flunky on attendance and other financial matters?" He arched his eyebrows and held his pencil poised above his notebook, ready to scribble my answer.

"That's exactly what I'm telling you, Mr. Murnane. For the third time! When it comes to that organization, I'm lower than a midget with a foot fetish."

He guffawed and rolled his eyes for Sean's benefit. "Just financial matters?" he said, making still another try. When I didn't respond right away, he turned to Sean, smiled broadly, and held out his hand palm, making beckoning motions with his fingers.

Sean winced, ceased drawing, and scrounged around in his pocket and extracted a coin that he slapped into Murnane's palm. Obviously, Sean Dennison had just lost a bet.

Murnane poked the coin into his vest pocket. "What about the player brought to the hospital? Was it Germany Long?"

The man was tenacious, I'll give him that. I knew I had to disengage. If I sat there longer it was going to be tougher and tougher to dodge Murnane's increasingly pointed inquiries. I straightened up, dabbed at my mouth with my napkin, and picked up my hat and dropped two quarters by my plate, enough to cover my meal and a generous gratuity for Molly. "I must excuse myself. I have an appointment with a jeweler—-a Mr. Ingram—about buying advertising on our outfield fence. I'm already late." I touched the brim of my hat with a finger. "Mr. Murnane. Sean."

"It's time you started calling me Tim," Murnane said, smiling, and bid me farewell with a gesture of his hand. Sean too waggled his fingers goodbye in the exaggerated motion of a vaudeville comedian.

I was almost to the door when Molly stopped me. She stood there beaming, vital, glistening with perspiration. The real berries.

"I'll be free after seven this evening, Mr. Beaman," she said, and locked her eyes on mine. When I hesitated, she added, "If you want to take a stroll with me, that is, Mr. Beaman." She said my name in an exaggerated, lilting, teasing way. The pale tops of her ample breasts rose and fell as she stood there seemingly looking into my soul.

I stared into the blue pools that were her eyes, seeing the moral lapses they promised, I remembered the soft strains of "I need thee every hour, most gracious Lord" I'd heard every Sunday as a young boy in the Lutheran Church on Gundersen Street.

Her eyes sucked me in, the promises becoming ever clearer. Despite my desire to turn over a new leaf and to become a better man, I heeded the words of the old Protestant hymn now as lightly now as I had as a youngster.

"Seven it is, then, Miss Muldine," I said, and stepped out into the boiling afternoon.

10

Mr. Ingram, the jeweler, would have to wait. I was determined to talk with Anna Anspach's parents. I didn't need Sean to remind me that parents frequently didn't know what their children were up to. My experience with my own father proved that often they did. I was going to talk to Anna's folks. Not one to believe in coincidences, I needed to see if there was any connection between the attack upon Long and Anna's death. Obviously, different weapons had been used in the two attacks. But too much violence in too short a time in too small an area, involving a small organization, troubled me.

I crossed the street and lingered in the shade to confirm that Tim and Sean weren't following me. Finally convinced they weren't, I swung up on a trolley. The ride to the Anspach's was brief, but time enough to contemplate my recent impetuousness in agreeing to meet Molly. I was determined to get to know Claire Denihur better. She was an absolute corker. But it wasn't going to be an easy matter. Clearly she had standards and a fixed attitude toward base ball and those connected with it. And there was always the possibility that she was spoken for, although Sean should know, and his actions suggested she wasn't. Molly, on the other hand, was a peach in the hand. A fetching, juicy peach. What with the look she'd given me, perhaps apple was a better comparison. Eden's apple.

On one level, the issue was clear to me. Claire represented what I hoped was my future. Molly was like many of the women who had soured relations between my father and me, and had led to my having to leave Minneapolis. But like most issues this one was murkier than that. Claire was cool, Molly sizzled. Claire appeared unavailable. Molly was not. My weakness was that I seldom deferred gratification. And, as with my promise just minutes before to meet Molly later today, I almost never acted on reason when it came to young ladies. By the time I reached the Mission Hill district, I still hadn't reached a resolution regarding Claire and Molly.

I found the Anspachs' residence, in a row of working-class clapboards in lower Roxbury. Bunched together as if no square of ground could be wasted, the homes showed age and wear. Eaves and roofs sagged, doorways were misaligned, some windows were boarded, paint was faded. Even the cursory glance I gave the neighborhood revealed much of its history, past and present. Older Irish and German families were being eased out by an influx of Jews. The small shops wore a variety of signs appealing to various ethnic groups. The newer signs were in Hebrew. I again consulted the address I'd gotten from Soden, and moved toward the Anspach's door.

Mrs. Anspach answered my knock immediately. She was a large, sagging woman whose size and gray hair did not fully obscure the beauty that once had graced her. She appeared exhausted.

"Mrs. Anspach?" I asked, "Mrs. Gertrude Anspach?"

She stared at me without speaking, her eyes red-rimmed.

"I'm Will Beaman from the Boston Base Ball Organization."

She continued to stare silently at me. Anna had had no accent when I'd spoken to her, but there was something 'old world' about her mother's looks and demeanor.

"Verstehen Sie mich, Frau Anspach?" I asked in labored German.

"Ja," she said wearily, "I understand. Vas iss it?" Though her German accent was heavy, her voice was soft, like that of a young girl's.

I gently explained that I wanted to express the team's condolences, and that I had a few questions to ask on its behalf.

Her tired, red eyes bore into me. "I haff alretty zee kvestions answert yesterday all evening mit der police."

"I understand that, Mrs. Anspach," I told her, "I'm sorry to bother you in your time of trial. But we want to find out what happened to your daughter. And this is the only way to do that."

"The police vill do dat."

I bobbed my head in agreement. "They'll try, Mrs. Anspach. But they're very busy. They have a good many incidents to investigate."

She stepped back in resignation. "Come," she said in an exhausted voice.

The inside of the Anspach home was as drab as the outside. But neat. Everything, shabby as it was, was dusted and in place. Furniture, lamp shades, and curtains were clean. The doilies on the sofa and chairs appeared freshly laundered, as did Mrs. Anspach's worn dress. This was the home of poor but proud people. The living room was as sweltering as McGreevey's. Two small windows stood open, their curtains hanging slack, as if they too were suffering from heat exhaustion.

A woman, virtually a twin of Gertrude Anspach, appeared from what I supposed was the kitchen, wiping her hands on a large white towel. She said nothing, merely stared at me as if she'd never seen a visitor in the house before. Mrs. Anspach pointed at her.

"Herr, ah, Beaman, this ist mein Schwester. My sister. Sonia. Sonia Kruetzer."

I smiled and bowed slightly. "Mrs. Kruetzer."

The woman tipped her head, but said nothing.

Mrs. Anspach motioned me to a threadbare easy chair. On the table next to my right arm was a photograph of Anna and her mother. Anna's stylish suit and flower-covered summer hat accentuated her mother's plain attire.

Mrs. Anspach and her sister sat on a sofa across from me. Getrude Anspach held a small paper fan in her hand. She asked if I'd like tea, but I declined, encouraging her and her sister to have some if they wished. Apparently, they didn't.

"You knew my Anna, then?" Gertrude Anspach asked, fluttering the fan to cool her face.

"I met her once, briefly. She struck me as a fine young lady, and very pretty."

She smiled shyly. "She vas pretty, ja. Und gut." Her eyes lost their focus and she seemed to retreat within herself.

I leaned forward, using my movement to focus her attention. "Mrs. Anspach, forgive me for prying, but Anna lived here with you and your husband, yes?"

She started. "Und mit Sonia. Ja." She shook her head as if to shake the German words from her brain. "Yess."

"What did Anna do in her free time, away from her job?"

Mrs. Anspach spoke slowly, deliberately. "Visited zee church every Zonday. The Mission Church. Joint her church friends zumtimes for zocial oc... what you say, party." She shrugged and again fanned herself. "Just zocials und der like."

"She went out often in the evenings?"

Gertrude Anspach looked at her sister as if to confirm the answer she was about to give me. "Mit church friends. Ja." Again the impatient shake of the head. "Yess."

"Did she have a young man?"

After a lengthy pause when I thought she'd retreated once again, she shook her head. "Nein. Just boice in the church group." The fan now hung limp in her hand, seemingly forgotten.

"Just church boys? No steady beau?"

She looked uneasy. Glanced at her sister. "Nein."

"No young gentleman at work?"

Her eyes widened slightly and flicked toward the door. "Nein. . . No."

I nodded, as if in understanding. "Again, I apologize for being so inquisitive, Mrs. Anspach, but it might help us find out something that will explain Anna's death. Do you know anyone who might do her harm?"

She shook her head no.

"No one had threatened her?"

Both women shook their heads. "But someone killed mein daughter," Gertude Anspach sighed.

"Did she seem depressed recently? Worried?" I asked.

"No."

I recognized in her expression and gestures the same evasiveness and duplicity that doubtless my father had seen many times as I tried to deflect his questions about my comings and goings. "She wasn't moody? Or angry?"

She hesitated and her eyes shot toward the door. Again, the frown and the slow shake of her head.

Sonia Kreutzer stirred, leaned forward. "Zumtimes."

I shifted forward, hoping to encourage her to say more by my body language.

"Sometimes?"

Gertrude Anspach put a hand on Sonia Kreutzer's shoulder and eased her back against the sofa. All the while shaking her own head in the negative. "Nein. No. No. No more than any utter girl her age. Nein."

Gertrude Anspach's actions and Sonia Kreutzer's now clamped jaw convinced me of the futility of pursuing that line of thought. I changed the subject for the moment. "What did she spend her earnings on?"

As if she'd suddenly made up her mind about something, Sonia Kruetzer pushed forward, eyes bright, eager to share. "Mr. Beaman," she said in a surprisingly strong voice, "You must unterstand. Our Anna—"

She never finished. The front door swung open and a huge man tumbled into the room. A muscular man with matted, carpet-thick gray hair covering his arms, chest, neck and head. He wore heavy canvas pants, held up by wide green braces, and a heavy, soiled work shirt rolled at the sleeves and unbuttoned at the collar to reveal a badly discolored undershirt. Large perspiration stains hung like bags under each arm. Clinging to him was the strong odor of beer and hops and sweat, suggesting he had come directly from his shift at the brewery. He was the boogie man of my youth.

Stopping in his tracks, he glared at me, then at his wife. "Vat der hell?" he sputtered. "Wer ist?"

Gertrude Anspach lurched from her chair, surprisingly agile, eyes wide. "He's from Herr Conant's und Herr Soden's office, Karl," she shouted, hastily. "Und he's trying to find vat 'appened to our Anna."

He glared at me and pointed to the door. "Rausmit'n. Mach schnell."

I stayed in my chair, afraid that he was in no mood for any sudden movements from me. I'd been in my share of brawls. I'd even won a few, what with my size and training. But now wasn't the time to resist Anspach. It was his living room and he looked like a man who'd be unimpressed by my size and youth. Instead of rising, I held up my hands in a conciliatory gesture. "Mr. Anspach, sir, I'm trying to help. I was asking your wife if Anna had been dep—"

His face darkened even further. "Gott! Sonia—"

Sonia bolted from the sofa, waving her hands and waggling her head in denial and shouting, "Nein. Nein, nein."

Gertrude Anspach stood beside her husband mimicking her sister with her hands and denials.

"Anna did not kill herself!" Karl Anspach raged.

The women were still fluttering their hands and loudly protesting Sonia's innocence as Karl Anspach lunged toward me. For a big man he moved swiftly, stepping in front of my chair, seizing my coat lapels and hoisting me out of the chair. Fearful that he'd tear my new suit, I didn't resist. I even tried to anticipate his intentions and move with him to minimize my chances of being hurt. Or my new suit being torn. Still, he jerked me up, without apparent effort.

"Raus, gottdammit."

My assessment of his strength was quickly confirmed. His hands were like steel clamps. He dragged me to the still-open door and heaved me unceremoniously out into the street. I'm a good-sized gent. I can handle myself, as I've said. But only my athletic ability kept me from being pitched headfirst into the gutter. I managed to stay on my feet and hang on to my hat, but with all the dignity of a naked man at a Shaker prayer circle. I heard the Anspachs' front door slam shut behind me.

11

So much for Will Beaman, super sleuth. Perhaps my lies to Murnane and Sean about my lack of experience in detective work were not as far-fetched as I'd imagined. I looked around to see if my brusque exit from the Anspachs' had been witnessed. Seeing no one, I straightened up and took a hasty inventory of my suit. Satisfied that my clothing was in better shape than my confidence, I considered the last few minutes. On one hand, as humiliated as I was to have been handled so easily by Karl Anspach, I could understand his reluctance to open his door to anyone with questions about his daughter. On the other hand, I didn't doubt for a moment that Sonia Kreutzer was about to confide important information to me when Karl Anspach interrupted. I'd have to return to their cramped, steamy home again and confront its secrets.

In the meantime, I had to put Molly Muldine behind me. Maybe Karl Anspach had shaken some sense into me. Sparking Molly made no sense. It was Claire who fascinated me. Considering my attraction for her, it would be unmanly to use Molly selfishly. And out of character with my hopes for personal reformation, and I was determined to take the high road for once in my pathetic life. This was going to be our first—and last—tryst, as much for Molly's sake as mine. Brimming with fresh resolve, I strutted toward the trolley line, chesty, like John Philip Sousa at a G.A.R. parade.

By the time I got to McGreevey's my shirt was clinging to me and my hair was damp under my skimmer. Clouds had rolled in, swollen and bruised. While the disappearance of the sun threw the city into shade, it did nothing to dissipate the humidity. Boston was a huge pewter-gray oven.

I stepped aside for a half dozen boisterous customers spilling from McGreevey's, and slipped into the dim, noisy tavern. There I quickly reviewed my strategy for terminating my relationship with Molly. The plan was simplicity itself, and compassionate, I thought: a cordial and harmless hour or so with her, then a gentle goodbye that would leave no doubt in her mind of my intentions to spend my time with others. There would be none of the complications of past liaisons, and hence, none of the heat and acrimony that characterized the end of those relationships.

Unfortunately, my scheme failed to fully take into account two critical elements, Molly's persistence and my own feeble character. To put it into base ball parlance: I was a wonderful batsman—had the proper stance and grip, good balance, kept my shoulders square and my keen eyes wide—until Molly starting throwing curves. Her curves.

I met her coming out of the McGreevey's backroom. She'd freshened up and changed into a dark blue skirt with a crisp white waist jacket. Her pale blue summer blouse was scooped at the neck and fluffed at the shoulders. She'd also put on a small, flowered bonnet with a half veil, and she carried a light blue, transparent parasol. Oh, my, she was pure pie. This was not going to be easy.

I greeted her, offered her my arm, and we moved through the catcalls and good-humored jesting of patrons and Molly's fellow workers. They were having us on, but we ignored them the best we could and stepped out into the heat.

We hopped a trolley to Copley Square, then another down Boylston to the subway under construction. Molly opened her parasol, flipped it over her shoulder, and began to gaily twirl it. In the face of the stifling heat, I suggested we find a cool creamery, but she insisted on a promenade. Bowing to her wishes, we strolled in and around the new Underground Station, viewed the spanking new monument to the commonwealth's Negro soldiers in the Civil War, and leisurely circled the La Tourain Hotel springing up on Tremont.

"It's absolutely beautiful," Molly said, craning her neck to view the hotel's top floors.

"It's mighty impressive," I agreed.

"Have you seen the Parker House Hotel on Bosworth?" she asked. "It's ten stories high and it's going to have water closets, curling irons, and telephones in each room!"

"And the room temperature will be regulated for the pleasure of each guest," I told her. "Sunday's *Globe* had a story on it."

"Oh, let's go look," she squealed. She urged me toward Bosworth and I let myself be ushered along. She was quite a tease as we perambulated, laughing and flirting, leaning into me, pressing her bosom against my arm. She kept up a steady stream of banter, stumbling to correct herself when her grammar or diction failed her, as they often did. Even as she bubbled and gushed she seemed aware of each person who passed us. She paid particular attention to hold her chin high and to beam at me when well-dressed couples neared us. She also made a concerted effort to say something witty to me once strollers were within earshot, speaking with more volume than necessary. Miss Molly Muldine was on parade, showing off her beau to her betters, it seemed, demonstrating she was every bit as clever and as well connected as they were. It was amusing to observe. I found myself joining in for the sheer fun of it, swaggering a bit and laughing too loudly when pedestrians approached us.

63

Despite the heat, we promenaded around the blocky, gray, limestone Parker House, admiring the five new floors that were being constructed upon the original five stories. Once our interest in the Parker House was exhausted, we rested on a bench in a grassy spot across the street from its massive Italian marble entrance. Workers and street peddlers had peeled off their coats, rolled up their sleeves, and opened their vests. Men tilted their hats back or used them as fans.

Seemingly oblivious to the heat, Molly closed her parasol and set it on the bench next to her. "Well, Mr. Will Beaman," she said in that teasing, formal way of hers, "And what is it you do for those rich bosses of yours?"

"I help them stay rich," I teased her back.

"And just how do you do that?"

"I sell advertisements and plan promotions to entice people to games."

"Like Ladies Day?"

"You know about Ladies Days?"

"Of course," she giggled, and snuggled closer. "Even the Park Theater has Ladies Days when the Bostons are out of town."

"Well, then, yes. Exactly like Ladies Days."

She snuggled closer, her face now but inches from mine. Her skin was flawless, her eyes as clear as a Minnesota lake. "And will you take me to the game on the next Ladies Day, Mr. Will Beaman?" Her breath was the sweetest cinammon.

My Sweet Aunt Maggie. She *was* cherry pie. A ball game wouldn't upset my strategy all that much, would it? I mean, I didn't have to dump her after a single walk to get my message across, did I? After all, she wouldn't read too much into an invitation to attend a ball game, especially on Ladies Day. Besides, my father used to tell me that flexibility characterized the great generals of his war. My grand strategy could remain intact, even if I had to maneuver a bit.

"Of course, I'll take you to the game," I told her. I suspected that there'd been few young men who'd ever said no to Molly Muldine.

Satisfied that that was now taken care of, she squeezed my arm and moved back to her original subject. "And do those rich employers of yours trust you with the money you collect?"

I waved off her implication that I was a confidant of Conant's or Soden's. "I get to touch the money for about five minutes," I laughed. "Before three other people stack it, count it, and tuck it away in a safe."

"Surely they pay you handsomely for your services."

Hers seemed an indelicate and indiscrete question. Determined to keep our conversation light and amusing, I scoffed. "Hardly. Mr. Conant and Mr. Soden are not noted for their generosity or philanthropy." I squeezed her arm in the same teasing way she'd squeezed mine. "You probably make more in gratuities in a single day than I do with the parsimonious owners of the Boston nine."

"You're funning me," she said, and dropped her head on my shoulder. "And I don't believe you for a single minute." Then, as if remembering something important, she added, "And do you have a business card, Will?"

"I do."

I was getting more than a little perplexed by her constant fishing into my business, but I dug into my vest pocket and withdrew one of the cards Mr. Conant had supplied me. I handed it to her.

She studied it with great interest and at great length even though it read, simply, 'Mr. Will Beaman. Assistant Treasurer, Boston National League Base Ball Club.' "May I keep this?"

"Of course." Conant had given me two dozen which he'd had printed up and I'd found few excuses to give them away.

She dropped the card in her purse. Looking at me with wide eyes, she said, "Tell me about your duties."

She was like a terrier with a rat. I began to wonder who was the sleuth here.

"There's really nothing to tell you. It's all very routine," I told her, affecting a bored tone.

"Still, I want to know," she pouted.

And so I told her. Some of it, at least. We sat there for thirty minutes as I dribbled out the details of my official functions. Molly continued to press against me, kneading my hand in both of hers. Whether she was taking in the details or simply content to hear the sound of my voice, I couldn't tell. Didn't really care, actually. When I finished, she said nothing.

My mind was already drifting back to the assignment Art Soden had thrust upon me. I knew little more today than I knew when Soden had surprised me with his demand that I investigate the assault upon Germany Long. Yet, I was sitting here with a young woman who worked in a pub frequented by ball players. It occurred to me that Molly might know a good deal about what the players did and talked about away from the South End Grounds. I'd be better off listening to her than sitting here explaining my job. I squeezed her arm to attract her attention.

"Lots of the Beaneaters patronize McGreevey's, do they?"

"Um hmm." It was more a sound than an answer, a noise uttered by a sleepy child.

"Do you know any of the players?"

Again, the sleepy acknowledgment.

'Which players?" Now I was the terrier with the rodent.

She pulled away and looked up at me, as if she'd just realized I was serious. "Most of them. Mr. Selee comes in. So does Mr. Bergen and Mr. Klobedanz. Mr. Tenny, too. 'Sweet Billy' comes in all the time. He's a sweetheart, and a sport."

Well, that was a start. Perhaps the hour or so with Molly wouldn't be a complete waste of my time. I remembered John Haggerty's remark to me about Billy Ewing's reputation with the ladies and decided to push further.

"You know Billy Ewing?"

"He took me to the vaudeville several times. We also attended a prizefight. It was sooo exciting."

"Was it, now?" It sounded to me like Molly and Billy Ewing were more than passing acquaintances. "He took you to a boxing match?"

"We saw a colored pugilist. Paddy Ryan licked him quick."

That sounded to me like one of those clandestine bouts one might stumble upon in the North End some weekend. As I mulled over her comment, I watched a matched pair of bays trot past, a beautiful lacquered chaise behind them, its passengers two handsome women, perhaps mother and daughter, in canary yellow outfits.

"You still do things together, you and Billy?"

She hesitated. "No. Not for several months."

"You see other players after work?" I could ask indelicate questions, too.

"No."

"Do you know Germany Long?"

She poked playfully at my arm.

"No. Oh, I know who he is. Why are you asking me all these questions?"

"Just making conversation."

She lapsed into silence and I let the stillness settle around us. I'd learned as little from her as I had from the Anspachs. When it came to investigative skills I was a pig at the grand opera. Mindful of all this, I decided to get Molly home and end this charade.

"We'd better fetch you a cab."

Molly straightened up and looked around. Seeing that I was right and that no one was paying attention to us, she swiftly brushed my lips with hers. "Now, Mr. Will Beaman," she whispered, "you *are* going to be a gentleman and see your lady friend home? The light is nearly gone, but we can walk."

"Absolutely, my dear Miss Muldine," I said, matching her teasing formality. I stood and offered her my arm. "And where is your home?" I asked gravely, bowing slightly. A gentleman can be gentlemanly, even when he's planning the cruel business of severing ties with a young woman.

Her apartment was south of the Parker House. We eschewed public transportation in favor of walking, though the light was fading fast. The street lamps were already on, causing our shadows to swing in half arcs at our feet as we passed.

Her apartment house was in poor shape, squalid in fact, as were surrounding buildings. A three-story brick affair, it contained apartments accessed from a single front door whose glass was cracked and partially covered with boards.

We stood briefly in front of the dilapidated building in the rapidly dying light and stared silently at the edifice. She pressed closer and encircled me with her arms. When I turned to her she rose up on her toes and bit my lower lip softly.

I stepped back, anxious to separate, to prevent any further intimacy. "It's been a lovely afternoon, Molly. Thank you."

"The stairs are dark, Will, will you walk me up, then?" she asked in a breathy voice.

I hesitated, alarmed by the tone of her question. "I suppose so, yes." What gentleman wouldn't see his companion to the door under these circumstances?

At the top of the stairs in the dim hall in front of her door, we paused. I stepped back to give her way to the door, but she held me, moved with me, and looked into my eyes, our faces only inches apart. She pulled my head down and kissed me, crushing my mouth against hers. Her tongue probed, and found mine.

Our tonsorial fencing ceased only when I pulled suddenly back. But I could retreat only so far, as she clung tightly to me. Her snowy breasts swelled out of the top of her dress as she flattened against me. The aroma of talcum powder and soap and warm flesh enveloped me, overpowering the stale, dusty odor of the hallway. My resolve to stand up to her took a decidedly familiar turn. I was standing up to her, all right, and as she wiggled against me, we both knew it.

"And would you like to come in, Mr. Will Beaman?" she whispered, her eyes soft and unfocused.

My resolve to be a better man dissipated quickly in the sweet intoxication of her cinnamon-scented question.

"I would, indeed," I told her, shame prickling my scalp.

12

The gathering was small. Less than two dozen people huddled in the shade of a sprawling hickory tree, before an open, freshly-dug grave. A cheap coffin rested at one side of the burial pit, a mound of damp soil on the other. Most of the attendees were elderly, doubtless friends of Anna's parents, perhaps relatives. They wore worn but formal clothes, the best apparel of working folks. The low, guttural sound of German wafted among them as they conversed somberly while waiting for the services to commence.

It was another brutally hot day, bright enough to make people squint and shield their eyes with hands and arms. Two large dogs lay sleepy-eyed in the shade, panting heavily. I struggled to ignore the lingering soreness in my back and legs, the result of keeping up with Molly's demands two nights ago. As tender as my body was, it was my injured conscience that tormented me. For a few hours of pleasure I had broken promises to myself, and to others. I didn't know which was harder for me to stomach, my embarrassment or my anger over my moral lapse. Or, perhaps my queasiness stemmed from a realization that I'd never met a woman as uninhibited in bed as Molly, and with my track record I knew it was not going to be easy walking away from her. So much for the reformation of Will Beaman.

I moved toward the gravesite. My hope was that I could spot someone among Anna's mourners who might provide a lead to her killer—if she'd been murdered—and perhaps a link between her death and the assault upon Long, if there was one. Near the gravesite, I found John Haggerty, large hands folded in front of him, his lumpy work shoes recently brushed. Sidling up to stand next to him, I nodded hello. He responded with a quick dip of his head.

"Well, boyo," he said, "There's less coal dust under your eyes today."

I absorbed his friendly sarcasm without comment or expression. Standing silently shoulder to shoulder with Haggerty, I noticed Tim Murnane and Sean Dennison across the grave from us, heads bowed. Each looked up briefly and bobbed his head in salutation. Sean's was a dark suit, like his others a mite short for him, but newer than any I'd seen him wear before. I slowly surveyed the remaining mourners, tugging at my collar which was damp and threatening to garrote me.

"I don't see Conant, Soden, or Billings," I whispered.

Haggerty screwed up his face. "There's labor and there's management," he muttered sourly.

"She was Conant's stenographer!" I seethed. "Surely *he'll* show up." I glanced toward the road to see if new carriages had arrived. None had. This was going to be a modest gathering.

"She was a dime a dozen as far as those bloody sods are concerned," Haggerty said. "Jayzus, lad, They've probably already hired her replacement." He watched me scanning the cluster of carriages out at the road. "A dollar says they don't show."

I rejected his bet with a wave of my hand. I knew he was right, but it irked me, nonetheless. It wouldn't' have taken an hour to attend the funeral, and it would've been a gracious gesture to make. So much for gestures. It would be easy to excuse my own failings in light of their incredibly bad behavior, but candor made me admit their failures of character did not diminish my own.

A tall, pale man with an impressive wart on the side of his nose stepped forward and in a surprisingly deep voice began the service. He spoke in German. Having worked and played with the sons of German farmers as a youngster, I could follow the gist of his comments, if not each word. When I concentrated, that is.

I didn't concentrate very well. I kept eyeing those who'd gathered to pay their respects to Anna and her family, as interested in some respects in those not there as those who gathered around the grave. A small group of elderly working men and two ruddy-faced grave diggers stood several feet away. The shovelmen, jackets off and sleeves rolled above their elbows, leaned impatiently on their tools, anxious to complete their hot and exhausting task and hustle off for a bucket or two of suds.

Haggerty nudged me. "There's Captain Hugh Duffy, Germany Long, and Kid Nichols."

I followed his gaze. The three players were standing off to the shovelmen's left. Long's hand was bandaged as were his cheek and forehead. The ball players, in fashionable suits, stood out in the crowd. They were the only members of the Beaneater nine there. Murnane had told me that Anna was an avid fan of the team, a genuine crank. She'd take breaks from her office duties to watch a few innings of each home game. Players, Murnane insisted, teased her about her interest in the bachelors on visiting teams. Strange that only three of her friendly kidders had deemed her funeral important enough to attend. Nichols, as Marty Bergen had told me at the game, was a churchman and 'had to be nice.' Duffy was captain of the team and probably was there in that capacity. I didn't know what to make of the fact that Germany Long was there.

The Anspachs stood to my left with Sonia Kreutzer. Gertrude Anspach's shoulders shook uncontrollably and she constantly reached under her heavy veil to wipe her eyes. Sonia Kreutzer clutched her close. On the other side of her, Karl Anspach stood absolutely still, eyes glued to the casket containing his daughter. His eyes stared in pain and confusion, like a bull smacked in the forehead with a shovel. His huge, powerful hands clenched and unclenched.

I was so mesmerized by Karl Anspach's stunned grief that the service was nearly over before I realized who besides Beaneater players and owners were noticeably missing from the mourners. Young people. There were no men and women Anna's age! No friends from her church she allegedly chummed with. No young men from the social clubs she supposedly frequented. Anna had been a very attractive young woman. Where were her men friends? Pretty Anna without young male mourners was like P. T. Barnum's dogman without fleas.

Questions regarding the absentees swirled in my mind. Swirled long enough to conjure up more guilt, I must admit. After all, was it any less disrespectful to attend a funeral and pay no attention, than simply to forgo attending in the first place? I tried to focus on the now impassioned words tumbling out of the clergyman's mouth, but the rapidity of his speech defeated me. After a few moments, my gaze drifted once again to Duffy, Long and Nichols.

It was at that moment I saw the figures. Halfway up a rise in the dark shade of a copse of trees stood two shadowy shapes. At first I did not realize what I was looking at. There was just something about the dark profile of the trees that was amiss. It was only after staring for several minutes that I realized two individuals—both males, I think—lolled among the trees. They appeared to be observing the service.

I squinted against the bright sun, trying to separate the deep shadows of the trees from the even darker shadows of the figures. Even though I could make out no details, there was something familiar about both. Something about their silhouettes, their posture. I stepped away from Haggerty and, slowly and as unobtrusively as possible, I worked my way to my right, hoping that a different angle might improve my view.

As if they were watching me, both figures slipped deeper into the copse as I maneuvered out of the crowd. Their movement provided me a glimpse of the person on the right. He'd moved quickly through a small patch of sun and the light momentarily caught his pale yellow suit. I strained to get a better look, but both figures retreated rapidly up the rise, for the most part keeping the trees between us.

I closed my eyes, struggled to bring up the quick photograph captured in my mind when the sun had momentarily revealed something of the man's line and color. I knew the man, I was sure of it. But who was it? The image of the man flitted about my consciousness just out of reach. And now the men were long out of my sight.

By the time I returned to Haggerty's side the service had ended, and mourners were drifting from the gravesite. The two grave diggers had already stepped forward to cover the casket. The dirt they methodically heaved into the grave drummed noisily on the casket below.

"Where'd you go?" Haggerty inquired.

"Just curious. Two people—both males—were watching the funeral from the hillside. I wondered who they were, why they didn't join us."

He patted his vest pocket searching for a smoke. "Find out?"

"No, although—" And then it hit me. The pale yellow suit! The mug at the ballpark! Mikey or Mickey something. Nichols and Haggerty had called him a small time grifter. Why would he be at Anna's services? And who was his companion?

"It was the bloke in the yellow suit you pointed out to me at the ballpark," I told Haggerty.

"Mikey Mul?"

"That's it. What would draw him to services for Anna?"

Haggerty made a dismissive sound. "Mikey knew Anna. I've seen 'em together at games, I have. 'N walking out of The Grounds together."

"Walking how?"

"Wha'?"

"*How* were they walking? Like two friends? Sweethearts? Lovers?"

Haggerty fumbled in his coat pocket before retrieving a dead cigar butt. He flicked the end of it with a stubby finger as if to remove a bug, and then shoved the stogie between his teeth. "Well, I —" He spread his huge, battered hands as if to say he had no idea. "They walked arm-in-arm, tha's all."

Well, well, I thought. Mikey Mul. A man who hung around the South End Grounds. A man with access to both Germany Long and Anna Anspach. Perhaps I'd found the fox in the hen house.

71

13

A challenge from Sean Dennison made me postpone my plan to sneak into Anna's chicken coop to look for traces of the fox. In the cool of the evening, he and I lounged in the Denihur backyard, our shoes off, our newspapers scattered on the grass by our lawn chairs. Three boarders who'd been sharing the large, shaded yard with us had wandered off, leaving us alone, dozing lightly. Aside from the chirping of birds and the sounds of children playing somewhere beyond the hedge that surrounded the Denihur property, the yard was silent.

"Are you a wheelman?" Sean asked, low and lazy, as if he were half asleep.

I looked over at him. His feet were crossed and his hands folded at his belt. His head was titled slightly back and his eyes closed. Except for the pencil stuck behind his ear, he looked like a cadaver laid out for a wake. Only the slight twist of his mouth, the hint of a smile, alerted me to the fact that he was not as unfocused or as sleepy as he appeared. I told him I could ride.

"Have you ridden one of Colonel Pope's new Columbias?" Again, his voice was sleepy, seemingly disinterested.

I informed him I was familiar with the safety models, but that I hadn't ridden one with pneumatic tires.

He rolled his head slowly toward me and gazed at me through half-closed eyes. He considered the sum of me for some time, a skeptical squint twisting his face. "In condition, are you?"

His seemingly innocent question about my physical conditioning swept the scales from my eyes. He was baiting me! Behind his innocuous questions was a challenge. His inquiry about my conditioning left no doubt about that. And his was not an easy question. At the moment I was in no shape to do anything. I was exhausted from the funeral and the heat of the day. But I knew even under the best of circumstances I couldn't compete with the conditioning of a professional cyclist like Sean. Especially if Tim Murnane's characterization of him as a scorcher was accurate. On the other hand, I prided myself on staying in fine fettle and I certainly had size—and, I hoped—strength on him.

"You bet I'm fit," I told him, and immediately prepared to go to bed early—without Miss Muldine.

He bolted upright, suddenly alert and grinning. "A dollar says you can't stay with me to Waltham."

A dollar is a dollar. "What do you mean, *stay with* you?"

"Say, keep within a quarter mile or so of me," he said, grinning mischievously.

"Done."

And, so, I found myself huffing and puffing in the cool morning air on an older Columbia that Sean used as a spare, my legs screaming, my back already sore. We'd started at King's Chapel, then headed up Beacon near the Commons. We'd stayed along the Charles River for a few miles, left Beacon Street at the Fens, wound through them, and circled back to the river. Now we were on our last leg to Waltham.

Most of our route was rural. Farm houses and haystacks dotted green fields. A hot, bright sun broke through the thin clouds over Brighton. It was going to be another blistering New England day. Fortunately for us, sprawling maples and elms shaded the roadway. Great numbers of cyclists joined us. Men. Women. Children. Beyond Brighton, the numbers swelled. It seemed that virtually every thoroughfare was crowded with bikers. I even saw several elderly men still riding the old penny farthings. Bone shakers, Sean called them.

"There's hardly room for horses and carriages," I yelled at Sean who pedaled double jig time fifteen yards ahead of me.

He looked back and grinned. He didn't appear intent on racing at the moment. "Oh, it ain't the horses and carriages that plague us," he shouted. "The political fight's with the damned trolley cars. The Council wants electric car lines on every thoroughfare. Wheelers hate 'em."

"Trolleys are great to get around."

"Give me a bike," he shouted back at me. "It'll beat an electric car any time, any day, sure."

Having expended most of my energy in our shouted exchange, I didn't respond. To double my trouble, as we neared Waltham, Sean accelerated, standing on his pedals but bending low to utilize his strength. I saw the power and skill that made him a professional. Despite my pounding heart and aching legs, I accelerated, too. Without much success. Sean opened up a half mile lead when, to my great relief, he topped Waltham's Prospect Hill and braked. When I finally caught up to him and dismounted, I was as wet and wobbly as old Grover Cleveland after a polka.

Sean chortled and shrugged generously. "Close enough to a quarter of a mile. We'll call it a wash."

I'd have appreciated his gesture more if I hadn't been so damned winded. I let his generosity pass without comment, preferring instead to scan the countryside while trying to bring my breathing under control. The view was magnificent from Prospect Hill. Even with my tired muscles and desperately sucking lungs, I could appreciate that. We leaned our cycles against a low stone wall that we sat on. Immediately before us was a precipitous drop. Beyond it, in the distance, lay Boston and its environs.

"It seems like everyone in greater Boston is riding today," I mused, running my fingers through my sopping hair. "I had no idea bicycling was such a popular rage. Art Soden and Bill Conant must wish base ball was as popular."

"The Beaneaters are a celebrated lot," Sean conceded. "But there's one thing more popular than base ball *or* cycling."

"And that is?"

He laughed mirthlessly. "Betting on both. Lots of money changes hands on those activities."

"Big money?"

"Mary and Joseph, biiiggg money." He raised his eyebrows a notch. "Wanna see? There's racing at Charles River Park tonight under lights.

"You're entered?"

"Not tonight. But the *Globe* wants sketches. I've got to be there."

I rolled my shoulders and stretched. I figure'd I'd want to sit and watch something tonight. And I'd never seen a sporting event outside after dark. "Why not? Sure, I'll go."

That taken care of, Sean paced slowly along the low wall, surveying the glorious expanse of farmland and villages below him. From our perch we could see dozens of roads, each filled with riders in colorful regalia. Occasionally Sean scooped up pebbles and idly flung them over the wall and down the steep hill. Clearly he was pondering something. After several minutes, he wheeled and approached me again. "You've had a chance to get to know our landlady, have you, Will?"

"Claire Denihur? No. Not really. I've talked with her briefly several times."

Sean made a face, exasperation evident on his features. "Sure 'n I didn't think a big, handsome devil such as yourself would let grass grow under his feet."

"What's that suppose to mean?"

He tossed another pebble down the hill. We watched its graceful arc and listened for the sound of its landing. "It means, boyo, that time is passing and other gents have their eyes on the fair Miss Denihur," he said.

I turned my gaze from the rock he'd flung to Sean. "Someone in particular?"

"Bradford Bent. Big fellow. Handsome devil, like yourself. But older. An operator and greasy slick. Lots of money."

I bent over, grabbed a small rock and hurled it where Sean had tossed his. Got better arc and distance than he had. "Should I leap off this cliff right now, or should I wait to hear the rest of your tale?"

"Your choice," he said, chuckling.

"What's all this to you? What's your interest in who sparks Claire Denihur?"

Sean idly tossed a small rock in his hand and eyed the area where I'd slung mine. "I don't like the man. And he wants Claire to sell out and move with him to New York."

The light dawned. "And that means Cait Denihur moves too?"

He didn't respond. He threw the rock with all his might down the hill. He sprang up on the wall and stood, his back to me, looking at where he'd tossed the stone. His posture and silence announced that he'd ended the conversation for now. And what more was there to say, anyway? I didn't have anything to add.

I didn't need Sean's urging to spark Claire Denihur. She was as attractive and as tantalizing a woman as I'd ever met. I'd hoped to overcome her obvious reservations with base ball people by biding my time. Letting her see my strengths and come to appreciate—even admire—them. Sean's information about Bradford Bent suggested that strategy might be self-defeating. Like assuming an egg would leap into a skillet and scramble itself. And, speaking of kitchen ware, I had to clear my plate of Molly before concentrating around Claire Denihur. It would not be easy to turn away from Molly. Sugar is no less addictive than opium or morphine.

Anticipating his calling an end to our rest, and not wanting him to realize how stiff and tired I already was, I paced up and down the wall, considering his comments, ostensibly taking in the vista. I managed to loosen up enough so that when he swung up on his bike I was able to mount my own wheeled machine and start back to the city.

Sean stayed beside me for the first hundred yards or so, pedaling easily and grinning conspiratorially. "Now that we're both loose, want to put a dollar on who can get to the boardinghouse first?"

My back and legs screamed "no," but I heard my voice holler "absolutely," and we streaked down the hill, startling nearby pedestrians and wheelers alike.

14

A long, hot bath helped relieve some of my soreness, but watching the Beaneaters lose once more to the Quakers stiffened me up again. By the time Sean and I had eaten supper following Boston's loss, and arrived at the Charles River Park, I could barely walk, although I did my best to disguise that fact. If Sean noticed my increasingly awkward gait, he didn't let on. I imagine it was like ignoring Teddy Roosevelt at a Democratic Convention.

The evening was humid and the air thick with winged insects. A slight breeze had arisen earlier, but by the time we arrived at the track it had died, and the air hung heavy and still.

Throughout our meal and trolley ride Sean bragged outrageously about the cycling track. I thought him the worst sort of exaggerator until I got my first look at it. Located by the Charles River, where Cambridge Street crosses it, it was in a spot bereft of structures during my Harvard days. The track was wide and banked sharply at each end. Poles were spaced evenly around the oval and hung with electric lights so that the raceway was well lit. I could easily see racers on the far side of the infield. Groups of brightly uniformed cyclists filled the grass patch inside the oval roadway and cyclists, as many as a dozen side by side, leisurely circled the track, warming up for their competition. From the park, you could see the Boston and Albany Railroad disgorging fans.

Sean waved his press pass at the gatekeeper. I paid my fifty cents admission, and we joined the milling crowd.

"There's got to be four thousand people—or more," Sean said, his eyes big. He may have underestimated the numbers. It was quite a throng. "And what did I tell you about the wagering?" Sean asked, sweeping his arm to take in the crowd. People everywhere were laying bets on individual cyclists and club teams.

"Put some coin on Little Jimmy Michael, the Welch Midget," Sean told me, leaning in close as if conveying some treasured secret. "He's a blazer; no one can touch him in the ten-mile race. He'll do it under fifteen minutes. Frank Rowe is wonderful in the half-mile sprints, too." He edged off a bit and held up his sketch pad. "I'll meet you by the front gate in an hour, boyo. I've got some drawing to do. *Globe* readers want to know what the layout looks like and who the new heroes are."

After Sean disappeared into the crowd, I purchased a racing card and studied it while meandering through the stands. Eventually, in deference to my tired legs (not to mention my increasingly painful bum), I found a space on the rail where I perused my card and shifted from one aching leg to another. The crowd continued to swell, hollering its delight for the winners, muttering at those whose poor performances lightened purses. As intense and hotly contested as the competition was, the betting was even more heated. Men and women alike, eyes bright with greed and hope, faces flushed with anticipation, screamed at the racers, waving and pointing at their favorites as if by their actions they could stir them to greater deeds. Those who'd learned (at least for the moment) the futility of such gestures wandered away from the rail, muttering to themselves, fingering their next card with the intensity of William Jennings Bryan searching for his favorite scripture.

A corpulent, rheumy-eyed man in a rumpled gray suit and the color and complexion of a week-old bowl of Quaker Oats joined me at the rail. "You're not betting, then?" he asked. He reeked of alcohol and his breath would take the paint off railroad boilerplate.

"Not me." I told him. But the truth was, I was sorely tempted. What would another vice mean to me? It would be the equivalent of adding another bean to a five-pound sack of 'em. And it just might bring me some much-needed cash. John Haggerty had lent me ten dollars against my first pay envelope, so I had some cash with me. In the end, however, fearing I might even lose my trolley fare home, I decided to content myself with observing. I considered it a tentative step in resurrecting my plans for reformation.

"Ya gotta put money on Wee James," the man insisted.

"Wee James?"

He pushed closer, thrusting his racing card in my face. "Little Jimmy Michael."

I remembered that Sean had mentioned Michael. Still . . . . "I think I'll pass," I told him. Jimmy Michael might be a wee sprout but he won easily, wheeling away from the others in one of the longer races of the night.

"Told ya," laughed the man, his mouth gaping with missing teeth. "Put some bills on Grimes. Bet him to place."

I searched my card. "Grimes?"

The man licked his lips and again pushed his card in my face. "J. N. Grimes, he's a professional from Cleveland. Weighs over five hundred pounds, but he'll hold his own even in the long races. Tends to fade, though."

"Five hundred pounds? A cyclist? I'll pass again, I think."

"Christ, ain't ya the tightfisted one?" my friend grumbled, "Ya could squeeze dust outtuva dime, you could."

When Grimes finished second the man beat his fists on the rail in disgust. "I tol' ya," he muttered, "You're a thick 'en, son."

I smiled ruefully, giving him his due. "You were right, my good man, absolutely right. Have you heard of a cyclist named Sean Dennison?"

"Sure. He's a good 'un. Ain't ridin' tonight, though." He glanced at his program to confirm that.

"You know your bikers," I said, shaking my head in admiration.

Obviously encouraged by my comment, the man seized my sleeve. "It's Eddie McDuffee now, son. Thas where ya put yer money. McDuffee, eh?"

I studied my card for McDuffee.

"I'm not a sharp for McDuffee, son. I'm telling you square. He's a scorcher." He clamped my arm in a fat hand, his breath nearly buckling my knees. "McDuffee'l win us green, son. Like Michael and Grimes woulda had."

"Us? When did we become partners?"

He glared at me as if I'd just spilt his drink. "You'd give sumpin' of your winnings fer th' tip, woodden't yer?"

I had to laugh. "McDuffee's a sure bet, eh?"

Suddenly terribly intense, he seized me by the lapel of my coat. "He *is* a sure bet, son. He ain't been licked in seven straight races. Seven straight. Agin' top competition."

An hour later, I disengaged from my newfound chum. He patted me on the shoulder and shrugged his shoulders in the time-honored fashion of those confronted with an unfair world. I'd lost nine dollars I could ill afford to spare, including several dollars on McDuffee. I slipped my alcoholic friend my last dollar, mustered a weak smile, and moved toward the front gate as I'd promised Sean. It hurt to give away a dollar but I figured his companionship had earned him a tipple or two. I shoved my way through the crowd, embarrassed by my empty pockets and chagrined at my puny resistance to my fire-breathing pal's promises of riches. In less than a week I'd taken two gigantic steps backward.

Moments later, I was standing by the refreshment stand when I spotted Deacon Bill Conant talking earnestly with several prosperous-looking gents. They were about thirty yards from me up against the grandstands. Though they were standing in the partial shadow of the stands, I could see that those in the light—and that included Deacon Bill—were exchanging bills, presumably settling bets.

"Made your fortune?"

I spun at the voice. Sean stood just behind me, grinning like a Cheshire cat, rifling through a handful of bills. His sketch pad was tucked under his arm and his pencil behind his ear.

"Not quite," I replied. I didn't tell them how much I'd lost.

"Well, boyo, this lad made a few extras." He folded the bills, waved them at me, and with exaggerated enthusiasm stuffed them into his coat pocket. "I placed a few dollars on Maj Taylor, the black sprinter 'n won a boodle. He's a whiz."

That hurt. "I don't remember you mentioning Taylor."

He grinned devilishly and his eyes sparkled. "Must've slipped my mind. Taylor is on Boston's team when it competes against other cities' teams. He's the only darkie on the squad." He clapped me on the shoulder. "Can't imagine I forgot to tell you about Taylor. He's one I was here to draw."

"You put any money on McDuffee?"

"Nah. I never bet on McDuffee. He's won a few recent races against inferior competition, but he's got no stamina. I've beaten him once. In a year or so, he'll be the real berries. Can't believe I forgot to tell you about Taylor. Loving you like a brother, as I do," he assured me in exaggerated concern.

"As Lizzie Borden adored her parents."

But by now Sean was through ribbing me. He was surveying the crowd. He jerked a thumb toward the group of men by the grandstand. "Didja see Conant there?"

I told him I had. I pointed to one of Conant's companions who was a head taller than the others, almost cadaverous, with sallow cheeks. Indeed, his cheekbones seemed to be pushing their way through his parchment-like skin, an Egyptian mummy in blue serge. A handlebar mustache obscured his lower face. His dark greatcoat accentuated his great height, as did his high bowler. "Who's he?"

Sean snorted derisively. "They're all moguls. Bankers, investors, speculators. The tall man is owner of the La Tourain on Tremont."

I *was* impressed. The tall man was one rich codger. I'd seen the architectural evidence of his wealth during my stroll with Molly. I indicated the gent standing to Conant's left, a large, handsome fellow in his late thirties or early forties, a well-trimmed but full mustache accenting his strong features. The cut of his clothes identified him as a man of Conant's social station. He was carefully counting out currency bills to Conant, laughing and joking as he did so.

"And the handsome fellow?"

Sean balled his fists. "That's Bradford Bent I was tellin' you about. Claire's beau. And the brains behind the Klondike Mining Syndicate."

I studied Bent. His clothes fit him impeccably and he was freshly barbered. His face was tanned and handsome, his manners animated. I could see why Claire might find him a catch. "He *is* an impressive specimen. He's investing in the Yukon gold rush?"

79

"He is."

"What's Conant's interest in him? Yukon gold?"

"Probably. Lots of monied men are putting cash into the Alaska Gold Syndicate and in the mysterious Bent's Klondike Mining Syndicate."

I studied Bent some more. "Why do you call Bent 'mysterious'?"

"Showed up out of the blue three or four months ago. Became a player in big money schemes right away. Word is he made his fortune in New York. Boston's finanacial circles embraced him like a puppy with a badly-singed tail."

Sean had a real knack for comforting me. First, he tells me that my love interest is being pursued by a gentleman who is rich and handsome. Now, he tells me that in addition to his wealth and good looks Bent is well-connected, hob-nobbing with some of Boston's most prominent movers and shakers. If that weren't enough to shrivel what little remaining self-confidence I had, he tells me that Bent is 'mysterious.' What woman is not fascinated by mystery?

My ruminations about Bradford Bent were broken by the movement of a man stepping out from behind Conant, a young sport in a flashy plaid suit and a boater. I saw him clearly when he stepped out of the shadow. The mug from the funeral! Mikey Mul. With his wise guy air and bold attire, he seemed an unlikely person to be hanging around Bill Conant, Bradford Bent and their expensively-dressed confederates.

"What's a pug like Mikey Mul doing with men like that?" I whispered to Sean.

He shrugged. "I can't imagine. Mul's a lowlife. He's more at home wagering in the rat pits in the North End than communing with Conant and Bent and their ilk."

"It's like McKinley inviting Debs and his Socialist pals to the White House."

"Maybe, boyo," Sean said slowly, eyeing the group with renewed interest. "But gambling and speculation, even more than politics, make for odd bedfellows. Bad business, like celery, comes in bunches."

Yeah. So did my failures, it seemed.

15

Will's comment about strange bedfellows rekindled an ember glowing in the recesses of my mind. Was gambling the link connecting the assault on Germany Long to the death of Anna Anspach? *Was* there a connection between the two incidents? The more Sean's observation flickered there, the more sense it made for me to check up on Anna Anspach's work habits. She was after all, as John Haggerty told me at her funeral, a friend of Mikey Mul, a chap who seemed to be everywhere that money was changing hands. Distressed by my continuing weakness for Molly, for "sure bets," and by all that Bent had to offer Claire, I was desperate to succeed in my professional duties. And that meant succeeding as well in my role as amateur sleuth for Mr. Soden.

My idea to check out Anna was sound. My execution was less so. Twenty-four hours after deciding to investigate her work records, I was sneaking up the stairs to my room at the Denihurs' much the worse for wear. My right eye was puffed almost shut and I could taste blood and feel it on my face and in my hair. My head throbbed and my kidneys ached. Concerned lest I'd have to share my ride home with gawkers, I'd hired a hansom for the ride to Denihur's boardinghouse.

To my mortification I met Claire coming down the stairs, carrying a bundle of dirty towels. Instinctively, like someone encountering a naked stranger in the jake, I pulled back. But there was nowhere to hide.

She gasped, eyes wide. "You told me there'd be none of this foolishness, Mr. Beaman. What in the name of heaven happened to you?"

A fair question. An even better one was, should I answer her candidly and forthrightly? On one hand, it was a wonderful opportunity to get to know Claire, to talk with her without a table full of boarders listening in. On the other hand, how much could—should—I tell her? How far could I trust her? I still hadn't confessed my sleuthing responsibilities to Sean or Tim Murnane, and I couldn't afford to have Claire spill my beans to Cait or Sean.

"The hazzards of my job, I guess," I mumbled, "I wasn't drinking."

"Hazzards of *what* job?" she asked, taking my arm. "Come with me. I'll put something on those cuts." Without waiting for an answer she led me down the stairs and into the kitchen. "You wait here," she said and disappeared. When she returned moments later, she carried a medicine box. "Sit down. Here." She stood in front of me as I sat. She took my face in her hands and tilted my head so that the lamp light shone directly on my swollen eye. "Look up at the light. Now, what kind of job calls for you to be beaten up, Mr Beaman?"

I took a chance. Criminy, I needed to start a new streak sometime. "Will you keep what I say between the two of us? I can't afford to have certain people knowing what I'm about. My activities aren't illegal, I just can't have them known right now."

She eyed me for a long moment, her brow furrrowed. "Sounds very mysterious, Mr. Beaman. But you needn't worry about me. I can keep a confidence. Now, what happened to you?" She began to rub ointment on the cuts around my eye.

"Mr. Soden hired me to investigate an assault upon one of his players."

She dabbed more ointment on my brow. "He must have a great deal of confidence in you."

I let that pass. "Yes, well. You remember the young woman who died in Mr. Conant's office the first night I was here? Anna Anspach? I'm also looking into her death. I'm trying to determine if there is a connection between the attack on the player and Anna's death. I can do this easier clandestinely. At least Mr. Soden thinks so. Obviously, I don't want Sean to know. He's too close to Tim Murnane at the *Globe*."

She put some gauze over a cut on my forehead and taped it there. Then studied her work. "Someone discovered your subterfuge and beat you up?"

I shook my head. "I'm not sure why I was attacked. I went to the South End Grounds after dark tonight to check the team ledgers. I wanted to see if Anna was keeping square books. Apparently, some one didn't want me there, or didn't want me to discover *them* there. Anyway, as I was leaving Conant's office, someone blindsided me, then thumped me good." I rubbed the back of my head.

"Why did you think Anna cheated on the books?"

I nodded to show that I knew that was a key question. "Because I wanted to see if her association with a known grifter had tempted her to embezzle funds. The man has been seen with her and with known gamblers." I didn't tell Claire that he'd also been seen with her Mr. Bent.

"So you *sneaked* into your employers' office?" She seemed horrified by the thought.

"I, eh, visited it after hours, yes."

Her eyes smiled. "A wonderful distinction, Mr. Beaman. Could you read in the dark?"

I had to laugh. "I used the electric torch I'd brought with me."

She dabbed away some blood under my eye, biting her lip in concentration as she did so. "Did you find anything incriminating?"

82

"Not right away. The first book was a daily account of home gate revenues. The receipts were totaled after each game by Mr. Conant, Mr. Soden, and myself. A third owner, J. B. Billings, oversees the turnstiles before and during the game. He brings the game's receipts to the office and places them in the safe. Following the game, the three of us—Conant, Soden, and I—count the ticket stubs and the money and leave a slip for Anna who then recorded the figures when she arrived the following morning. She would recount the money, check it against the slip, and return everything to the safe."

"Sounds thorough—and reliable."

"It's a check system that Conant and Soden insists upon. Because I was familiar with recent figures I easily determined that Anna faithfully recorded the numbers from the slips in the book, and saw that the correct amount ended up in the team's safe. The figures in the book corresponded to what I remembered of daily totals."

Claire wiped at dried blood in my ear. "So Anna was innocent?"

"Afraid not. The second volume gave her up. It took me an hour to spot it. I wouldn't have noticed it had I not been involved in selling advertisement. The first several times that I examined the book I had carefully checked to see whether Anna had listed each transaction. I checked each advertiser and the dates that he paid. Anna had dutifully recorded each of my transactions with the merchants."

"So why do you say she embezzled?" she asked with some exasperation while standing back to examine her work on my ear.

"Well, I looked more carefully at the far right column where she'd recorded the amounts paid. It was the notation for Mr. Ingram, a jeweler, that caught my eye. He'd recently given me twenty-five dollars that I'd brought to the office and placed in the safe. I had then left a notation in the book for Anna's successor to record formally. That was standard procedure. But Ingram had mentioned to me that the twenty-five dollars he'd given me was five more than he'd paid the previous year. He'd grumbled that he hoped he'd attract additional business to offset the additional costs. When I looked at the earlier recording for Ingram, made by Anna, I found a notation for fifteen dollars."

"Not twenty-five."

"Nope. I thought maybe Ingram had been mistaken. So, I went back an additional year and checked his listing there. Twenty dollars. I remembered another merchant, Theodore Bisetti, a tobacconist, telling me the thirty dollars he spent each year for the advertisement on our outfield fence was money well spent. I looked for mention of Besetti in the previous

83

two years. The figures appearing in the right hand columns was twenty-five dollars for this year, thirty the previous year."

Sadness crossed her face. "She *was* stealing."

"No doubt about it. She was skimming money from the club. Not gate receipts, but monies not directly monitored. She'd received monies, skim off a portion, then record and deposit the lesser amounts. All the time that Conant and Soden and Billings were concentrating on gate receipts, counting and recounting every penny, she was stealing them blind and queering the books."

Claire adjusted the tape under my eye, pressing it more firmly in place. "And what does that tell you about her death?"

I shrugged. "I don't know. Anna Anspach was an embezzler. Was she also a suicide? Had she become remorseful? Afraid that she'd been discovered? Did she kill herself rather than face the consequences of discovery? Rather than face up either to her own conscience, or the authorities? I don't know. That at least makes some sense."

Claire made a face. "Well, her thievery doesn't explain why someone else might want to kill her. Had Mr. Conant or Mr. Soden uncovered her duplicity, they would have fired and arrested her. Possibly even sued her for recovery. Why kill her? No one would gain by murdering her, would they?"

"I don't know. I don't think so."

Her eyebrows rose a notch. "Unless, of course, she had a confederate. One who feared she'd snitch on him."

"But that would suggest one or all the owners had been in league with someone directly stealing from the club, wouldn't it? The amounts that were taken were large enough to provide Anna with a sizeable supplement to her salary, but they were hardly sufficient to justify someone like Billings, Conant, or Soden conniving with her in crime. Could she be in league with a player? A manager? Her gambling companion? That's what I want to know."

She didn't respond. She wiped her hands on a towel and mulled over what I said.

"On the other hand," I went on, "while it's clear that Anna knew about the skimming, and even abetted it, that doesn't prove that she ended up with the money, or even a portion of it. Perhaps she was pressured, even blackmailed, into embezzling. I need verification that Anna was spending more than appropriate for her salary." I didn't tell Claire but of course the same is true concerning the owners. Checking that out would be harder.

She put the towel on the table and began to screw the cap on the tube of ointment. "You still haven't explained why someone assaulted you. Who knew you were there, examining Anna's books?"

"Don't know. When I was finished, I turned out the torch and stepped out of the room. Someone was standing in the dark, maybe ten feet from me. I lunged back into the room. But realizing how guilty that appeared, I stepped out again prepared to bluff whoever was standing there. No one was there. Who ever it was had bolted, apparently no more anxious for me to find him there than I was to have him discover me."

She boxed up her medical items. "What then?"

"I hurried for the gate. There were no lights on in The Grounds, but there was moonlight. As I rounded the corner of the pavilion, it felt like I'd run into a wall. Someone slammed into me, knocking me down and knocking the wind out of me. Before I could catch my breath, whoever it was pummeled me." I shook my head slowly.

"You didn't see who it was."

"No. Whoever it was knew how to even the odds, and also to use his dukes. By the time I cleared my head, he was long gone."

She fingered the taped gauze above my eye. "It must have been terrible."

"Well, I wish it hadn't happened. Still, there's some good news. My new suit weathered the attack. It's in better shape than I am."

Though she playfully tapped my nose with her finger, her voice scolded. "Very funny. Just like a man to make light of violence." She scooped up the box of medicines, bandages, and tape. "What are you going to do now? Besides get some rest?"

I shook my head slowly, afraid to move abruptly. "I really don't know," I told her truthfully. "I've got some thinking to do, for certain."

16

I decided to start with Long whose assault had triggered my dilemma. I'd seen him at Anna's funeral following his beating, but I met him formally for the first time on Tuesday, before the opening game of a three game series with Chicago. While continuing to recuperate he'd come by to watch his mates practice before they contested Cap Anson's Colts.

Hoping to identify players who might be at odds with Long, I shucked my coat and hat and walked around the field pretending to check the infield, kicking the bases to see they were secure, and raking around home plate. All the while I kept my eyes open to see who visited Long—and who didn't. First baseman Fred Tenney, breaking in a new glove, asked me to throw to him. For twenty minutes or so, I fielded ground balls he threw to me and fired tosses to him. I'd spent four years as a minor league player and it felt good to fire the ball to Tenny. My play on the field was more crisp and professional than it was in my recurring dreams. Nonetheless, I continued to pay heed to players who commiserated with their indisposed chum. Players approached Long singly or in groups. Not a single player failed to speak to him. No doubt about it, Long was a popular man. Sleuthing was not all it was cracked up to be.

The fielding and throwing with Tenny raised my spirits. It felt good to loosen up and relax in the warm sun. Between cycling with Will, my amorous adventures with Molly (no, I hadn't gotten around to ending our relationship), and the beating I'd taken, I'd achieved little as Conant's assistant or as detective, though I knew a bit more about Anna Anspach than previously. At the moment, I just wanted to work the kinks out of my body, let the hot sun heal me, and figure out whom on the team might have targeted Long.

I almost missed this chance. Sean had caught me at breakfast and cajoled me into helping him move furniture for Cait and Claire, who were cleaning. It had turned into longer and more arduous work than I'd expected. Moving furniture didn't help my battered body, but the opportunity to spend time with Claire was not to be passed up. Knowing what she did, she didn't remark upon my wounds. However, several times I caught Cait furtively studying me and sneaking questioning looks at her sister. Upon seeing my bruises, Sean merely made a face and shook his head. He said nothing about my injuries then, or later, while we rearranged furniture.

The cleaning stint at the Denihurs, for all its heavy lifting, turned into a fun-filled and amusing morning. The women scurried about, chatting and giggling, weighing options for furniture moves as seriously as President

McKinley contemplating policies in Cuba. Sean and I exaggerated the heft of the items we were asked to move, groused in mock seriousness about the demands made upon us, and guyed the women about their indecision, then their choices. Whether I made the kind of progress with Claire that Sean had suggested I make during our bike ride to Waltham, I couldn't judge. Still, I'd been able to complete my labor for the sisters, get to know them better, and make it to The Grounds in time to observe Long.

I'd barely finished with Tenny and walked to the bench when I was confronted by Soden. He was sitting directly behind the bench, hunched over, hands folded before him, holding a rolled scorecard. He wore a dark three-piece suit and tie, his high collar bent at each tip. With his round head and nearly bald pate, he looked like a children's illustration of Humpty Dumpty. "Your father might have been right, after all," he said.

"Sir?"

Soden snorted. "Oh, your father's letters were complimentary enough about you, but they also sounded to me like they were written by someone trying to convince himself of what he was saying." He seemed prepared to say more about my father's evaluation, but stopped and shook his head in apparent disgust. "I hired you in spite of your father's letters, not because of them. I thought I saw something in you. Perhaps what your father hoped to see."

"Sir, I assure you—"

He didn't let me finish. "You look like you've been run over by a beer wagon. Just what is going on, Mr. Beaman?"

"I'm sorry, sir, I—"

"You haven't done a lick of work on increasing our attendance—or on our little understanding. You're as useless as a one-eyed umpire."

"But I have made progress," I protested.

Soden wasn't listening. He stood and strode away. When he was thirty feet from me, he stopped, turned and pointed a stubby index finger at me. "I want results," he growled. He paused, then after a moment added, "I thought you had sand." He half-ran up the stairs, taking two steps at a time. He was surprisingly agile for a big man.

I sat there for several minutes contemplating what Soden had said about my father and me. I knew my father wanted desperately to be proud of me; he made no secret of that. He kept insisting that I was short-changing myself, that I always set my sights too low for a man of my education and gifts. There is no heavier burden to live with than to know someone's criticism of you is justified.

"Well," I said aloud to my tired stems, "if you blokes are still in working condition I will wind my way over to Mr. Long and introduce myself. Perhaps ask him a question or two." My body responded as gallantly as it had in my previous encounter with Molly, and I headed toward Long.

Long was as unlikely a person for a base ball star as one could imagine. He looked younger than the thirty-one years I knew him to be, and much too young to be a veteran of seven years with the Boston nine. Not an especially imposing man—he was probably 5' 9" and one hundred fifty pounds—nor an especially handsome gent, he nonetheless offered to the world an intelligent and pleasant countenance. He was fair-skinned and fair-haired, like me. For a fact, he looked like the serious and honest chap and respectable husband and citizen I'd heard him to be.

I sat next to him and exchanged nods with him. However, before I could speak second baseman, Bobby Lowe, known to mates as "Link," leaned against the rail separating the field from the bleachers. "How's the cranium, Fritz?" he asked. "Feeling more bully, are you?"

Long made a face and gently touched his bandaged head. "I got pounded around a bit, Link. But it's my hand that concerns me more." He held up a still bandaged left hand.

"Ah, hell, you'll be catching smokers with it in a few days," Lowe assured him.

"Hope so," smiled Long, not too convincingly.

Lowe backpeddled to his position. "We need you back on the field, pal," he shouted.

As Lowe retreated to the infield he passed Sweet Billy Ewing. It was the first time I'd seen Ewing up close since our meeting in Conant's office. He stretched over the rail and shook Long's good hand. "You're looking fit, Germany."

He glanced at me, then pointed. "You've met Conant's pup here, have you?" he asked Long, flashing me an easy grin.

"I don't consider myself anyone's pup," I said frostily. "Not in size *or* inclination."

"Just guying you, friend," he said, holding up his hands in surrender, then turning to Long. "This is Will Beaman, assistant to old man Conant. Looks big and athletic enough to play, don't he?" He peered at my swollen face, but said nothing.

Long nodded and reached out to shake my hand, eyeing my bruises. "You look like you ran into the same bastard who conked me."

I shrugged and waved off his remark in embarrassment. "Willing to introduce me to him? I'd like to meet whoever it was face to face."

"Me, too, but I can't help you, friend."

Taking him at his word, and not wanting to share my personal troubles with Ewing, I changed the subject. "You fellows seem to be a close-knit lot," I said, waving at the other players to include them.

Long appeared to appreciate the shift in conversation. "Oh, like any team early in the season, we have some knots to untangle," he said, "but generally we are a close outfit. We'll get closer as the season rolls on and everyone finds out they have to pull together."

In for a penny, in for a pound, I thought. "Do the Bostons fraternize off the field?"

"Lots of us go to the theatre, or hang out at Tommy McCarthy's," put in Ewing. "Or go to the races. Horses, dogs, bicycles, sculls, it don't matter."

"Make any money on them?" I asked as innocently as I could manage.

"Helllll, yes. Won a pile on the trotters last week." He winked at Long. "I told yuh to put your money on that gray nag, Germany."

Long yawned and rubbed the back of his neck. "I prefer to save or invest, thanks."

"Hell, it's all gambling, Germany, Ewing sputtered. "Don't matter whether you put your money on base ball games, horses, bicycle races, or the chance of finding gold in the Yukon. It's all one big gamble." He grabbed me by the arm. "When *you* muster the courage to go for the big money, let me know. I'll introduce you to the right people."

He moved away from the rail, heading back to the field, but stopped to point back at Long. "You 'n me are as likely to lose our shirts on the promise of the Klondike as I am betting the ponies or mutts." He laughed lightly and trotted back to the infield.

"Investing in the Yukon gold rush?" I asked Long.

He grunted. Whether he grunted in assent or denial, I couldn't tell.

"I'm a timid man when it comes to money," he said. "So's the little woman. We put a little in properties, stocks, and so on. Small investments for our autumn years."

"Hell's bells," I said, "I'd like to find a way to expand my meager income." And I meant it.

He looked at me, idly probing his battered left hand with the fingers on his right. "Well, be careful, Mr. Beaman, there's as many scams out there as opportunities."

"Billy says he knows the right people."

Long shrugged.

I decided to take advantage of the growing familiarity that I sensed between us to return to my previous inquiry. "*Do* you have any idea who assaulted you, Mr. Long?"

He looked down the left field line where the clank, groan and squeak of railroad cars could be heard connecting and disconnecting, and clouds of white steam periodically floated above the fence. A sudden belch of black smoke, smelling of oil and gas, rolled over the fence and blanketed left field, momentarily obscuring the players shagging flies there. Long stared for a good while, seemingly lost in thought. "No," he finally drawled. "I have no idea."

I'd started with Long. Apparently I'd also dead-ended with him.

17

Following the game, I sat across the desk in Conant's office from Conant, Soden, and Dillingo, counting the day's receipts. The total again was disappointing. Soden glared at the final figure, stared balefully at me for a second or two, crushed his cigar in a large brass ashtray, and stalked from the room. Billings followed him, but more calmly, leisurely pulling on his greatcoat and civilly wishing us good day before pulling the door shut behind him.

Conant leaned back in his chair and relighted his cold cigar. He inhaled deeply and blew a stream of blue smoke toward the ceiling where it slowly dissipated. "It's going to change," he told me. "This is a good team, perhaps a great team. The pieces just aren't in the right places yet. Selee'll fix that." He eyed me for a long moment, a man seeing P.T. Barnum's bearded woman for the first time. "You come up with any ideas for booming the attendance?"

I fingered my cheekbone where the swelling and discoloration was now minimal. "I have a few in mind."

"You'll keep me posted?" he asked, with just a hint of sarcasm. He slammed shut the big gray ledger with green leather corners and hoisted it.

It was as good a time as any to tell him about Anna's embezzling, but I let it pass. I wasn't yet ready to open that can of worms with him. "Ewing played well today," I said instead.

Conant nodded. "He did. But, Judas Priest, to win consistently we need Germany." He stood, holding the ledger under his arm.

"When'll that be?" I asked.

He shrugged.

"I was talking to Germany today. He tells me players are investing in the Yukon."

Conant looked over at me, taking another puff on his cigar and exhaling a burst of blue smoke. Before becoming part of what the sporting press labeled the "triumvirs" which included himself, Billings, and Soden, he had grown rich selling hoopskirts, corsets, and other female unmentionables. "Watch your coins, young man," he said. "Investments are for men of means, or at least for those with steady incomes." He rolled the cigar between his lips. "You're not yet in those circles."

"I'd better stick to wagering on the ball games, horses, and cyclists, then?"

"My boy, you'd be much better off banking your savings," he said, shaking his head. "And that's my advice to you: live frugally and bank your savings."

"Do as I say, not as I do?"

He raised his eyebrows a notch and seemed to take a second appraisal of me. "That's right, son. Do as I say, not as I do. I bet the races. Win some, lose some. I can afford to. I invest in some iffy projects. I can afford to." He pointed his cigar at me and gave me a paternal smile. "You can't afford to. Not yet, anyhow. You don't want to end up like a shuttlecock in a cyclone." He headed toward the annex with the ledger.

"Still," I pressed on, "if a young man was determined to stay away from the precarious life of the gambler, how would he go about finding solid opportunities to invest in?" At the moment I honestly didn't know whether my own question was prompted by my growing inclination to make some of the easy money other Bostonians were raking in, or by my growing belief that somehow gambling and speculation lay at the bottom of the attacks upon Beaneater personnel.

Conant stopped halfway through the doorway. Again the curl of blue smoke from his pursed lips shot toward the ceiling. And a third, long appraisal of me. "I'll let you know when you're ready."

My response, a grunted 'hmmph,' hung between thoughtful reflection and angry disappointment.

He paused to appraise the meaning of the noise I'd made before stepping into the annex, where he shelved the ledger. He returned, removed his coat from the coatrack, and pulled it on. Without another word, he let himself out.

I was still furious at what I judged to be Conant's condescension and my own pathetic docility in the face of it when I left the office. I was so engrossed in my own self-pity that I did not at first realize that Sweet Billy Ewing and Marty Bergen had emerged from the area leading from the dressing room and were walking some twenty yards in front of me. When I did recognize them, my words just popped out. "Hey, Billy," I yelled, "I'm ready to be introduced to those important friends of yours."

Ewing and Bergen stopped and looked back at me. "You serious?" Billy asked me.

"As J. Pierpont Morgan counting gold."

Ewing and Bergen exchanged glances while waiting for me to catch up. Apparently Marty was in a more civil mood now than he was when I'd tried to talk to him my first day at The Grounds. If he was sorry for his bad manners on that occasion, however, he gave no indication of it. He did point to my face. "What happened to you?"

I waved off his question and directed my comments to Billy. "What about those friends of yours?"

Ewing capped a reassuring arm around my shoulder. "Tell you what," he said, "Me and Marty have been invited to a promotional dinner tonight. The men I was talking about will be there. In fact, there'll be two presentations, two syndicates vying for your fortune. You take my invitation."

"No, Billy," Marty broke in, "he can take mine. I want to get back to North Brookfield. My wife's poorly. If it's not one thing, it's another. Hell, I'm already in, anyways. I don't need to hear their spiel."

"You're sure?" I asked Bergen.

He tugged a white card from his coat pocket and handed it to me.

"Liberty Tree Restaurant. 5 Essex Street. 8:00 p.m. sharp," Billy said. "Keep your mouth shut and your ears open." He looked at Marty. "You okay with this, Marty?"

Marty nodded. "Yeah. I've got to check on the missus."

Billy stabbed a finger into my shoulder. "This is your lucky day, friend."

I waved the ticket at him. "About time I had a lucky day."

18

That evening, I arrived at The Liberty Tree just as Billy stepped from a hack. He was quite the dandy, dressed in a smart dark suit and vest, black bowler, accentuated celluloid collar, gold cuff links, and a diamond tie stud. His lapel held a fresh flower. With his fancy duds and his long slender fingers, looked like no base ball player I'd ever seen. He greeeted me with a hearty wink and an even heartier hand shake.

We were ushered to one of two long tables tastefully set and decorated. A half dozen couples were already seated at the far table. A surprising number of men were accompanied by women. With so many well-dressed and prosperous men and women it looked more like a society bash than a sales promotion. Seated at our table, puffing on his ubiquitous cigar, was Deacon Bill Conant. Several of the gentlemen sitting with him were the same men I'd seen him with at Charles River Park although, not suprisingly, Mikey Mul wasn't one of them. To my dismay, Bradford Bent was. And next to Bent sat Claire Denihur.

Sweet Billy spotted her at the same time I did. "My, my," he gasped, "Ain't that pie." His eyes never left Claire as he leaned toward me and tugged at my sleeve. "You know that skirt?"

Mesmerized as I was by Claire, I ignored his fresh language. Claire was more than pretty; she was beautiful. She wore a pale yellow dress high at the neck and puffed at the sleeves. Narrow strips of white lace circled her neck, highlighting a brooch, and both wrists. Her black hair shone and her eyes were shards of crystal. There wasn't another woman in the room that stood comparison with her. Bradford Bent's smug smile suggested he was very much aware of that fact.

"That's Claire Denihur," I told Billy. "She owns a boardinghouse."

He stared at her in silence, his appreciation of her beauty obvious. "My, my," he said again, his voice trailing off.

He and I were seated across the table from Conant, Claire, and Bent, catty-corner, perhaps twenty feet from them. Conant's eyebrows soared when he spotted us. He smiled enigmatically and dipped his head in recognition. Claire and Bent saw us just after Conant did. Claire's eyes widened and she bobbed her head in salute, a surprised smile on her lips.

Upon observing Claire's brief greeting to me, Bradford Bent stared at me, curiosity pinching his handsome face.

I wish I hadn't come. Sean told me Claire was seeing Bradford Bent but hearing and seeing it were two different things. Bent was annoyingly attentive to her. Every time I looked their way, he was leaning close to her, whispering intimately, patting her hand, caressing her arm. If she ever looked my way after her first glimpse of recognition, I missed it. And I checked often.

Dinner conversation around me was as stimulating as a McKinley State of the Union address. Chiefly it consisted of brief introductions and insipid observations regarding the weather, the Beaneaters' recent lack of luck, developments in Cuba and Greece, and, of course, the Yukon. Apparently conversation across the table and down from us was more stimulating. Conant, Bent, and Claire were very animated, chuckling and toasting each other frequently.

It was only after the meal was consumed, the table cleared, the cognac poured, and the cigars and pipes fired up that the group turned to the real business of the evening, the presentations by the rival syndicates. I expected the women to excuse themselves at this point and retreat to quarters of their own. A surprising number of females stayed on, including Claire. If they were offended by the clouds of blue smoke from the men's tobacco burners, they hid their displeasure well. One regal-looking but ancient crone lit up a slim cheroot and puffed away. This was no society bash; it was a business meeting of largely prosperous individuals, male and female, nakedly eager to enlarge fortunes.

Conant stood and tapped his glass with a fork. He addressed the assemblage briefly then turned to a large florid man whose few strands of red-gray hair lay on his bald pate like worms crawling across a sidewalk. "Mr. Reed," Conant asked, "Do you wish to speak for the Alaska Gold Syndicate?"

Mr. Lawrence Reed did. For almost forty minutes he laid out his syndicate's schemes to profit from the recent discovery of gold in the Northwest Territories. "Farmers and tradesmen all over the northeast are flocking to the gold fields," he told us, "and thousands of others are sure to follow in their wake. Women, too. In great numbers they are leaving Boston and other eastern ports for the gold fields—and for personal riches."

Reed began to sweat freely. Drops of perspiration flew from his large head as he abruptly swiveled it to take in his many listeners. His voice rumbled and his arms swept in dramatic arcs. "Those who supply their means of transportation and their supplies are going to get every bit as rich as those who find gold in their Canadian adventure. Additional gold discoveries are occurring daily and the possibilities for massive returns are unlimited. Many prominent New England men have already invested in our syndicate."

After twenty minutes of facts and figures, he bowed slightly to show his spiel was concluded, pulled a large white handkerchief from his back pocket, and with a flourish, mopped his face. "I'd be happy to entertain questions."

A flurry of questions spewed from those around the tables, their faces flushed with the prospect of riches. I listened intently, but did not participate. It's amazing how empty pockets can dry up a man's conversation. I remained content to observe Claire. She listened to Reed with rapt attention as well as to the questions posed to him.

It was another forty minutes before Bradford Bent had an opportunity to celebrate his Klondike Mining Syndicate. He whispered something to Claire, then backed away from the table and took a briefcase from a young man who hustled up to hand it to him. He rummaged briefly in the valise, then passed out copies of two maps. In a deep bass voice, he told us, "Ladies. Gentlemen. The number that will spell riches for us is 5,035."

He paused dramatically. "That's the number of miles from where we sit tonight to Dawson. It is 3,283 miles from Boston to Seattle, and another 1,000 miles by steamer to Juneau. From there it's 130 miles up the Lynn Canal and over the Chilkoot Pass. Finally, it is an additional 600 miles through the lake country and down the Yukon River to Dawson." Again, he paused to let the numbers sink in. He pointed a finger slowly around the circle of rapt listeners. "Each mile represents an opportunity for us to make money. Five thousand and thirty-five opportunities."

Billy Ewing nudged me with his elbow and raised his eyebrows a notch.

In a voice and cadence reminiscent of old time intinerant Evangelicals, Bent laid out his syndicate's strategies besides purchasing mining claims on the Yukon and building stores in Dawson. Among them was to provision ships to San Francisco, Seattle, and Juneau. The syndicate also was prepared to construct a tramway capable of hauling goods from Skagway over Chilkoot Pass. "Currently," he informed his audience, "the price of carrying the one ton of supplies required by each person heading for Dawson over the pass is one dollar a pound. A tramway will be a gold mine."

Bent chuckled. "We're also constructing a snow train, able to scale the pass, but also capable of traversing the six hundred miles of lake country between the pass and Dawson. The ability to transform a steam-propelled ship to carry a steam-powered eight-to-ten car snow locomotive driven on runners is already within our reach. The syndicate is excited enough about its proposed snow train that plans are already underway to sail to Alaska, then carry men and supplies over Chilkoot Pass to the gold fields. After the tramway replaces the locomotive as the prime mover of goods over the pass, the snow train will provide the principal means of transportation of men and supplies.

"Our syndicate is moving quickly to exploit these opportunities," Bent assured us, his right hand pumping in the air, "but time is of the essence. Shortly, the first of the syndicate's ships, with more than a thousand berths, will arrive in Boston to take on passengers for the Yukon."

His bushy brows furrowed menacingly. "Those of you lacking the courage and foresight to invest in the next few weeks are going to be closed out. Closed out–and passed by."

Billy was nodding his head vigorously, in agreement with Bent's assessment. He punctuated Bent's points by tapping his fist on the table. Finally, leaning over to me, he whispered, "Better get in on it, pal. The train's leaving."

I absorbed his oddly chosen metaphor without comment.

Forty-five minutes after he began, Bent had persuaded most that his syndicate could produce quicker and higher returns than Reed's Alaska Gold Syndicate. He elicited more questions than had Mr. Reed, and those who'd been fingering checks following the first presentation, now thrust them at Bent. I had no money for such adventures, but Billy passed a check forward.

The issue for me, since I couldn't rake up enough money to buy a bicycle let alone invest in a mining syndicate, was discovering how many of the Beaneaters, like Billy and Bergen, were investing substantial sums. That might lead me to who was desperate enough to bet on games to bankroll investments, desperate enough to attack team personnel in order to affect the outcomes of games. If anyone.

Later, after most of our table mates had drifted out of The Liberty Tree, Billy, and I stood outside waiting for the doorman to hail carriages. The cool, fresh air felt good after hours in the sweltering heat of The Liberty Tree, and the thick smoke that engulfed the room. Mr. Conant spotted us and came over.

I looked for Bent and Claire, but didn't see them. Whether they had left the restaurant before us, or were still inside, I didn't know.

I turned to Conant. "Lawrence Reed and Bradford Bent are wonderful salesmen. I wish I had the resources to invest in each of their companies."

He nodded noncommittally.

I remembered seeing Conant with Bradford Bent at the races. "How does someone who does have the money decide which to invest in?" I asked. "Or do you invest in both?"

"You weigh character, son," he said. "A man in my position learns to gauge integrity. I invest with the man I trust."

"And which is that, sir, Reed or Bent?"

97

He wagged a finger at me. And confirmed my worst fears. "That, young man, is what you're going to have to figure out for yourself," he said. "If you have character, you will readily recognize it in others."

19

My days fell into a routine. Each morning I rose early, joined Sean for breakfast, then hopped a trolley to The Grounds where I did everything from helping John Haggerty maintain the field to carrying out dozens of office chores, including selling advertisements. When on rare occasions crowds backed up, I took my turn at the turnstiles. In spare moments I wrestled with ways to get more folks to come to games. I had several ideas that I had not yet broached to Conant or Soden.

My hopes that Sean had forgotten about my cuts and bruises were quickly dashed. "By all that's holy, man, what happened to you the other day?" he asked, on the first occasion we were alone. "Where'd you get them bumps? I figured you didn't want to discuss it within earshot of Cait and Claire."

I gave him a highly edited explanation of my bruises and scrapes which seemed to satisfy him. I didn't share with him details on where the attack had occurred or what I'd found out about Anna Anspach. I still didn't trust his close relationship with Tim Murnane.

Whenever possible, I worked out with the players before games. Most days during the games I sat on the bench with Frank Selee, soaking up information about base ball and the team. Selee made some changes in the nine, moving young Chick Stahl into right field and replacing Tucker at first with the more agile Fred Tenny. Both brought defense as well as speed and quickness to the lineup. Ten days after being attacked, Germany Long took back his position from Billy Ewing. Wins came more frequently. There was even talk of a pennant.

With each passing day, the assault on Long drew less comment. And Anna Anspach's death faded in people's minds. The police, still not sure whether to treat her death as a suicide or a homicide, achieved nothing so far as I could see. My own efforts to advance the investigations into those incidents turned up little more, except for establishing in my own mind that she had embezzled funds.

Molly remained as attentive and as curious as ever. When she wasn't making love to me, she was pushing for details of my work. She seemed insatiable at both tasks. Her apparent absorption with me eventually made a habitual liar of me, as well as a scoundrel. I found myself conjuring up a slew of lame excuses to ensure that our rendezvous were not an every day thing.

Curiously, the more available Molly made herself to me, the more I yearned for Claire. Our nurse-patient routine the night I was attacked aside, the specifics on how to approach Claire continued to elude me. I seldom saw her at breakfast because Cait served us. I ate near the ballpark most evenings. Generally, by the time I returned to the boarding house, Claire had retired for the evening—or was out being wooed by the rich and handsome Bradford Bent.

As it turned out, while we were at breakfast one morning, Sean showed me how I could spend more time with her. "Heard an editor at the *Globe* yesterday tell a reporter to lay off the Anna Anspach death. That it was yesterday's news," he told me. "If it was *my* business to find out about her, I would start with her family. I've said that from the first."

I figured that I wouldn't give away too much about my agreement with Soden if I admitted that almost two weeks before I had done just that. "It wouldn't help," I told him. "I've done it."

His eyebrows soared. "Oh?"

"For the team, you know, as a representative of the nine."

"And, you learned what?"

I was relieved that he didn't ask me what business I had questioning the Anspachs, team representative or not. "They told me nothing worthwhile," I told him. "And Karl Anspach threw me out of his house."

Sean threw his head back and laughed. "Sure 'n that must have been a pretty sight." He fiddled with his silverware, got more serious. "Me mother always talked more forthrightly when me da' weren't around. Or when she was talking to a woman like herself."

At that moment, Claire entered the room, blessed those of us at the table with a radiant smile, conversed briefly and privately with Cait, and turned to leave. With Sean's words echoing in my ears, I stood and beckoned her. I'd already confessed my clandestine activities to her. What would it hurt to have her learn a little more? I cleared my throat. "Perhaps you would do me a favor?"

"A favor, Mr. Beaman?"

Sean understood what I was up to. He grinned. "Well, the lad bent his back for you 'n Cait for several hours Monday, shuffling furniture around 'n all," he said.

She nodded, a smile flirting with the corners of her mouth. "That's true enough. Mr. Beaman was a great help. You both were."

Sean 's carrot-colored head bobbed in agreement, nearly dislodging the pencil wedged behind his ear. "So, will you do him a favor?"

Claire looked at me, eyes curious, though she addressed her question to Sean, asking, "And what favor might that be?"

"Would you be willing to accompany me to the Anspachs, to add a woman's touch to my return visit."

"Anna's the lass who died in Conant's office," Will blurted.

Claire ignored his contribution. "A woman's touch?" she asked, puzzlement showing in her eyes.

"Anna's mother might find it easier to tell you things she would not tell me, a man, a stranger," I told her. When she hesitated, I quickly added, "You'd be doing all of us a favor—even the Anspachs. It isn't right that a young lady's death be dismissed unexplained."

She held a hand before her, palm down, fingers spread, and studied her nails. "I know nothing about criminal investigations."

"You wouldn't be investigating, merely making Mrs. Anspach comfortable while I ask questions," I assured her.

She weighed my argument for a long moment, her eyes darting to Sean. "To make Mrs. Anspach feel more comfortable?" She paused. "To show the team's concern?"

"That's it," I said. "It would put her at ease and encourage her to be frank, I think."

"Yes. Well. All right. That might be quite an adventure. When do you propose we visit the Anspachs?"

By mid-morning the following day we stood before the Anspachs' door. We'd made small talk on the trolley. Most of the time, however, we listened in silence to the hum and screech and rumble of the car, lost in our own thoughts. The ride was a wonderful chance for me to explain myself further and to wedge myself more firmly into Claire's life. But I let it pass, my head uncharacteristically devoid of ideas, my tongue tied in her presence. Somehow the familiarity that I'd felt while she ministered to my wounds and I'd described my discovery of Anna's perfidy, was missing on the trolley. I was like the medieval army that, having laid seige to a city, had neither the wherewithal or cleverness in the end to breach the walls.

Gertrude Anspach answered our knock immediately. She looked at me then held her eyes on Claire. "Ja, vat ist it?" she asked, irritation clear from her tone and expression.

I introduced Gertrude Anspach to Claire. My rambling explanation of my return was making no appreciable impact on Anna's mother when Claire leaned forward, touched her arm and spoke softly. "We've come to talk to you about dear Anna, Mrs. Anspach. And to help you and her."

The woman sagged as if from a body blow and retreated into her home, leaving the door ajar. We followed her into the dim room. Dark as it was, I could see that the room was as immaculate today as it was on my previous visit.

As if on cue, Sonia Kreutzer appeared in a doorway. Mrs. Anspach introduced her sister to Claire and reminded her who I was.

101

"Tea?" Mrs. Anspach asked us.

"Please," Claire told her. As Gertrude Anspach and her sister disappeared into the kitchen, Claire picked up the photograph of Anna and her mother and examined it for a long moment.

Mrs. Anspach brought the tea, her sister the cups and saucers. For the next thirty minutes or so I pressed Mrs. Anspach for details of her daughter's life away from the South End Grounds. I interrogated her particularly hard on Anna's spending habits.

She gave me the same answers she had before. Her furtive eyes and fidgeting hands told me she knew more than she was telling me, but I couldn't wrench it from her. Watching her conceal the truth from me brought back images of my own father's look of skepticism and pain at my disingenuousness as he questioned me on my often (to him) disgusting activities.

Sonia Kreutzer fidgeted almost as much as her sister. Several times she opened her mouth to speak but apparently thought better of it.

"No one threatened Anna or was a threat to her?" I asked.

The women shook their heads.

"No one who might want her dead?"

Again, denial by both women.

"And she wasn't depressed or moody just before her death?"

An emphatic 'no' from Gertrude Anspach.

"Anna had no accesss to guns?"

A still more emphatic 'no' from Gertrude Anspach.

"The .22 calibre pistol wasn't hers?"

Vehement denial by both women.

I had begun to repeat my questions—and Gertrude Anspach her answers—when Claire put down her cup and saucer. "Thank you for your courtesy and hospitality, Mrs. Anspach, you've been most generous with both—and with your time," she said. She paused, looked at me, but continued to address the women. "Mr. Beaman has another appointment. He assures me it'll take but a few minutes, a half hour at most. Would you mind if I stay and enjoy your company while he conducts his business?" She flashed a knowing smile to Mrs. Anspach and made a small face. "His business has to do with base ball. It's of no interest to me."

I prayed the women did not see my mouth go slack.

"Vy, ja," Mrs. Anspach said, pausing as if hesitant to commit herself. "Dot vould be fine." She glanced at her sister. "Ja?"

Sonia Kreutzer shot me a quick glance, then nodded.

Claire stood and indicated the door. "Mr. Beaman?"

Claire managed it with greater finesse than had Karl Anspach. Still, it was the second time I had been unceremoniously dispatched from the Anspach home.

20

An hour later I returned to the Anspach home, picked up Claire, and persuaded her to have lunch with me. It had taken me only seconds to appreciate her strategy in getting me away from Gertrude Anspach and her sister. Now I was eager to find out how successful it was, and what she'd learned. Lunch together would prolong my time with Claire, and that counted for something, too.

"Where to?" I asked, as we boarded a trolley for downtown.

"Wherever you want is fine," she said, "I have a great deal to share with you."

I chose the Park Theatre, a popular gathering spot for cranks. For twenty-five cents, on afternoons when the Boston nine was on the road, the Park Theatre provided electrical play-by-play accounts of the games—The Compton System, it was called—and posted scores from other games as they arrived by telegraph. Rooters crowded in to take advantage of the large selection of sandwiches, beverages, and cigars as they watched the progress of their team or teams. I was eager to introduce Claire to my world and the excitement associated with it, and I thought the Park would be a suitable initiation.

We found seats with an unimpeded view of the electric base ball apparatus on stage, and ordered sandwiches and lemonade. A series of lights signaled individual movements on the mock diamond so patrons could visualize plays on the field. A master of ceremonies provided running commentary. The game against the Giants in New York was in the third inning when we took our seats. Amos Rusie, the Hoosier Thunderbolt, was whitewashing the Beaneaters.

As we unwrapped our sandwiches and waited for our lemonades, I could no longer contain my curiosity. "Tell me about Mrs. Anspach."

She held up a hand, signaling me to hold that thought. Her gaze swept the theater, taking in the swarm of people who sat with eyes glued to the electric display. "My, I had no idea that base ball was so popular," she mused.

"And not just among the rowdies and bulldozers," I reminded her. I indicated those around us, many of who were respectable couples and single working girls. One section of seats was set aside for unaccompanied females.

A lad brought our lemonades. I tried once more as Claire took a first sip.

"What did Mrs. Anspach tell you?"

Still preoccupied with the automated display on the stage, she did not heed my question. "Who are the Bostons' opponents today?" she wanted to know.

I studied her, trying to determine if she were as fascinated by her new surroundings as she seemed to be, or, as I was beginning to suspect, she merely meant to tease me by delaying her account of what happened at the Anspachs following my departure.

"The New York Giants," I told her, playing it straight.

"And are they a formidable team?"

"When Mr. Rusie pitches they certainly are."

"He throws the ball swiftly?"

"As swiftly as any man alive."

She peered at the wall game, squinting prettily. "How many points do the Bostons have?"

"Runs."

"Pardon?"

"Runs. In base ball teams score runs, not points."

"Oh, yes. Runs, then."

"So far none. They're being bested, 2-0."

'And which is the most formidable team? Of them all?"

"In the National League? Presently, the Baltimores are. But they are being challenged by the New Yorkers and the Cincinnati team. And our Boston nine is coming up." My strategy wasn't working. She now seemed more intent on the game than on what had transpired at the Anspachs'. "Tell me about Mrs. Anspach," I repeated.

This time it was the game that conspired against me. At that moment, the crowd roared and we again swung our attention to the electric recreation. "What happened?" Claire asked.

With my free hand I pointed to the flashing lights. "See the lights on the diamond? They show that Billy Hamilton is now on third base and Hugh Duffy on first. None of the lights below the diamond is on, telling us that there are no outs yet. Boston has a chance to tie the game or go ahead this inning."

I had barely completed my explanation when the lights blinked again. Claire rose half way out of her seat, squeezing her sandwich and almost spilling her drink. She hugged her food and drink to her chest and pointed to the board. "Look!"

Duffy had scored and Hamilton had raced to third. Fred Tenny now perched on first. People all around us had jumped to their feet, doffed their caps, and screamed, flailing their arms, and pounding each others' backs.

Women squealed, clasped their hands and hopped around like participants in a sack race. Unfortunately the Beaneater rally fizzled quickly.

As the rooters glumly settled back into their seats, Claire seemed to lose interest in the lights. She sipped steadily at her lemonade, her cheeks forming dimples each time she drew on her straw.

I tried once more. "Tell me about Mrs. Anspach."

She grinned mischievously. "That's right, this *is* a business meeting,"

I waved off her insinuation. "Trust me, Claire, no time with you is ever strictly business." Her cheeks colored and she opened her mouth to speak but I gave her no opportunity. "You implied that Mrs. Anspach opened up to you."

Completely serious now, she raised her eyes to me, cupped her glass of lemonade with both hands, and nodded thoughtfully. Her half-eaten sandwich lay in its wrapper on her lap.

"Does she believe Anna killed herself?" I asked.

"She doesn't know. But her sister is convinced of it. They needed someone to confide in. Ten minutes after you departed, we were talking like long-time friends. They took me into Anna's room. We sat on her bed and chatted about her and her friends. The aunt showed me Anna's clothes and photographs"

"And?"

"Her mother was more worried than she acknowledged earlier to you or, apparently, to the police," Claire said. "Mrs. Kreutzer is convinced Anna took her own life."

"Why?"

"Anna was running with a fast crowd and living far beyond her means."

I told her with my hands that I wanted to hear more.

"She spent much more on clothes than she made. She rode cabs to work rather than walk or use the trolley as most working girls in her neighborhood do. She told her mother and aunt that her days of working were going to end soon."

Aha. "Meaning what, do you suppose?"

"Anna didn't say—and her mother doesn't know what she meant. Perhaps she was already thinking of suicide. Her mother hoped she'd met a suitable man to marry her and free her of the need to work."

"But Mrs. Kreutzer is convinced that Anna took her own life?"

"Yes. She's been worried about Anna's recent bouts of crying, new clothes, new habits, new mood. Her shadowy beau. All the secrecy, for that matter."

"Shadowy beau?"

"Though the women haven't confided the fact to Mr. Anspach, they'd found out Anna went out in the evenings, not to attend church functions but to see some man. Her mother prayed that was a hopeful sign. Mrs. Kruetzer was convinced it wasn't."

"They never knew who Anna was seeing? Or where she was going with him?"

"No."

"Well. That doesn't help us."

"Mrs. Kreutzer saw him. Once. She went out on the stoop after Anna left one evening and saw the man join her niece several blocks away. He stepped under a street lamp."

"She describe him?"

"Young. Slim. Flashily dressed. He was about a block away."

"Not much to go on."

She shrugged. "That's all she saw."

It was suddenly enough for me. I slapped my open hand on the armrest. "Mikey Mul." It had to be Mul, he of the brash suits. And it confirmed what John Haggerty told me at the funeral about Mikey and Anna.

Claire frowned. Our faces were now only a few inches apart. Her skin was unblemished ivory, her teeth pearls. "Who's Mikey Mul?" she asked, breathlessly.

"Remember the night you gave me first aid? I told you that Anna had a friend who had gambling connections? The grifter who I'd seen at ball games and bike races? And perhaps at Anna's funeral? That Mikey Mul."

"And you think that it was he who supported Anna's ostentatious behavior?"

"Perhaps. But Anna was skimming money from her bosses and queering their books. She was probably giving money to Mul, not taking it from him."

"Oh, my heavens," she whispered. "She killed herself for fear of being discovered?"

"That's what I'm determined to find out."

Her face was now flushed with excitement. "Could *he* have killed her?" She grabbed my arm and squeezed. Her eyes were bright. "Is that what we have to find out?"

Her use of "we" sent chills up my spine. In that brief second when I considered how to respond to her comment, a particularly exuberant outburst from the crowd jerked our attention once more to the game. Though the emcee was shouting into his megaphone, the crowd noise drowned him out.

107

The Beaneaters had rallied to within one run of the Giants and now had the bases loaded with Hugh Duffy facing a probably tiring Amos Rusie.

Claire's attention was now fully on the stage. "How exciting," she said breathlessly.

I saw my opportunity and leaped at it. "It's even more exciting at the games themselves," I told her. "The Baltimores come to town tomorrow. Would you honor me by being my guest?"

She seemed to ponder the implications of my request. Then her eyes sparkled in anticipation. "Why, yes, that would be . . . fun. Will Mikey Mul be there, do you think?"

"I'm sure he will."

"Oh, my," she sighed, her eyes bright.

For the moment, I put Anna Anspach and Mikey Mul out of my mind. I also swept aside thoughts of Molly Muldine and Bradford Bent. Tomorrow was going to be my day with Claire.

21

The following day, the South End Grounds was bathed in bright sunshine as players shuffled out to loosen up. The park wasn't packed yet, but the crowd promised to be one of the larger gatherings to watch a Beaneater contest. The Orioles always drew crowds. The Bostons' current winning streak obviously had also increased interest in the contest. The Boston players sported white uniforms with a gothic red B on their chests. Their caps were white with bills matching the players' crimson stockings.

It wasn't the players or their uniforms that interested Claire Denihur. Only seconds after taking our seats, she tugged at my sleeve and gazed around expectantly. "Is Mikey Mul here?" she asked.

He was. And with his flashy attire, easy to spot. Today the cluster of gamblers was larger than usual. And in its midst was Mikey Mul, wearing what for him was an unusually subtle, pale, lima bean-green suit. He hustled the crowd tirelessly, shaking hands, slapping backs, exchanging slips of paper, laughing gregariously.

I pointed at him. "There he is."

Even as I pointed at Mul, my attention was drawn to first base by 'Nuff Ced' McGreevey and his Royal Rooters who began jeering the Orioles' Dirty Jack Doyle. Rooters leaned out from the rail, stretching their arms as if to strike Doyle, jaws jutted, necks corded. Like their ancestors in Salem who'd shrieked disapproval of the town's witches, they seemed on the verge of hysteria.

Claire paid them no heed, content to keep her gaze glued on the affable Mul. Nor did she pay any attention to the commercial activity around her. Customers flung nickels that glinted in the sun toward vendors who snatched them expertly from the air and flipped bags of peanuts back to buyers' outstretched hands. Several bags soared over her head to customers behind her. "Peanuts! Get your peanuts," hawkers bawled.

She sat quietly, back charm-school straight and hands clasped demurely in her lap, her mouth puckered and a small frown pinching her face.

"Doyle, ya slacker," bellowed one of the Royal Rooters, "ya field like a kitten playing with grandma's yarn!"

"You'd muff an apple dumpling if youse was starving!" added another.

Doyle glared at the source of the derision and snarled something I couldn't hear. The crowd pelted him with additional scurrility.

Attracted by the growing cacophony around her, Claire finally lost interest in Mul and looked toward Doyle, her face as white as new-milled flour. "Such coarseness," she muttered. "Why don't they leave the poor man alone?"

"Well," I began, "Dirty Jack Doyle . . . " I didn't finish. She was now staring across the field, toward third base. Suddenly, she pointed excitedly. "There's Mr. McGraw," she said, "I saw his picture in last evening's newspaper." Clearly, she had done her homework. The slight, intense McGraw stood near the third base rail, exchanging warmup throws with a stocky catcher. Claire leaned forward in her seat. "Where's Mr. Jennings? His picture was also in the newspaper. And I remember him from last year."

I indicated a slim red-headed player strolling toward the infield. "There's Hughie Jennings, McGraw's partner in crime," I told her.

The first three innings went by quickly and uneventfully. The Boston hurler, Ted Lewis, and Baltimore's Arlie Pond, retired each batter they faced. Claire watched the proceedings without comment, content simply to make occasional small sounds of approval or disapproval.

Eager to have her enjoy the game and my company, I kept up a running commentary on individual batsmen and game strategy. It was my impression that I was successful on neither front. She listened respectively but did not comment. She merely watched and occasionally made her mewling noises.

Without making too much of it, I kept track of Mikey Mul. I wanted to make sure that I observed each person he contacted. If he were part of this mess with Long and Anspach I needed to know if he had confederates. I watched as he made his way behind the Beaneater bench and lolled against a grandstand post.

In the fourth inning, McGraw bunted but Boston third base man, Jimmy Collins scooped up the ball in his bare hand and snapped a throw to Fred Tenney who stretched far off the base to record the out.

"That was a wonderful play!" Claire told me, her eyes wide. "Just marvelous!"

The fiery McGraw kicked about the call, waving his arms and hopping angrily from one foot to the other. He shouted violently, the tendons of his neck bulging out like rope, but I couldn't make out individual words over the roar of the crowd.

"Stop kicking, Mr. McGraw," Claire said, "The ball beat you to the base." She spoke in a normal voice, apparently not caring whether she was heard, but believing her comment was pertinent. She was getting into the game, no doubt about that. When, in the fifth inning, Germany Long lunged to his right to stab a hard bouncer off the bat of Joe Kelly and threw the Oriole out from his knees, Claire sprang to her feet. "Well done."

"He's the stuff, isn't he?" I said, teasing her. "There's no flies on him."

Though Mul was now leaning over the fence talking to one of the Boston players, he was between me and whoever he was talking to and I couldn't make the player out.

It was in the seventh inning that Claire's reserve collapsed. By that time Mul had moved down the right field line. With one out, Hugh Duffy hit one between the outfielders and raced toward second. As he rounded first, Doyle threw a shoulder into him. Regaining his stride, Duffy scorched around second only to find Jennings blocking his way. Duffy swerved around the devious redhead, again struggling to regain his speed. At third, McGraw squatted to block Duffy, but the diminutive left fielder slid wide, then used his momentum to pivot and grab the bag with his hand. Safe! The crowd was on its feet, as was Claire, cheering Duffy's triple.

"Oh, Mr. Duffy's swift!" she squealed.

"He certainly is," I concurred over the roar of the crowd, leaning in close to her so that she might hear me. I could smell her. The sweet smell of lilacs and talcum.

She turned to me, inches away, eyes bright, face flushed. "Did you see what the Baltimores did?" she asked, her face and hands displaying her exasperation. "They did not play square!"

"No, they certainly did not," I huffed.

"They purposely hampered Mr. Duffy!"

"It's play typical of those ruffians," I noted piously.

Her eyes were wide and her cheeks were flushed with excitement. "We must best them," she said angrily.

Boston did best them. Duffy scored later that inning to put the Bostons up 1-0, and they went on to score four more runs in the eighth. The only unhappy note for the local nine occurred when Sweet Billy Ewing, playing for an injured Bobby Lowe, swung widely at a Pond curve ball, lost his grip on the bat, and slung it wildly behind him. It struck Germany Long, waiting his turn to bat, and sent him sprawling. The pain was great enough that Long had to step aside for a change batsman. Still, Boston prevailed, 5-1.

Claire walked out of The Grounds with me, beaming. She took my proffered arm and leaned in against me as we strolled from the South End grounds with other happy Boston rooters. "The Baltimores are so . . . pugnacious," she marveled. "It's satisfying to see them routed."

Seeking to maintain the momentum in our relationship that I sensed developing, I pressed her to have supper with me.

"I must help Caitlin prepare dinner," she told me, seemingly in disappointment.

"Have coffee with me, then."

She paused only briefly before saying, "Just a coffee, then."

I couldn't believe my luck. And it got even better. Our coffee house conversation went well; I managed to clasp her hands several times during our review of the game. She didn't bring up Bradford Bent's name and I was reluctant to. Naturally, I wanted to know more about her feelings toward him, but preferred to pick my spots. Now wasn't the time. My strategy seemed to work. Later, following our trolley ride, but before we entered the boardinghouse, she bussed me chastely on the cheek and thanked me for taking her to the game.

Though hers was a perfunctory kiss, quick and dry on my cheek, it sent an electric charge through me. For all my experience with women, with Claire I felt like a schoolboy. As she entered the house, I remained on the porch momentarily, smiling smugly, idly twirling my hat in my hands. Full of it as a bull in a field of cows, I tossed my spinning hat easily into the air, then caught it. I'd sent it spinning into the air a second time, higher, when I glimpsed a figure leaning partially behind a tree across the street and several doors down from me. Even in the poor light I recognized the pale green suit. The man moved around more than Nellie Bly in her race against Phineas Phogg.

I stood there dumbstruck, my hat rocking at my feet. Who was watching whom, I wondered, as the figure slipped from behind the tree and quickly disappeared down the darkened street.

22

The following morning Marty Bergen intercepted me just outside The Grounds. A brief thunderstorm had left streets glistening and sidewalks damp and clean. The air was fresh and cool and smelled of the sea. Pedestrians on Columbus seemed to have a bounce in their step, peddlers optimism in their spiels.

Not me. I had not slept well, tossing and tumbling, suffering a series of nightmares. The base ball fields were different in each dream. A few were hardscratch and pebbly, the grass dry and spotty. Others were manicured, green and soft. The results were the same. My mother, still slim, dark-haired and young, would find her seat in the vacant stands and sit impassively, watching my father and me. My father, jaw set, face grim, would take a few tentative swings, then begin to hit ground balls. Despite my years of low-level professional experience as a shortstop, I could not catch the routine bouncers my father sent my way. They richocheted painfully off my ankles, knees, thighs, arms, chest and glove. One particularly awkward—and unsuccesful—lurch in pursuit of a daisy cutter woke me. Rather than endure more, I pulled myself out of bed. Despite my early rising, I came to The Grounds later than usual, still distracted, my eyes scratchy from lack of sleep.

Standing with Marty was Bradford Bent, impeccably dressed and barbered, looking alert and rested. The man was handsome and the last person I wanted to see at the moment. Rumpled and preoccupied, I had no desire to stand comparison with the urbane and confident Mr. Bent.

Marty hailed me. "Will, could I have a minute?"

He took Bent's arm and approached me, smiling broadly, or at least as broadly as I'd ever seen him smile. "What a surprise, Will. I thought you'd be busy in Conant's office. I generally don't see you when I come in." He clamped my arm, a long lost friend.

For reasons that I couldn't put my finger on at the moment, I didn't buy his surprise—or our fortuitous meeting. As for his enthusiasm, Marty wasn't the type to be effusive about anything. In addition, he commuted from his farm and seldom showed up at the Grounds before noon. He'd been waiting for me, and so had Bradford Bent, I had no doubt of that. The question was why.

"What can I do for you, Marty?"

Marty stepped back from Bent and held out his palm toward me. "Will Beaman, Mr. Bradford Bent. You remember Mr. Bent from the dinner at The Liberty Tree? He's a, uh, business associate of mine."

Bent gripped my hand and pumped it vigorously several times, all the while beaming at me. "A pleasure, Mr. Beaman, I'm sure."

Saying nothing, I looked expectantly at Marty.

Marty read my look. "Mr. Bent wanted to meet you," he said with a shrug.

Bent continued to beam. "I'm sorry we didn't have the opportunity to speak at The Liberty Tree. By the time Miss Denihur and I worked our way through the crowd, you had already departed." He looked about as if he'd suddenly forgotten where he was. "Perhaps we could retire to Cosgrove's for a coffee? Or tea? You look like you could use a hot drink."

I wasn't in the mood for this. "I don't think so, Mr. Bent. Perhaps some other time."

"Mr. Bent wants to talk business with you, Will," Marty said. "He thinks you have real promise."

"Marty," Bent smiled graciously and urged the catcher away. "Perhaps you could leave Mr. Beaman and me alone for a few minutes? We can meet after the game." He turned to me. "Give me a few minutes, Mr. Beaman," He gave me a knowing wink. "I'll make it worth your while."

Well, why not? I didn't know what was on his mind but I wasn't about to pass up an opportunity to get to know him better. I had a lot of questions for Mr. Bent and only part of them had to do with his business. I wanted to size up this pitchman for the Klondike Mining Syndicate and suitor to Claire Denihur. And, God knows, I needed coffee. "A few minutes, then."

We strolled in silence to Cosgrove's, dodging streetcar and horse traffic on Tremont. The crowd at Cosgrove's was sparse. We easily found a table and ordered, strong black coffee for me, tea for Mr. Bent.

I saw no reason to beat around the bush and barely waited until the waiter had placed our drinks before us before asking, "You can make it worth my while? How?"

He smiled knowingly. "Ah, a man after my own heart, gets right to the point." He sipped his steaming tea, looking at me as if he were eyeing me over a pair of eyeglasses. "I've heard very good things about you, Mr. Beaman."

I took several swallows of the black coffee, feeling ever more alert as the hot liquid surged through my system. "From whom, Mr. Bent?"

He dismissed my question with a wave of his hand. "You're young, intelligent and ambitious. I like that. Exactly the kind of chap I want in the Klondike Mining Syndicate."

"You want *me* to be part of your syndicate?"

"Precisely."

"Doing what?"

"Supervising my New York operations."

"New York?"

He nodded enthusiastically. "New York. It's a great opportunity for an energetic, ambitious young man. A chance to do *very* well, indeed."

"And you think *I'm* the man for the job?" I asked, smiling sardonically.

He pushed forward, eyes narrowed, jaw set, intense, all business now. "Oh, I know you are. You have the skills and character and personality to serve the Syndicate effectively in New York's sporting community. You're accustomed to athletes. You can talk to them, show them the benefits of investing in our venture."

"I know the Boston sporting world better," I protested.

He pushed his hands toward me, palms out, like a man stopping a train. "Of course, but the Syndicate is in excellent shape here in Boston. I have several outstanding associates here already. *I* can oversee progress here. It's New York where investment capital is slow in coming."

Bent was intense, locking eyes on mine. But I wasn't buying his sincerity, not by a jugful. I'd seen those same eyes in the mirror. "I already have a job, Mr. Bent."

"I'm prepared to double your current salary," he said without hesitation.

"Double my salary? Do you even know how much I earn?"

He didn't blink. "I'll double your salary, sir."

This was getting more and more curious. "I'd have to leave Boston? And my, uh, friends?"

"Opportunity beckons in New York, Mr. Beaman. There would be commissions and bonuses, of course."

Could it be? *Was* the man sincere? Could I afford to be cavalier regarding his offer? After all, my current job wasn't all that secure. And my bank account was as empty as a tax collector's heart. "That's a good deal of money."

He dipped his head, one confidant to another, and examined his perfectly trimmed and buffed finger nails. He tugged out his cuffs and examined them as well. "It most certainly is, Mr. Beaman."

"You're sure, I'm the man for the job?"

He checked the edge of a nail with a finger and eyed it again, exuding vanity and self-assurance. "Absolutely."

The man was persuasive, I had to give him that. "When would I have to take this job?"

"Immediately."

"Pack up and leave for New York?"

"That's where opportunity awaits you."

"And you'd double my salary and provide commisions and bonuses?"

"And provide you stock at preferred rates."

Libby's knickers! I suddenly felt like J.P. Morgan at a Republican Party fund raiser, wooed and slobbered over.

"But I need to know quickly," he told me. "There are several very qualified young men eager for the position. I need to made a decision."

"How soon?"

"Let me know by the weekend."

Why so soon? Why me? What had I done to impress this man? What did he really know about me? These questions brought with them a wave of depression and the suspicion that Bent's concern for my welfare was a sham. The more he talked about business opportunities the more convinced I became that it was not business at all between the two of us. More than wanting me in New York, I had the nagging feeling that Bent wanted me away from Boston. Why was that? My interest in the assault upon Long? Anna's death? My interest in Claire?

"This is all very sudden, Mr. Bent," I told him. "I have a job I like here in Boston. My friends are here. It would be difficult to leave."

Bent's eyes hardened; he looked like a gentleman asked by a maid to empty the chamberpot. He clasped his hands before him, knuckles white, and hunched forward. His mustache twitched. "I'm a generous man, Mr. Beaman. But my generosity has limits. As has my patience. Opportunity does not wait. No, sir. I have no truck with those who do not have the ginger to grasp opportunity when it presents itself." His knuckles cracked under the pressure of his grip. "Don't disappoint me, Mr. Beaman."

As he delivered those last admonitions, I thought I glimpsed the real Bradford Bent—a man who did not like to be crossed. And I suspected that included being crossed in his romantic goals.

23

The first opportunity to impress the Boston ownership with my promotional skills came on Wednesday with the arrival of the lowly Louisville Colonels. Baltimore, last year's pennant winner and a favorite to repeat—and notorious for its dirty play—drew crowds like bees to honey. The turnstiles spun when the Birds were in town. Louisville was another matter. Mired in the cellar, the Colonels offered fans few star attractions. They did boast a hard-hitting outfielder in Fred Clarke, but sharps knew their best player was newcomer Honus Wagner. Unfortunately for Louisville— and for me, as I tried to seduce viewers to watch them play—the Colonels were struggling while waiting for Wagner to blossom.

Sputtering teams did not draw fans—either at home or on the road. And that's where I came in. Under mounting pressure from Soden, I organized a combination Ladies Day and Field Sports Day to entice rooters to the opening game of the Boston-Louisville series. Knowing that my job might be on the line (maybe both jobs, as I'd made little progress on the Long-Anspach investigations), I worked tirelessly to guarantee the promotion's success. I didn't see Claire for two days. It was longer than that since I'd talked with Sean. Despite my hard work and careful planning, I was as jumpy as a kid with a wasp in his pants.

Adding to my discomfort was the fact that weeks before I'd promised Molly I'd take her to the Ladies Day game. Obviously, I would rather have asked Claire, but a promise is a promise. And so, I found myself sitting next to Molly watching people meander into the stands. And on the alert for Mikey Mul. At the Baltimore game I had been intent on observing Mul. Now, I was more concerned that he was watching me. His interest in me was disconcerting to say the least. I preferred the role of the hound to that of the stag.

My discomfort with Mul notwithstanding, I was even more anxiously watching the lowering and darkening skies. Rain would bite deeply into the numbers drawn to the park to enjoy the pre-game high jinks. When the field events began, the crowd did not look promising. Fewer than fifteen hundred people had pushed through the gate. I nervously wiped perspiration from my palms.

Though I had organized the pre-game activities, arranged for particular participants, and publicized the contests in the previous week, John Haggerty was to oversee the on-field details. The first contest pitted players from each team in a race from left field to home plate. The husky, bow-legged Louisville youngster, Honus Wagner, surprised fans and players

117

alike by outpacing everyone. A second contest matched players in a race against bicyclists. To my growing chagrin, the crowd's reaction to the races was lukewarm. A contest where players and fans tried to lob base balls across the infield into a bucket, brought greater approval.

I began to relax. Not only was the crowd warming to my program, but the sky began to lighten. The stream of fans, a slow trickle when the pre-game ceremonies began, was now a steady flow. It looked to me that the total might go above three thousand. Unlike most days at The Grounds, this crowd was laced with bonneted and beribboned female rooters, taking advantage of tickets at half price.

Molly could hardly sit still. She clasped her hands in her lap and scooted to the edge of her seat to watch the milking contest. Having seen my share of similar contests in minor league parks, I let my eyes wander. Most of the seats in the pavilion and grandstands were taken now, and the left and right field bleachers were filling rapidly. The always easily-spotted Mikey Mul was standing behind the Boston bench.

A sliver of sunshine highlighted bright red hair on a man in a row twenty yards to my left. Sean Dennison? I sprang to my feet to look, but at that moment the cow bellowed and broke free from its handler, tumbling a Louisville player trying to milk it, and trotted toward the outfield. The crowd stood and hooted, blocking my view of Sean—or whoever it was. I craned to see if it was Sean, and if so, who he was with, but without success.

Nor were my attempts in the next half hour rewarded. Even when the cranks sat following the cow's capture, I didn't spot the man I thought was Sean. Worse, the more I thought about it, the more I became convinced that Claire and Cait were surely with him.

The game itself eventually took my mind off the man to my left. Although Molly asked me a hundred questions about the game and players, it was not an easy task providing answers what with her bounding to her feet on virtually every play to bellow her excitement or derision. She was no Claire Denihur. Nor were Molly's the restrained mutterings of most females in attendance. Hers was the earsplitting assault of the true crank. She was as demure as a rogue elephant.

"You're off your feed, Lowe!" shouted a large, red-faced man when Bobby Lowe muffed a bounder in the fifth inning.

"You're a lobster!" cried another. "Yuh couldn't pick blackberries."

"That ball ain't a greased-pig, you bum! That's damned loose work!" brayed a third.

Molly rocketed to her feet. "You hooligans," she seethed. "Lowe plays to the limit. He's plucky! Don't you dare roast him."

"He plays like a schoolboy," the florid-faced man retorted.

"He's steady and nervy," she insisted. She turned to the field and screeched. "Come on, boys, ginger up!"

"Ah, clam up, lady," growled the florid-faced crank two seats away. "What d' you know about base ball?"

Molly plunged at the man, leaning angrily into the man next to her and clawing at her detractor. "Don't you dare tell me to shut up, you liver-faced, simian . . ."

I circled her with my arms and pulled her back into her seat. "Simmer down, Miss Muldine," I admonished her in exaggerated formality. "This is a base ball contest, not a public riot."

But Molly was not to be mollified. Her face a deep scarlet now, she struggled to free herself from my grasp and lunge at the man two seats away. "You snotty-faced horse's bum!" she screamed, "You wouldn't know base ball from pig pokin'—"

I grabbed her and muffled her mouth.

The game forgotten, the crowd now stared at Molly and me, and roasted us good.

"You got a lot more 'n you can handle there, sonny," one man shouted derisively at me.

"By Christ, he's got more woman than *any* man could handle," laughed another.

"That's ain't no woman, that's a flaming banshee," roared a third.

By now half the people in the pavilion and right field stands seemed to be pointing at us, staring and laughing. I was afraid to look toward Soden's and Conant's seats to see if they were aware of our exhibition. I don't know whose face was redder, Molly's from anger or mine from embarrassment. I knew that Claire would never embarrass me like that. I needed to end my relationship with Molly the unbridled. I couldn't think of a serious relationship with Claire until putting my life in order. And that meant ending it with Molly.

When she finally settled back to watch the game, I swung my gaze in search of the red-headed man. And for the next half hour or so, I kept my attention divided between the field and my search. By the seventh inning I was desperate for an excuse to indulge in a more thorough search for him. I had to know if Sean was there, and if Claire and Cait were with him. In the eighth inning, determined to find out once and for all if Sean were there, I excused myself and pushed to the main aisle. By now I'd forgotten about Mikey Mul.

Before I could move to a better locale, Haggerty yelled up at me. He was standing on the field, leaning over the rail, motioning and bellowing at me with that fog horn voice of his. I jogged down the aisle toward him, all the while looking to my left, trying to spot Sean. Haggerty grabbed me in one of his huge paws and patted me on the shoulder. "Just talked to Soden. He's as happy as a boar with two dicks. You done well, laddybuck. Soden'll be wanting you fer a son-in-law, you don't watch it." He shoved me roughly but playfully away. "I've got some ideas of me own for the next time, m'boy."

I waved my thanks, told him we'd talk about his ideas, and headed up the aisle. When I finally reached a point where I had a clear view of the section, there was no redhead. I stood frozen in the aisle, letting my eyes pan a second section. As my gaze reached the top of the aisle, perhaps one hundred feet above me, my eyes locked on those of Mikey Mul. Clearly, he'd been watching me for some time.

Enough of this nonsensical game of hide 'n seek, I thought, and bolted up the aisle toward him. I'd hardly moved, however, before he disappeared. By the time I reached the top, I knew I had no chance of finding him. Frustrated and more than a little angry, not to mention badly winded, I found my way back to Molly.

Boston scored a run in the ninth on Hamilton's triple and Collins's single to salt the game away and the happy crowd began to drift out of the park. Eager to get Molly on a trolley and to continue my search for Sean and, possibly, the Denihur sisters, I pushed through the crowd. At the trolley, I urged Molly up into a car.

Gripping the leather strap, she beamed down at me. "It was a lovely day, Will. Thank you." She leaned down, cupped my neck in her hand, and kissed me deeply. She giggled and swung into the car, waving to me, handkerchief in her hand.

I retreated a step, speechless, abashed by her public display. As I stepped back and turned toward the park, I saw them. Sean, Claire, and Cait. They stood there staring at me, their mouths open in amazement.

Twenty yards behind them, mouth grim, eyes unreadable, was Mikey Mul.

24

What was wrong with me? I couldn't sustain anything. I generally overcame my bad luck and poor decisions. But I too frequently squandered my good luck and progress. I'd made strides tying Long's assault to Anna's death, but then lost my focus when Mikey Mul turned the tables on me. I'd offended my friends with my bad behavior, only to have Bradford Bent promise me wealth and influence. I'd made headway courting Claire, then lost her through my stupidity with Molly. What I needed to do was manage four steps forward, not one forward and three back.

With the Denihur sisters giving me the cold shoulder and Sean being polite but frosty, I decided to spend my evenings away from the boardinghouse, hunting Mikey Mul. With Bent's proposition—and my ambivalence about the man—swirling in my head, I needed to keep busy. I determined to confront Mul. Enough of this cat and mouse stuff.

I didn't find him on Thursday. Friday evening, I popped into McCarthy's. There, upstairs, the dozen or so pool tables were in use, and clusters of would-be players huddled behind competitors shouting insults and waiting their turn. Publican Thomas Francis Michael (Tommy) McCarthy circulated among his customers, loud and gregarious. The atmosphere was casual. Men shucked coats and jackets; many unbuttoned their vests and discarded their hats. A few had rolled up their shirt sleeves. With virtually everyone smoking, the air was thick and blue. Dozens of conversations created a loud buzz in the room, punctuated occasionally by sharp laughter, pins being toppled in the bowling alley below, and the clacking of billiard balls.

I peeled an eye for Mikey Mul. No luck. It seemed as if everyone was there *but* Mul. I did spot Tim Murnane, and pushed my way through the crowd toward him. He was talking to a half dozen ball players waiting their turn at a table. Marty Bergen, Germany Long, Billy Ewing, Kid Nichols. Also, Chick Stahl. Ewing was jawing with Cy Young and Bobby Wallace from the Cleveland club, in town to start a series tomorrow. I grabbed Murnane by the elbow. "Seen Mikey Mul?"

"Not tonight, I haven't," he said, shaking his head and disengaging. He shoved his way toward a newly-available table.

For the next two hours, the crowd milled, smoked, quaffed huge quantities of alcohol, and took turns at billiards. Clumps of men formed and reformed. The evening wore on and the numbers thinned. Mikey Mul did not appear.

Having been soundly thrashed at billiards by Bobby Wallace, the diminutive Cleveland shortstop, I sprawled on a bench next to Murnane at the rear of the room. Bergen, Long, Stahl, Nichols, and Ewing also were there, taking a smoke. As usual, the moody Bergen seemed somehow removed from the others. Frankly, I was surprised to see him. Billy Ewing probably invited him; he was the only Beaneater who chummed with Bergen. Wallace, following his triumph over me, had refilled his stein and joined us. Apparently Cy Young had departed.

"Everything go all right with Mr. Bent?" Marty asked.

I waved him off. "Fine. Everything's fine." I didn't want to talk to Marty about Bent. I fanned the few bills remaining in my hand and decided I was through playing for the night.

"It's a good thing the wagering was modest on your play, darlin'," Murnane ribbed me, "or you'd have to get a second job. And maybe a third."

The men chuckled knowingly.

"The key is learning how to recoup your losses," laughed Billy Ewing.

"Billy's right," added Bergen, "if you're lousy at billiards—and you are, Will—bet on something that's more a sure thing."

"Like what?"

"Like dogs, or nags, or sculls, or sulkies, or bikers," sneered Bergen, his tone making it unclear just how serious he was.

I sat back, loosened my tie, and shoved my remaining bills into my pocket. I pulled my sweaty shirt away from my body and remained silent.

Bobby Wallace picked up the slack, directing his comments toward Bergen. "I've lost enough bills on the mutts to build a palace. I hear everyone in Bean Town is putting their dough on the Yukon."

"People around here are going crazy over prospects there," Bergen conceded, nodding his head vigorously. "A boatload left for the gold fields last week."

"Hell, I don't want to *go* to the Klondike," Wallace scoffed. "I'm a ball player. I just want to make money *investing* in the gold rush."

I was easing myself into the group to hear better what was being said, when Chick Stahl, spoke up. "I'd throw my money away before I invested in those chuckleheaded schemes. I've heard some are crookeder than a snake."

Billy Ewing grunted like a bee-stung bull and leaned past Bergen. "Horseshit. Cowards never hit it big and they always piss about companies being crooked."

Stahl's face reddened, but he didn't back down. "I heard that the Klondike Mining Syndicate is a scam. Pure and simple. It has about as much credibility as a peach in a bucket of elephant dung."

"Oh, horseshit!" seethed Ewing, unaware of the humor of his retort.

"Rookies," Bergen mumbled disparagingly.

"Where'd you get that idea?" I asked Stahl. Rookie or not, he had always impressed me as an intelligent and thoughtful chap.

"This oughta be good," Ewing sniffed.

Stahl glared at him. "Scuttlebutt at the Base Ball Exchange. Some gent said Bradford Bent was behind a scheme that collapsed in New York two years ago. Bent got rich. Everyone else got soaked."

Bergen pushed toward Stahl, teeth bared. "That's crap. Bent is up and up and the Klondike Mining Syndicate is as sound as gold." He shoved roughly at Stahl.

Little Bobby Wallace and Kid Nichols moved quicker than I did to wedge themselves between Stahl and Bergen. "Gentleman," Wallace laughed, "I should let you beat the shit out of each other. It'd make my job easier tomorrow at the ball park."

Ewing snatched Marty by the coat and jerked him away from Stahl, saying, "Easy, Marty, easy."

I edged next to Stahl and nodded toward Wallace. "Mr. Wallace is right. You fellows are team mates. Don't let a disagreement over where to invest your money hurt the team."

Germany Long had remained a silent observer. Now he stepped forward and put his hand on Stahl's shoulder. "Chick's right about one thing," he said. "There are lots of schemes out there and lots of grifters eager to scam us. A guy's got to be careful where he puts his dough. I don't know whether Bent's Klondike Mining Syndicate is legit or not, but an investor'd better look very carefully at whatever company he drops cash in." He looked at Billy and Marty in turn. "There are some funny stories going around."

"I've heard some of the same stories Chick mentioned," I put in, adding fuel to the fire, hoping to encourage others who might've heard stories similar to those Long alluded to.

Bergen, his face still flushed and his eyes wide, sneered. "I *have* looked at Bent's company carefully. And I have money in it. It's a sure thing." He turned and addressed me directly. "You've talked with Bent. You know he's square."

Billy Ewing didn't let me respond. "I've put my money in Bent's syndicate. And I may put more," he said.

"Suckers," Stahl snickered, wheeling and heading for the door. "You're gonna lose your shirts."

"To hell with you!" Bergen shouted at Stahl's back.

Long and Nichols circled Bergen and Ewing with outstretched arms and herded them toward the bench. "Hey, hey," Nichols said, "Calm down. Chick's one of us."

"You guys have this much ginger on the ball field?" kidded Bobby Wallace, doing his part to calm Ewing and Bergen and defuse the situation. "The next brew's on me."

Ewing, Bergen, and Wallace slumped on the bench, but Long and Nichols remained standing, still alert to trouble. Long's warning against Bent's syndicate intrigued me. I wanted to hear more about stories he referred to. I sidled up to him and eased him away from the others. "Want to elaborate on those funny stories you mentioned?"

He tugged out his pocket watch and studied it for a long moment. "Hmmm. Not tonight I don't. Told the little woman I'd get home early."

I filled my lungs as if ready to hold my head under water in an endurance contest. Then I let my words out in a rush. "How about dinner tomorrow night? After the game? Bring Mrs. Long. On me."

He stared at me, trying to make up his mind. "Dinner tomorrow night. Seven o'clock at Doherty's Oyster House."

He squeezed my shoulder and excused himself, but he paused after a few steps and looked back at me. "Just the two of us. And I'll take care of the tab."

I expelled my breath again in relief, and waved at a waiter. Now I could afford at least one more beer.

25

I arrived at Doherty's before Germany Long. It didn't take me the five-minute wait to guess why he chose this eatery. Here our privacy would be assured. Ball players generally didn't frequent Doherty's. Too plush. Too expensive. And the restaurant certainly didn't solicit ball players as customers. Players' reputations as rough, uncouth, and violent men preceded them.

Long asked the maitre d' for a secluded table and we were seated in a back corner, not far from the kitchen. Long had the waiter trim the lamp near us. We sat in dim light. Someone would have to get pretty close to recognize either of us. In addition, business was slow. We had all the privacy and anonymity we might wish. The waiter took our orders crisply and scurried off.

I studied Long. Well-dressed, clean cut and clean shaven, his blue wide-set eyes were bright with intelligence. I was reminded again that he was not a handsome man but, rather, uncomplicated looking, a man's man. Scars from his beating had healed to the point they were barely visible. In his finely-tailored suit, he looked more the prosperous businessman than ball player.

"You've had a wonderful career," I said.

"Well, it ain't over yet!" he said, in mock asperity.

"No. No. I just meant, I've followed your career—."

"I know what you meant," he said, holding his hands up, palms out, in a placating gesture. "Yeah, I've had a good career. Had some rocky years early on, but once I got to Boston, things looked up."

"You're the best short stop in the League."

He didn't dispute that. "Having Collins on one side and Lowe on the other hasn't hurt. They're quick as kittens."

Our meals arrived and we attacked them with gusto. During dinner our conversation strayed from base ball to the topics of the day. Long was well informed and talked easily about American policy toward Cuba's Butcher Weyler, the American Cup Race, the switch from gas to electricity in the city, the proposed elevated, and plumbing innovations in hotels. Only when our plates had been cleared away and the brandy poured, did I bring up the reason behind our meeting. "I take it that you have not invested in the Klondike Mining Syndicate."

"No."

He tugged a cheroot from his inside coat pocket and offered it to me. When I waved the cigar off, he stuck the cheroot in his mouth.

"But you've heard stories about it?"

"Just rumors," he said, lighting the stogie and taking a long pull on it. "Some of the same ones Chick Stahl mentioned."

I made motions with my fingers for him to continue.

"Well, one is that Bradford Bent baled out of a New York investment company several years ago, letting investors take the fall," he said, blowing a stream of blue smoke over his right shoulder. "I've heard, too, that he has a jail record in the Midwest. All hearsay, of course."

"What about the Klondike Mining Syndiate?"

He shrugged and made a face. "Nothing other than that Bent is the brains behind it. And that Billy and Marty seem convinced it's going to make them rich. They're probably not alone in thinking that."

"You've not looked into Bent or his syndicate personally?"

"I'm a ball player," Long snorted and waved his cheroot at me. "I don't have the inclination, ability, time, or resources to investigate Bent's syndicate."

"Heard anything suspicious about Lawrence Reed's Alaska Gold Syndicate?"

"Nope," he said, exhaling a thin stream of smoke away from me.

"Or Lawrence Reed himself?"

"Nope."

"You think Bradford Bent's company is a scam?" I asked again.

"Don't know."

"Think Billy and Marty are working for him?"

"Don't know that either, but I've heard enough about Bent to make me reluctant to put my savings or salary into his company."

Thinking about Bent's offer the previous morning to me, I asked Long if Bent had ever offered him a piece of the syndicate or any job connected with it. He told me no.

"I appreciate your willingness to talk to me about the ball club," I told him.

"I'm interested in anything that will help our nine win," he said, shrugging.

Because I hadn't sensed in Long any inclination toward evasiveness, I opted for even more direct questions. I leaned toward him, resting my arms on the table and making a steeple with my fingers. "Do you think that the recent attack on you was designed to put you out of the lineup so that the team would lose?"

He didn't blink. Just nodded as if to tell me he understood the question. "I've thought about it." He shook his head suddenly and drew on his cigar. "But it makes no sense. Our team is too well balanced. One man can't make that much difference. We've got the best depth in the League."

I noted the obvious: "The team hasn't done well without you."

He conceded my point with a canting of his head. "It's had some tough breaks."

I again pointed out the obvious. "Billy has caused some of those breaks."

"What're you suggesting?" he asked, his pale blue eyes squinting.

"Billy's erratic play has come at unfortunate times."

He swiveled slightly, looking at me out of the corners of his eyes. "You're suggesting Billy's deliberately making errors? Throwing games?"

I separated my hands and wiggled them at him. "When you're out, he's in, and when he's made errors or failed to hit at crucial times, Boston's lost."

He stubbed the unfinished cheroot into the ashtray and twisted it roughly. "Yes, but—"

I didn't let him finish. "And it was Billy who let the bat fly that injured you again once you returned to the lineup. Against Baltimore."

"He's had a run of bad luck, that's true," he said, continuing to stab the crumbled cigar into the ashtray, now with more vigor.

"As you've had. What do you know about Billy? Known him long?"

Long pursed his lips. "It's his first year in Boston. He played some minor league ball in New York."

"No stories about him? No special connection with gamblers?"

"None I heard of. Like every player, he knows gamblers, sees them every day at the park."

"No dressing room grousing about his queering games?"

Long blinked and shook his head more slowly, thoughtfully. "Most of the awkwardness in the dressing room centers on Marty. He's a troubled man."

I let that pass. I knew about Marty's volatility. "Ever see Billy with Mikey Mul?"

"They've talked before games. I've also seen them together at McCarthy's. And at McGreevey's with Mikey's sister."

It was my turn to blink. "*Mikey's sister?*"

"Molly."

"Molly Muldine and Mikey Mul are *brother* and *sister*?" I croaked. Sweet Jesus, I'd been sleeping with the sister of a man possibly deeply involved in . . . God knows what? I suddenly couldn't catch my breath. "Molly Muldine is Mikey Mul's sister?" I repeated stupidly. I could barely control my voice.

His brows edged up a notch. "Didn't you know?" he asked, "Mikey Mul is Michael Muldine."

Sweat popped out on my forehead. I swallowed and tried to slow my heart beat.

The mind is a funny instrument. No sooner than Long told me that Mikey and Molly were siblings, then I remembered Haggerty telling me on my first day that Mikey had showed up at games about a year ago. I also recalled Sean informing me during our first meeting at McGreevey's that McGreevey had hired Molly a year ago last summer. The fact that they'd surfaced in Boston at the same time had meant nothing to me until now. And now was too late. What else had I missed? "And you were aware that Mikey Mul—Michael Muldine—knew Anna?" I asked Long. "Even that they were close?"

He nodded. "Un huh."

"How'd you know that?"

"Oh, I knew Anna pretty well. Among other things, she talked to me about investing. Said she wanted to put some of her savings into investments."

"Why you?"

"She came to a team party at the Selees. Met my wife who introduced her to me. The three of us—and, later, the Lowes—talked about investment possibilities. Mostly in generalities." He shrugged his shoulders. "Lots of players and their wives are looking for ways to make additional money. Our careers aren't very long."

"What advice did you give Anna?"

"I told her what I tell anyone who asks—that there are lots of shady characters and cons around to stiff people like us. Told her she'd better be careful who she associated with, and where she put her money."

"You weren't surprised that a simple working girl like Anna would be plotting investments?"

He shrugged. "*Everyone* in Boston is plotting how to get rich. Besides, she was talking modest sums." He leaned forward and locked eyes with me. "Why are *you* so interested in all this?"

I gave him a neutral smile. "I don't want team personnel getting hurt, or it costing the team."

He made a low, snorting sound. "And because of that you're looking into gambling among the players and Billy's possible link to them?"

"Something like that."

He lurched back, his hands flat on the table, his arms straight and rigid in front of him. "Son, you be careful you don't end up hurting the very people you're trying to help. You show Soden and Conant that players are gambling, even betting on the team, and they'll force us into even more restrictive contracts."

"I don't follow."

He waved vaguely. "They'll write tough moral clauses into our contracts and limit what we can do outside baseball."

"They'd do that?"

"Damned tootin', they would—they have—and will again." Suddenly animated, he pounded a fist on the table, then scrunched down and looked around to see if the noise had attracted attention. "Look, man, you've got to understand something. Players bet on anything and everything. Players bet on their own games. They always have. Mostly, it involves chump change. The owners claim there's no betting in league parks but it goes on. They know about it; hell, they do it theirselves. But, if they come to believe it's *big* money players are putting down, and that it's compromising the game, they'll tighten up our contracts, sure."

We talked for another twenty minutes before Long paid for our meals and we left. By the time we departed Doherty's, a thunderstorm had lowered on the city and was drenching it. The streets, black and shining, were deserted as we moved toward the corner to hail a cab.

We were walking into the rain, heads down, hands stuffed in our pockets, when we neared an alley separating Doherty's from a furrier's. In the silence that had settled between us, I thought about what I'd learned today. Molly and Mikey were siblings. Anna and Mikey were lovers. Anna was investing, maybe in the same schemes Mikey was. Mikey and Billy were acquaintances. Perhaps Ewing was responsible for the Beaneaters' slump. Despite limiting myself to two glasses of wine, my head spun in confusion as I sorted through the pieces of the puzzle.

At the byway, dark forms shifted in the shadows and lurched toward us. Instinctively I threw up an arm to protect myself and tumbled away from the mouth of the alley. Pain seared through my brain as something hard slammed against my head. Strength left my legs like air from a punctured balloon. I toppled sideways, only dimly aware of Germany Long pitching downward. Then everything went black.

26

Cobblestones bit into my knees and the chill dampness soaked my trousers as I slowly regained my senses. Breath as sour as turpentine assaulted my nostrils and chin bristle scraped my cheek. Somebody was holding me from behind, arms under my armpits, hands clasped before my chest, his cheek against mine.

Long was on his feet, but being pressed flat against the building in front of me by two rough-looking plug-uglies. The two men restraining him looked like footpads who'd just burgled Shuman's Clothier and helped themselves to his finest. A stern fellow in a smart-looking suit and expensive bowler, clearly more accustomed to fancy threads, faced me, feet spread. His fists, encased in expensive leather gloves, were on his hips. He stared at me as if he were trying to judge the intellectual capacity of dirt. "You understand how it is, do you not?" he asked me pleasantly and politely—and in precise, clipped English.

I tried to raise my arms but had no strength. I did manage to shake my head, trying desperately to clear the cobwebs from my mind. "Understand?"

The ape supporting me hoisted me slightly, gripped me tighter with his left arm, and cuffed me savagely on the ear with a rock-like right hand. He addressed me in terms that would have made stevedores blush. Blood oozed from my nose and dribbled down my chin and onto my shirt. My head rang. Bright colors danced before my eyes.

The gent facing me acted as if nothing had happened; he remained studiously courteous, almost bored. "Mr. Beaman," he said, pointing a leather-gloved finger at me for emphasis. "You simply cannot continue to talk rot publicly about the syndicates. It is not in our interests to have you spreading false alarms. Or, in your interests, either. Surely, you understand that?"

He turned to Long still pinned to the building by the dapper thugs, and spoke conversationally. "And, you Mr. Long, do you understand, sir?"

Long bobbed his head.

I shook my head, blinked my eyes, and tried to make sense out of what was going on. A horse nickering drew my attention to my right where a half block away a four-horse carriage waited at the curb, the animals dancing nervously in place. A man wearing a cutaway Prince Albert coat and topper leaned casually against the large, dark carriage, watching us. He looked vaguely familiar. Before I could figure out where I'd seen him previously, the gent in front of me stepped forward, leaned down and lifted my head by putting a leather finger under my chin, and tilting it up, turning it toward him. He peered intently into my eyes. "There will be no further calling into question the legitimacy or trustworthiness of Alaskan syndicates," he said, tilting my head up farther. "None, sir. Not a single utterance. Understand?"

His smooth, cool finger holding my chin helped me shake my head, yes. He retreated a step and smiled, satisfied. "Then good evening to you, Mr. Beaman." He spun around and raised a forefinger vaguely toward the brim of his hat. "And to you, Mr. Long, sir."

He nodded brusquely to his henchman and strolled casually toward the carriage. His associates trailed after him, a hunter and his hounds. The gentleman who'd been observing us stepped into the carriage, the men in tow.

When the thug released me, I fell forward on my hands and knees and remained there, dazed. Long continued to lean against the wall as the carriage pulled away from the curb and passed us at a fast clip. Fittingly, one of the horses dropped a ripe trail of steaming road apples before us. Only one of the two carriage side windows was shuttered. As the carriage clattered past, under the street light, I glimpsed a large, florid man with the gray-red, worm-like strands of hair hanging from beneath his topper. Lawrence Reed! The Alaskan Gold Syndicate man!

Long and I had surprisingly little to say to each other once the carriage turned the corner and we were again alone in the rain-slickened street. My hands shook, whether from fear or rage I don't know. I would like to believe that I'm physically intimidated by no man in a face-to-face confrontation. My father and I had spent many a happy hour practicing boxing skills when I was young and it had been he who had encouraged me to box at Harvard. But apparently man-to-man frays weren't popular in the streets of Boston. It was damned frustrating.

Long seemed more embarrassed than cowed by what had happened. He hailed a hansom and gave me a lift to the trolley tracks. We rode in silence, each content to brood inwardly about our recent impotence in the grasp of the plug-uglies.

"Did you recognize the man in the carriage?" I asked after a long moment. "The one who was obviously paying the mugs to rough us up?"

"No," Long muttered. "I don't know who it was. But, it was obvious those guys were pros."

"The dapper gent who did the talking knew you. Think he was behind the earlier attacks upon you?"

Long pursed his lips. "Maybe. But lots of people recognize me. Anyone who's interested in base ball." He lapsed into silence again, a man perplexed.

As he left me at the trolley tracks, I called after him, "We'll talk more about what happened later?" He didn't turn around.

At Denihur's boardinghouse it was dark on the main level. I let myself quietly in the rear door and crept up the stairs. I had just inserted my key in the lock on my door when Sean's voice startled me.

"Saints preserve us, what happened to *you*?" he asked. He was striding down the hall in his robe, coming from his bath, looking pink and refreshed. It was one of the few times I've seen him without a pencil in his hand or behind his ear.

"Why do you ask?" I inquired as innocently as I could.

He snorted. "Normally you don't come in drenched to the skin and looking like you've gone twelve rounds with Sailor Tom Sharkey."

"That bad?"

"Worse, boyo." He dropped the jocular banter and moved in close. He reached up tentatively and touched my right cheek lightly. "Hurt?" I could smell soap and talcum.

I probed my face gently, winced in pain. "Now that you mention it."

My cheekbone and eye socket were sore to the touch. My ear still burned and my head rang from the cuffing I'd received at the hands of my brutish companion.

"Who did it?"

I wasn't in the mood to talk about the attack. Besides, I didn't *know* much about it, really, except that it hurt. I mumbled, "Don't know. A random attack, I suppose."

Sean nodded. "A lot of that going arouund." He tugged at my sleeve. "Come to my room. I have some medicine that'll fix you up."

Suddenly the idea of a stiff drink was very appealing. "Medicine, is it? Do Claire and Caitlin know about your medicine?"

"Don't even think thoughts like those," he said, making a face and baring his teeth. "Or I'll be sharing the dog house you currently occupy." He opened his door and motioned me into his room.

A half hour later we were sprawled in his chairs, stomachs glowing and heads buzzing from Sean's generous portions of medication. A fine physician, John Barleycorn.

Sean held up his glass in a gesture of toasting. "To this fine healing broth."

I returned his gesture. "Speaking of healing, has Claire spoken of me?"

He closed one eye and pulled away as if he had been punched. "Don't go down that alley, boyo. There's only more pain fer you there."

"Still upset, huh?"

"Madder than a farmer with a fox in his chicken coop."

"Well, I suppose the good news is she cares enough about me to be wounded by my stupidity," I said, trying to smile.

Sean made a dismissive sound and muttered, "Ah, wishes are wasted things, Will lad. And you are a stupid man." The liquor blunted the sharpness of his observation.

"So, I'm 'bout as popular around here as Booker T. Washington at a Klan rally, eh?"

Sean belched loudly, then watched the invisible belch float across the room. "'Bout as popular as the Pope at a Baptist deep-water dunking. Or an alcoholic toast at Carrie Nation's birthday bash."

"Or a Japanese diplomat at America's Hawaiian Annexation Celebration," I blurted.

We both laughed louder and longer than our exchange warranted, then lapsed into glum silence, each of us lost in our own thoughts and the buzz of the liquor. It was several minutes before Sean took another healthy swig of his wonder elixir and pointed to my puffy face with his glass. "So, what will you be doing about that? It wasn't willy-nilly was it?"

The liquor had altered my mood and fed my candor. "No, it wasn't haphazard," I confessed, gingerly fingering my cheek. "They wanted me. And I'm sure as hell going to find out what this is all about. Thugs are starting to queue up to beat on me."

"The city's full of toughs who'll bonk a pedestrian fer a farthin'. What makes you think you were a picked target?"

"I recognized Lawrence Reed."

"Who's Lawrence Reed?" Sean asked, raising his eyebrows a notch and staring at me with uncomprehending eyes.

I told him about Reed and his Alaskan Gold Syndicate.

"So, again: what are you going to do about it?" he asked after a long moment of mulling over what I'd told him.

I held up a hand. "First, did you know that Mikey Mul and Molly were brother and sister?"

He looked like I'd just told him that Sarah Bernhardt was a fine actress. "Of course."

"I didn't. Until tonight."

Sean puckered his lips. "I just assumed that you knew. They live in the same apartment building."

"They do?"

"Un huh. So what?"

"So, you asked what I'm going to do about all this. First, I'm going to visit Molly Muldine, ask her a few questions, then put an end to our association."

"'Association' is it? That's what they call it now?"

I ignored his sarcasm. "*Then* I'm going to see Mikey Mul—or Michael Muldine—or whoever he is—and find out just why he's been tailing me. I'm not convinced it has only to do with Molly. And I want to know why he's so friendly with Bradford Bent and Conant. And Billy Ewing. And I want to know what his connection was with Anna Anspach." I held up a finger. "And when I've done *that*, I'm going to call upon Mr. Lawrence Reed."

"I can help," he said, hoisting a clenched fist. "I'll go with you."

"That's your medical elixir talking."

"No sir, it ain't." He giggled. "If I can recover sufficiently from tonight's medical treatment by morning, I'll go with you. I'm a reporter. Tim has taught me how to ask questions and how to run down information. I can help, boyo, you'll see."

I wasn't sure whether it was the bonding effect of the liquor or my growing affection for Sean that finally made up my mind. But the idea of Sean accompanying me was suddenly appealing. I held up my glass in a toast.

"I'll drink to that." Again we howled with laughter.

27

I was shakier than Sean the following morning at breakfast. He looked wan and distracted, his face fish-belly white. Still, what with my swollen cheek, now discolored eye, enlarged lump behind my ear, and the massive throbbing in my head, I undoubtedly looked worse than my red-headed chum. Cait said not a word to either of us, serving us in silence, a scowl pasted on her pretty face. Claire was nowhere in sight.

We took our time to the Muldines' apartment house, stopping twice for additional helpings of strong black coffee. The building where Molly and her brother lived looked shabbier in the bright light of day than it had during my evening visits. Paint was peeling from its walls. Its sign, sprawled across the front, could barely be made out. Someone had left indecent scribblings near the front corner. Windows were filthy and hung with even filthier curtains. Plyboard had been nailed across the front door where once there'd been plate glass. The wind had piled litter in the corners by the stairs and left it there.

Two barefooted toughs lolled insolently by the entrance, their skimmers tugged low over their eyes, thin, sun-browned arms folded across pigeon chests. I took them to be maybe eleven or twelve years old, trying to be eighteen.

A beefy policeman in a uniform a size too small for him leaned against the front of a pharmacy across the street, surrounded by giggling youngsters. The kids were barefooted and dressed in ill-fitting hand-me-downs. Even as the bull teased his young admirers, his eyes remained glued on Sean and me and the two toughs.

Seemingly oblivious to the scrutiny of the copper, the toughs watched us with sullen eyes as we ascended the steps and entered the building.

The interior was even dingier than the exterior—and much dimmer. Pale gas jets hissed in the gloom. As we started up the stairs shadowy figures passed us coming down. We could hear the sound of babies crying and mothers scolding children. I couldn't make out the source of many of the sounds drifting down from the floors above, but a few of the thuds and crashes were ominously loud.

Molly's apartment was on the third floor. With Sean standing patiently behind me, I knocked on the familiar door and waited. When several minutes passed without her responding, I knocked insistently. Again, what seemed a full minute went by without us speaking, and without Molly opening the door. I turned to Sean and gave him a questioning look.

Without speaking, he leaned past me and twisted the doorknob. The door swung open. He looked at me, made a funny face, and pushed me gently into the apartment. It was silent and empty. Not only was Molly not in sight, there was no evidence she'd ever been there. We walked slowly around the small apartment, idly touching things, opening cabinets, peering under towels and blankets, looking for signs of Molly. Her personal effects, familiar to me by now, were gone.

"What now?" Sean asked in a whisper.

He had me. I glanced around the apartment again, ambivalent at best. If Molly had ducked out it would certainly simplify my life. No Molly, no need to cut off our relationship. On the other hand, she held the answers to dozens of questions I had. "Well, I suppose—"

Sean wasn't paying any attention to me. He'd frozen, his eyes on the door into the hall. Standing there were the two toughs, posed like they were when we'd first spotted them: hats pulled low, eyes sullen, mouths grim, arms crossed defiantly, legs spread. Neither looked liked he'd been within a mile of a bathtub in the past year.

"Whatta youse guys doin'?" the taller one snarled. The shorter one curled his lip in an exaggerated but silent sneer. We're tough whipper-snappers their posture cried.

I didn't know whether to be amused or angered. Here were two spindly waifs, half our age and size, thinking to intimidate us—with words and scowls, no less. Maybe my bruised and swollen face encouraged their sense of our weakness. But I wasn't in the mood for this little theater production. "Shouldn't you be a bit bigger before you talk to people in that tone of voice?" I asked.

Sean waved off my question and pushed past me. He greeted the urchins like pals. "Hey, chums," he said, reaching into his pocket and pulling out several coins. "We're looking for friends. Think you could help us?"

Their eyes riveted on Sean's hand that clutched the coins. "Who youse lookin' fer?" asked the shorter one, now more inquisitive than threatening.

"Do you know Molly Muldine?" I asked.

"Yeah, but she ain't around," replied the taller one.

"When did you see her last?"

They looked blankly at each other. "Two days ago?" the smaller one ventured.

"What about Michael Muldine? He lives somewhere around here."

The boys exchanged puzzled looks.

"Mikey Mul," I said.

Realization dawned in both the boys at once. "Down at da end of da hall, on da left," said the taller one, as he waved vaguely to his right. "Treedee."

What the hell was 'treedee'? I looked imploringly at Sean.

"3D," he explained, and handed the coins to the boys whose wide grins collapsed their poses as thugs. They romped down the hall, whooping and yelling. We could hear them racing down the stairs, their bare feet slapping on the linoleum, presumably on their way to the ice cream shop to spend their newly-gotten fortune.

We closed Molly's door, walked down to "treedee," and knocked. I didn't wait for Sean to take the initiative when Mikey didn't respond immediately. I tried the doorknob. The door swung easily open. Didn't people bother to lock their doors in this place? It wasn't exactly the kind of neighborhood to inspire this kind of confidence.

I was still thinking about how odd it was that both doors had been unlocked when Sean entered Mikey's rooms. "Hello?" he called. "Anyone home?" When no one answered, he walked deeper into the apartment, circling its small living room. The windows were closed and the room was already uncomfortably warm. An even smaller alcove held an ancient ice box and a filthy, crusted stove. The smell of boiled cabbage and something else was thick in both rooms, and plates and pans were piled, unwashed, in the sink. Sean looked at me and rolled his muscular shoulders.

"Mother o' mercy, what now?"

I motioned to a closed door. "We check the bedroom, then hunt up the Super. He'll know what's going on."

I stepped to the door and opened it. The smell that boiled from the bedroom immediately overpowered that of the cabbage. I lurched back and saw Sean wincing too, even though he was several yards away. I knew the smell of death instantly, having encountered corpses while working for my father. And sure enough, sprawled on the bed, face up, arms and legs spread wide, his chest a mass of dark blood, was Michael Muldine. And Mikey Mul was just as dead as Michael Muldine was. He was staring at the ceiling as if bewildered by what he saw there. The bed was tossed and a badly rumpled blanket lovingly cradled the corpse. Mikey was wearing his flashy plaid suit, but didn't look sporty at the moment.

"Oh, Sweet Jayzus!" Sean moaned, peering around me, his hand over his nose.

I moved to the bed and bent over the body, waving Sean away. "Make sure the front door is shut and our two friends don't come back."

No expert at these matters, I had enough casual experience at my father's agency to know a few things about homicide and what occurs to

137

bodies in death. Mikey looked to me liked he'd been there awhile. Probably all night.

So where was Molly? Had she killed her brother and then disappeared? Why would she murder her own kin? Mikey was a wiry man but muscular enough to protect himself against his sister—or any woman—I should think. On the other hand, a sister could get close to him, catch him off guard, stab him before he realized what she was doing. I couldn't tell with all the blood whether Mikey had been stabbed once or several times. The killer, whether it was Molly or someone else, apparently had taken the murder weapon from the apartment. It wasn't anywhere on the bed, unless it was under Mikey and I wasn't about to look.

Could someone other than Molly have done it? Of course, and probably did. More likely than her killing her brother, was her finding him and then fleeing in fear for her life. She doubtless was in hiding this minute. Perhaps her brother was in debt to loan sharks, and they had killed him. Maybe a wager had gone wrong and the loser had killed Mikey. Maybe he'd queered one too many deals.

Sean touched me on the shoulder and mumbled, "Will, we've got to get the police. We've been seen here. Those two would-be mobsters can identify us. So can the bull. We can't just walk away 'cause it'll come right to our doorstep, sure."

He was right, of course, and I nodded my agreement. "Okay. See if you can find that policeman we saw across the street."

He moved toward the door, then seeing I wasn't following, paused.

"Coming?" I saw the flicker of doubt and suspicion in his eyes. He wasn't completely satisfied that I was an innocent onlooker that I appeared to be. "We came in together, we ought to leave together," he said. "It'll make the police work easier."

"Probably. But it doesn't take two of us to find a policeman. I'll stay and look around."

"Look around for what?" he asked, eyes narrowing.

"Nothing. I don't know. Just look around."

Sean's eyebrows suddenly rose dramatically. He prodded me in the chest with an accusing forefinger. "Tim was right about you, wasn't he? Sure 'n you're more than you seem to be."

I made a face at him as if he'd just told me that Tom Thumb and Buffalo Bill Cody were twins. "What does that mean?"

"Are you investigating Mikey?" he asked, moving closer to me.

"Hardly," I insisted, throwing up my hands and scowling.

His expression told me he didn't believe me. "First the Anspachs, then Mikey. Now you want to 'look around.' That's a lot of curiosity for an assistant treasurer."

"Sean, find the copper. We'll talk later." I wanted time to toss the apartment without Sean looking on, and before the police arrived.

He left. But only after pointing a finger at me and mumbling, "And we *will* talk, Will, pal o' me heart."

As soon as he departed, I began a more thorough search of Mikey's apartment. A battered couch in the living room was covered by small slips of paper and I rapidly sorted through them. Betting slips. The chaff of a gambler's life. I hurriedly looked for familiar names, but found none.

Several notebooks were on the sink. I quickly scanned them as well. Most of the pages were missing from one of them and, like the betting slips, they contained no names familiar to me. I was moving toward the bedroom to make another survey of that area when I heard heavy footsteps on the stairs. I'd hardly returned to the living room when Sean burst into the room, trailed by the huffing and perspiring policeman, his gray bullet-cap under his arm.

Fifteen minutes later, the apartment was crowded with police and medical people. Sean and I were standing with the neighborhood patrolman in the dangerously-stretched uniform and a lanky investigator. The tall, thin detective—Dennis O'Dwyer—who I'd seen at Anna's death, had shed his coat and stood in shirtsleeves and gray fedora. The pipe he'd smoked at Conant's office was still screwed into his face. He had a narrow face and a perpetually furrowed brow, as if he were thinking hard on some subject— and not quite figuring it out. He turned suddenly to Sean and me. "I've met you boys before," he said. "Where?" Before either Sean or I could answer, he snapped his fingers. "Anna Anspach's death. William Conant's Office." He raised his eyebrows as if to say, good memory, eh? O'Dwyer apparently expected no confirmation from us and we gave him none. "What're you doing here?" he asked.

Sean and I told our stories several times and were, like him, now staring silently at Mikey, each of us lost in our own thoughts.

"Can we take him?" an ambulance man asked the detective, gesturing toward the corpse.

"I suppose," O'Dwyer muttered, then snapped his head up. "No, Wait."

He approached the bed again, paused briefly, then pointed to Mikey's left hand. A blanket fold partially hid it. That is, it hid it from a person standing close to the bed, looking down. But from where we now stood we could see under the fold. For the first time, I noticed a white object beneath Mikey's hand.

O'Dwyer inched the fold away from Mikey with his index finger. With the same finger he moved the hand. Like the rest of those crowded around the bed, I leaned forward and squinted at what O'Dwyer had uncovered. It was a badly bent business card. O'Dwyer pinched the card between thumb and forefinger and held it up. He stared hard at it, then locked eyes with me, and displayed the card so that I could read it.

I gulped and blinked. The card the corpse had been clutching was mine.

28

Pedaling furiously, Sean and I plunged down the nearly deserted bike paths around Chestnut Hill Reservoir. A few strollers braved the boiling sun, mostly bonneted mothers and nannies with small children. Ancient gentlemen lounged on benches in the shade, poring over newspapers, playing chess, exchanging gossip, dozing.

Sean hunched low over his wheeled steed, brows narrowed, mouth a grim line. It took all my effort to stay within sight of him as he sped in petulant silence over the maze of paths circling the reservoir, his red hair a brilliant crown in the noonday sun. There was no hint of his usual leprechaun self in his visage or actions.

He had insisted on the ride after O'Dwyer finished grilling us and permitted us to leave. Though he claimed he needed the exercise, it was obvious what he really needed was an outlet for his mounting anger with me. The more I had protested my innocence to the detective, and the more I had insisted that I was nothing more than an acquaintance of Molly, interested in her whereabouts, the more Sean had seethed. But he kept silent. He meant to confront me, and needed the ride to calm himself before doing so.

He braked near the fountain at the bottom of a long, sloping path that had taken us around the top of the reservoir. Uncharacteristically, he slid off his bicycle and let it slam to the ground. He strode briskly to the fountain, bent over, scooped up water in cupped hands, and splashed it on his reddened face. He did this several times before I pulled up.

I strolled up to him and sat on the small wall that enclosed the fountain. "Okay, Sean. Let's hear it. What's eating you?"

He wiped his eyes clear with his sleeve and glared at me. "What's eating me, is it? Well, I'll tell you, boyo. The more I listened to you horseshitting that detective, the more I wondered just what was going on. I don't like being played the fool."

Heat rose in my cheeks and the familiar heat prickle skated across my scalp, but I kept my voice low and calm. "What do you mean, being played the fool?"

His face darkened as he jabbed a finger at me, bringing it to within inches of my nose. "You heard me. You've lied to me from the beginning, 'n I'm tired of it."

I brushed his finger away from my face. Gritting my teeth, I tried to keep my voice neutral. "I didn't lie to you, Sean."

"An' *that's* horseshit!" he fumed. He held up his right hand, fingers spread and used the other hand to count. He pressed the little finger on his right hand with his left index finger, bending it back to the point where I heard the knuckle crack. "One. You lied to me and Tim about your duties with the Beaneaters."

"I didn't."

He ignored my denial and bent a second finger back. "Two. You lied to me about your interest in the assault upon Germany Long."

"I didn't lie to you about my interest in Long," I protested.

Again, he swept aside my denial and pushed a third finger back. "Three. You lied concerning your feelings about Claire."

"Dammit, Sean, I didn't—"

His voice became thin as he continued to count. "Four. You lied to me about your interest in Anna's death."

"No." I was boiling now, whether at Sean's accusations or their merit, I wasn't sure.

If Sean recognized my growing anger, it didn't slow him. He emphatically bent his right thumb back. "Five. I think you probably lied to me about why we went to see Mikey Mul by what you *didn't* tell me. He had your business card and Lieutenant O'Dwyer found that mighty odd. So do I." He strode over and jerked up his bike that he'd left on the ground. He bounced it on the ground as if to knock the dust off it. "How much else have you lied to me about? Are you palling with me to help you with Claire, or to learn what Tim knows?"

That was it. "Well, you're not exactly Snow White yourself," I shouted, sounding more than a little like a schoolboy arguing with mates, I'm afraid. But I plunged on. "You lied to me about why you introduced me to Claire. You were much more interested in seeing that Claire didn't end up with Bradford Bent, and that Claire and Cait didn't move away with Bent, than you were in pushing my interests. What about *that*?"

"I wanted you and Claire together," he muttered.

"You wanted Cait to stay in Boston. Period." I was really hot now.

Sean's freckles were almost white against his reddened face. "I just didn't tell you the whole story. You lied to me constantly—and knowingly. And played me like a fiddle, you did."

Sean's accusation defused my anger like a pin striking a balloon. This was getting out of hand. Sean was a pal, the best friend I had in Boston and he thought me a liar and a weasel. I knew I'd better come clean with him.

"Look, Sean, it's not what you think." When he made no response, I moved toward him and rested my hand on his sleeve. "It *isn't* what you think. I couldn't tell you about my real interest in what happened to Long and Anna. I promised Mr. Soden I wouldn't tell anyone. I also didn't want either you or Tim looking closely into my activities because of what you might find out—and spill to Soden and Conant."

The flush left his face and he seemed to slump. "Like what?" he asked, quietly.

I bit my lip, tearful that I was stepping into a morass, but afraid if I didn't take the step I'd lose a valued friend. "Can I trust you?" I asked.

"Trust me with what?" he asked, suddenly full of anticipation.

I took his bicycle from him and placed it against a tree with mine. Grabbing his arm, I pulled him back over to the wall on which we'd first sat. "Sit down, I've got a lot to tell you."

I told him the full story of my embarrassing conduct in Minneapolis and my rift with my father. I told him about my hopes to reform on a personal level, my entanglement with Molly, my deep attraction for Claire, my private assignment from Soden, and my hopes that I could establish myself with the Boston club without Soden and Conant discovering my odious past and current impropriety. I told him about Bent's proposition to me. I told him everything. I told him things I hadn't admitted even to myself before today. It was not an easy thing to do—or pleasant, either.

He listened silently and impassively, apparently without judgment. Occasionally he'd nod as if he understood, or had been guilty of the same failings himself. When I'd finished, he stood and asked, "And what is it you want now, Will?"

Well, that was the question, wasn't it? A question not easily answered. A question that had plagued me for years and had lain at the heart of my difficulties with my father. How many times had I heard that question from him, his face flushed with anger and frustration? And how many times had I fumbled with answers? I didn't *know* what I wanted. I understood well enough the pleasure of women, the merriment of wild high jinks with college chums, the attraction of the bottle, and the pull of self-absorption. For heaven's sake, I was still sucked in by them; that ought to be obvious. However, I also knew the sour dissatisfaction that followed those pleasures, and the nagging suspicion that something was seriously amiss with me, something crucially missing in my life. But what, exactly?

"Well," I muttered, thinking I could give Sean one of my immediate goals. "I want to do the right thing by Molly and Claire. I want to tell Molly how I feel about Claire. And I want Claire to trust me and to know how much I care for her."

"That it?" His eyes panned the park and the men on the nearby benches that slumped and wilted in the afternoon heat, then bore into mine.

"I want to find out if someone killed Anna. And who killed Mikey. And I want to know who's responsible for the assaults and threats, including

143

those directed toward me—and why they're doing it. That way, I'll do my job. I want to do my job."

He looked at me, his eyes suddenly gentle, his mouth forming a small smile. He made beckoning motions with his hands. "And?"

I nodded to acknowledge that he was right. I did want more. "I want to—"

"Yeah?"

"I want . . . my father to respect me. And Claire, too." I swallowed hard. This was getting tough. "And you."

Sean guffawed cynically.

"And I want to find out how square Bradford Bent is," I added quickly, eager to get back on a less sentimental path.

He snorted. "An' do you want world peace an' free beer to boot? Would you judge me a heartless man, Will, if I suggested that, while it's a grand thing you lust for, you're as likely to pull it all off as pigs flying? You being a philandering sod, an' all."

I felt my cheeks and neck redden. "I have been," I protested. "That doesn't mean I can't change."

"Your record to this point ain't all that impressive," he pointed out.

I started to protest but quickly gave it up when it was apparent that neither of us wanted to hear further rationalization. Besides, until I really knew what I wanted for myself, how could I explain it intelligently to Sean?

One of the great things about Sean was his ability to read people and to sense their discomfort. He obviously knew that I was floundering. He provided a termination to my confession of failures, slipping his hands under his racing shirt and loudly patting a tune on his hard, bare stomach with wet, open hands. A thin, mustachioed gent in a top hat on a nearby bench, paused in his reading of his newspaper to peer over his eyeglasses at the sharp, slapping sounds. Sean glanced at him and slapped his stomach a few more times before turning back to me. "You asked if you could trust me. Isn't the question, whether I can trust you? I've been up front with you. You certainly haven't been very candid with me, least not 'til today."

I knew he was right, but if he thought I was going to grovel and wallow in contrition, he was wrong. "I've confessed my sins, friend—and have repented sincerely; I'm not going to drive nails in my hands or don a hair shirt."

"Good man," he said, clapping his hands. "Let's figure out how to get you what you want. Or most of it."

"And why should you care about whether I get what I want."

The leprechaun re-appeared. "Well, then, b'hoy, you won't be such a brooding pain in the ass. Besides, I'm as eager as you are to prove that Bent is a slimy slug. And to make sure that Cait and Claire sees him for what he is. This whole affair with the assaults has turned ugly. Now people are being killed. We need to separate the good lads from the bad."

The old man two benches down was snoozing noisily, his newspaper scattered at his feet.

"So what's our first step, do you think?" I asked.

" I'll get Tim to put the word out on Molly and Mikey and those they hung around with. He can also check up on Bent's New York career. He has contacts there. I'll check on Bent's interests here in Boston and pile on the sweet lies to Claire about you. The last thing I want is for Bent to sweep Claire off her feet." He canted his head at me. "What about you?"

"I'll look into Reed and his syndicate. I'll also try to find Molly. Okay?" I raised an eyebrow.

Apparently it was. Sean walked over and retrieved his wheeled steed. "Sure. And you're going to trust me, right?" he asked, wiping the dust from his crossbar.

"Right. Incidentally, where does our Mr. Bent reside?"

"He lets rooms at The Quincy near Brattle Square."

"I need to talk to him. I promised him I'd give him an answer to his proposal."

"And what's your answer going to be?"

I didn't know what I was going to tell Bent, so I could hardly tell Sean. "I'll tell you when I decide. Let's go."

We ran a short distance, then leaped astride our bicycles. My left foot missed the pedal and I briefly swerved off the path onto the grass before regaining my balance and control.

Startled, the old man on the nearby bench looked up, his feet scattering his newspaper. "You're a mite wobbly, son," he rasped.

"Nah," Sean shouted back at him, "He's been a mite wobbly, but he's steady now."

29

It was one of those bright, windy days in Boston that sailors love and base ball players despise. Gusts of wind swept through The South End Grounds, tossing gulls wildly about the sky, white confetti against a pale blue backdrop. Banners and flags fluttered and popped in protest. Blasts of wind whipping across the diamond confounded pitchers' efforts to control their curve balls and off-speed pitches, and drove outfielders nappy as they tried to shag fly balls. After six innings the wind had been the better ally of the Cincinnati Red Stockings and their hard-throwing southpaw, Ted Breitenstein. They led 4-2, against Fred Klobedanz whose soft curves sailed everywhere but over the plate.

While the ball players held their caps on tight and battled the wind, I struggled with my own predicament. My talk with Sean had cleared the air between us, I thought. I was now more confident in confiding in him than I had been previously, and convinced that his primary allegiance was not to Tim Murnane or the *Globe*. On the other hand, the murder of Mikey Mul and the disappearance of Molly had persuaded me I was badly out of my depth when it came to carrying out Soden's assignment. And more and more my queasy stomach told me that the assaults upon Long were the least of my worries, that Anna's death and that of Mikey Mul were linked in some indecipherable way to the attacks upon Long and me.

Equally troublesome was Bent's offer. It gave me the opportunity to walk away even as I doubled and maybe tripled my salary. No small temptation, though at what price? Selling out? Joining forces with a possible sharp? Losing whatever chance I had with Claire?

My welcome in Boston seemed to be wearing thinner than Lillian Russell's shift. I'd spent an earlier hour in Lieutenant Dennis O'Dwyer's office answering questions about my connection with Mikey Mul and why I'd been in his apartment when he was found dead. In no uncertain terms O'Dwyer let me know that he didn't think much of my answers, and that he'd do his best to tie me to the murder if I were involved. He impressed me as a man who'd pursue Nellie Bly around the world if she were guilty of a crime. And catch her in less than eighty days, too.

To top off my problems, the light attendance at today's game was sure to disappoint Soden and Conant and undermine further their already limited confidence in me. John Haggerty and I had spent days putting together and advertising a between-games exhibition I was confident would draw well. With the help of Haggerty's contacts, we approached former Beaneater players who lived in the area. The great George Wright and John Clarkson were among those who'd agreed to participate. Players and spectators alike enjoyed these Old Times contests but, disappointingly, today's was apparently going to be viewed by less than two thousand cranks.

The Reds hung on to win the first game. Klobedanz never did control his curve in the gusting wind. The Old Time Game began almost immediately. I was still brooding about my poor luck at drawing fans when Billy Ewing and several Beaneaters ambled out by the first base bleachers to watch the former players struggling to exhibit their previous prowess. Billy was leaning against the short wall that separated field from bleachers, slightly apart from the other players. On impulse, I wandered down to bait him about Mikey and Molly.

He saw me picking my way toward him through the scattered fans and made eye contact. He nodded without warmth when I reached him. "Mr. Beaman," he said, He deliberately pronounced it Bayman and drew it out slowly. "A first rate promotion," he added sarcastically, gesturing toward the field.

I tried to turn his criticism of the Old Time Game to my advantage, telling him, "It's hard to concentrate on amusing fans when people close to me have disappeared—or been killed."

He glowered at me without comment.

"You heard Mikey Mul was murdered?" I asked.

He nodded, almost imperceptibly.

"You knew Mikey Mul didn't you? And Molly?"

Suddenly very interested in his glove, he held it up and carefully studied its seams. He fingered several rawhide knots, then pounded his right fist into the glove. "Seen Mikey around the Grounds. Didn't know him well."

I picked up on Ewing's obvious lie. "You didn't know Mikey well?" I let him see—and hear—my skepticism.

"Laid a few wagers with him. 'At's it."

"And Molly?"

He shrugged. "I knew who she was. Saw her a couple of times at McGreevey's. Sweet little cooze." He punctuated his observation with a lewd wink.

I let both the disparaging comment and gesture pass and again let him know by my posture and tone that I didn't believe him. "That's it?"

It didn't faze him. He met my eyes. "'At's it."

"She's disappeared," I told him.

"Oh?" He glanced out to the field as John Clarkson pitched to a gray-haired Andy Leonard, once one of the better outfielders in professional base ball. "Johnny Clarkson can still throw," he sighed in admiration. He turned

147

back to me. "What's your interest in all this? It's a police matter, ain't it? And ain't you a suspect?"

My heart accelerated. "Where'd you hear that?"

"Someone mentioned it," he said, his eyes flicking toward the field. "It is a police matter, right? Why're you poking around?"

I let my breathing slow, then added to the lies and half-lies that we'd already exchanged. "Just curious. I'd seen both Mikey and Molly around."

The look he gave me said he didn't believe me any more than I believed him. He drifted away from me. Then stopped. "I've got to change my undershirt before the next game. Have you given any more thought to the Klondike Mining Syndicate? Mr. Bent tells me the deadline is getting close."

"Still thinking about it."

He winked and pointed at me. "Don't wait too long. Oh, and Marty tells me you have another big decision to make—if you're out of jail and free to make one."

I let the implication of his snide reference to my future freedom pass. "What else does Marty tell you?"

He spun and walked off, looking briefly over his shoulder at me and laughing.

"'At's it."

By the time the Old Time exhibition game was over and the second game of the double bill finally ended, it was nearly dark. I helped Conant and Soden count the day's take, all the while listening to Soden grumble about the pathetic turnout. When the tallies were completed and the ledger shelved, I pulled on my coat and stepped out into the night. Though the wind still buffeted The Grounds, it had changed direction and the smell of salt and tide was strong. A light fog had crept in.

I stood in the dark passageway that led from the pavilion underneath the grandstands to the fountain and dressing room area. Billy Hamilton and Hugh Duffy, fresh from their baths, strolled past and grunted goodnight. I stayed in the passageway and inhaled the brisk, salty air. Leaning against the wall in the dark, I pondered my life, wondering if Claire would ever forgive me my indiscretions—hell, my lack of character, that's what it was.

"Give me a hand down here, will you?"

The voice startled me. I thought everyone had left from below the grandstands. Duffy and Hamilton were notorious for being the last to leave after games. I didn't recognize the voice and I'd been in such deep thought that I really didn't fully absorb the message. I stared down into the unlighted area. "What's that?" I shouted.

"Down here. Give me a hand, will you?" The voice sounded strangled, full of tension.

I moved toward the voice that seemed to emanate from the area of the fountain. The fog was thicker now. Having been waylaid several times already, and being damned tired of being thumped on, I bunched my fists, hunched deeper into my topcoat, and moved cautiously toward the fountain. "Who's there?" I shouted. No one responded.

As I rounded the corner, a dim yellow light from the small window in the dressing room softened the fog. The fact that I could see a little better relaxed me, but not enough to drop my guard. Though I saw no one there, someone had called to me. I knew I hadn't passed anyone. I stepped on the planking that had been put down so that fans could drink without standing in the mud around its base. After a full day of heavy use the mud was deep enough to cover some of the planking, and to slicken others. As I stepped back and turned to look behind me, my foot slid off the plank and plunged into the muck, throwing me off kilter.

At the same moment I toppled backwards, someone plowed into me, swinging an arm up, then driving it toward my chest. I wasn't even aware the hand held a knife until I felt it slice through the hand I instinctively thrust up to protect myself. My attacker's momentum and my own awkward stumble carried the knife past my hand and over my shoulder, ripping through the heavy material of my coat. The two of us pitched into the muck with a splash, pinning his arm and knife hand under me. My face was wedged sideways, crushed under the chest of my assailant who struggled to extract his knife and stab at me again. The smell of his damp wool overcoat engulfed me.

Even before I fully comprehended what was happening, my attacker released the knife, struggled to his feet in the slop, and kicked me in the head. I clamped my eyes tight, in defense against the impact, and to shield them against flying mud. While I tried to clear my eyes of swill, the man kicked me a second time, this time in the ribs. Fortunately, my heavy overcoat absorbed some of the impact and the ooze slowed his kicks. Still, I was only half-conscious when the kicking stopped.

"Hey!" I heard the word yelled as if someone had shouted in an empty beer vat.

I tried to clear my head and made another swipe at my eyes. I was more angry than hurt. Oh, I hurt, all right. My head pounded and my ribs felt like the Boston Strong Boy had used me as a punching bag. My hand now throbbed and burned. But as much as the pain wracked me, it was my own anger that I was aware of as I struggled to my feet. This was the third beating I'd taken in recent days and I'd yet to have a fair chance at any of my assailants. It was like being in a boxing ring blindfolded.

John Haggerty had my sopping coat gripped in his huge hands and was hoisting me out of the slop. My legs weren't sure they wanted me to remain upright and I was pleased that Haggerty maintained his grip on me.

"What happened?" I stammered.

He moved his hands under my arms so he could hold me up by my armpits. I'm a big man and he did it easily. The man was strong. "Well, b'hoy, I was in the dressing building getting ready to hose it out. I heard scuffling outside. When I opened the door to see what was going on, someone bolted around the corner. I saw you lying there. Snoozing like a baby, you was."

"Funny."

He chewed on his ubiquitous unlit stogie. "Well, lad, you was all curled up like a babe, sound asleep. All ya needed for a nursery scene was to have your thumb in yer mouth."

"Haggerty," I warned. "Enough. You're as amusing as a depression."

He removed the dead cigar from his mouth and spat a piece of tobacco at the ground. "Lost yer sense of humor, have ye?"

I worked my jaw and swiveled my neck. I stretched, twisted, felt my ribs. I slowly flexed my shoulders. Examined my bleeding hand. Apparently, I'd sustained no permanent damage.

Haggerty took out his handkerchief and pressed it into my hand to stanch the blood. Then, like a doting mother, he licked his fingers and began to wipe the mud from my face. When he'd done the best he could with my face, he removed the handkerchief from my hand, examined the cut briefly and tossed the soggy handkerchief aside.

"It'll keep," I said, studying the cut that still oozed blood. I walked slowly around in a small circle, studying the mud. "Did you see who did it?"

Before Haggerty answered I spotted the knife, partially submerged. I bent and retrieved it with my good hand.

Haggerty peered at the muddy knife I held. "Nah. I didn't see who it was," he said. "As soon as I opened the door your friend hoofed it." He straightened out my suit and scraped mud from my coat. "Pretty athletic, he was. Reacted quicker than most could. He had only seconds to escape before I slung the door open."

"I'm getting awfully tired of this," I groused, pressing my own handkerchief to my bleeding and throbbing palm. A wound that I'd barely felt when the knife first struck me was now a searing pain.

"Any idea who did it?" Haggerty asked, making a last swipe of my face with his thumb.

I had a whole list of people who would like to punch me. I didn't know how many hated or feared me enough to have done this. My first thought was that Lawrence Reed had sent one of his goons to finish the job he'd started outside Doherty's restaurant. Or that Billy had brooded over my insinuations earlier today, and had decided to shut my mouth. Heck, any number of players, including Marty Bergen, could have been riled by my comments at McCarthy's and wanted me quiet. I even toyed with the thought that Bradford Bent may have concluded his job offer wouldn't do the trick, so decided to get rid of me once and for all. But, I wasn't ready to share my candidates with Haggerty. Not yet, anyway. "I haven't a clue," I told him.

He snorted. "Well, I wouldn't recognize you anymore without all them wounds."

"Is this your vaudeville audition?"

"Not at all, lad." His voice dripped with sarcasm. "I wouldn't put myself in competition with a hilarious chap like yourself. Here you are, a big fella. An' minding your own business, you tell everyone that'll listen. And yet, someone keeps beatin' on you like a dusty carpet. Or trying to cut you into confetti. They've given you more cuts 'n bruises than Billy Sunday has homilies. Strange, all this."

"My Sweet Aunt Maggie! Out with it, John. What're you saying?"

He shrugged. Got serious. "I'm saying, b'hoy, me da' told me never to believe in coincidences. One attack, I could buy. Two? Maybe, lad. But three? Nah. No coincidence there. Now, the question is, is someone jest beatin' the shit outta you to discourage you, or because they find you an obnoxious sonuvabitch. Or"—and here he paused—"are they trying to do worse 'n have just been interrupted before they could put yer lights out fer good." He splayed his hands as if to say, which is it?

I didn't know which it was either, but like Haggerty's pa, I no longer believed in coincidences. Someone wanted me dead.

30

I did not awake the following morning until after 9 a.m. Between my throbbing hand and my usual fitful dreams, I'd tossed all night and gotten up a half dozen times. I didn't finally fall asleep until five or six in the morning. I would not have awoken when I did but for someone pounding on my door like a man desperate for the privy.

"Just a minute," I shouted grumpily, and struggled to pull myself out of bed. I shuffled to the door, every muscle sore and protesting. My bandaged hand felt as if I'd seized a hot iron. Opening the door, I squinted out. It was Sean.

"What do you want?" I demanded.

Sean beamed at me in exaggerated exuberance. "Will, pal o' me heart, it's cycling we're going!"

His bright, clear eyes and unbounded enthusiasm appalled me. I tried to shove the door closed with my good hand. "No, Sean, we're not."

He blocked the door with his foot and leaned in, his stocky frame slowly pushing both me and the door back. He peered at my bruised face and bandaged hand with a pained expression. "Holy Mother of God, what happened this time?"

"Got mugged at The Grounds."

He looked at me as if he didn't believe a word I uttered, but all he said was, "Again? Sweet Jaysus. You've had an impressive run of bad luck an' all, lately. "

"Yes, and I'm going back to bed to recover. Leave me alone."

"No. No," he protested. "Come on, Will. You can tell me the details of your thumping later. We're going to cycle down to the wharves." He arched his eyebrows in expectation. "Your legs aren't broken are they?"

"The wharves," I croaked, "why'n hell ride to the wharves? What's there?" I stepped back, knowing that trying to hold the door against Sean was futile.

He brushed past me and sat on my bed, bouncing there like some kid at Christmas. "The *Marshfield* leaves for San Francisco. They'll be loading more than one thousand people heading for the Yukon. A third of the klondikers are women, Will! Heading for riches."

I shook my head—slowly so as not to increase the pain. "Not today, Sean. I'm in no shape. Even my pain has pain. There'll be other ships, Bradford Bent is scheduled to have two ships here next week heading for Juneau."

"Fine," he said, holding up his hands in resignation. "You go back to sleep. I'll go talk to Tim about Bradford Bent."

Talk about Bent? I scowled. "What has Murnane and Bent to do with the *Marshfield?*"

"Interested, huh? Well, Tim's been investigating Bent's New York career and he's going to be at the *Marshfield* to talk about what he's discovered."

I tried to fight the line Sean had snagged me with. As much as I wanted to know about Bent, I ached all over and my hand hurt like blazes. I needed time to recuperate.

"You go, Sean. Tim can tell you and you can tell me later. I need sleep."

Again, Sean held up his hands in apparent surrender. "Just thought you'd want to join me and my friends for the ride."

I looked hard at his now expressionless face, but couldn't read him. "Friends?"

The corners of his mouth moved ever so slightly. "Cait and Claire are cycling with me. They want to see the big sendoff. And the women adventurers."

"Claire know that Tim has been investigating Bent? And is going to tell us what he's found? She's not going to like that."

Sean wagged his hands like a trainman trying to flag down an engine. "No. No. She doesn't know a thing. We'll work around that once we get there."

Twenty minutes later, still without breakfast, I joined the three of them. The Denihurs sported the latest fashions for female cyclists: silk bloomers, denim, laced leggings, silk waists, blouses with leg-of-mutton sleeves, and golf caps. Cait was in blue and white, Claire in pale yellow. Sean wore green and tan checked plus fours, green stockings, and a tan golf cap.

I was the least colorful in gray plus fours, light gray stockings and dark gray golfer, offset, as they say in fashion circles, by my red and blue cuts and bruises and white medical wrappings. I nodded solemnly to each woman. "Claire. Cait."

Cait stared at my bruised face, reddened eyes, and bandaged hand. "You look chipper today, Mr. Beaman," she said, eyes mischievous.

I smiled lamely.

"Chipper, indeed," sniffed Claire, "I remember you telling me that you and the current Boston men were different from my former boarders—being university men and all. I don't recall quite so many bruises on my former base ball boarder—and he was a drunk and roustabout."

I could read neither her eyes nor the inflection of her comment. Or whether she was commenting for my benefit or that of Cait and Sean. If the corners of her mouth moved upward, as they usually did when she teased, I missed that, too. But then she leaned over and touched my arm. "Are you all right?" she asked, then more quietly added, "again."

"I'm fine," I assured her.

"Shall we go?" Sean asked innocently, breaking the silence that followed. We mounted our bikes and headed for the wharves, first along heavily-traveled Dorchester Avenue to South Bay, then winding through back streets to Atlantic. Fortunately for myself, and probably for Cait and Claire, Sean made no effort to show off. One look at his bike and ours would tell anyone that he took cycling more seriously than we did. But if he toyed with the idea of showboating for Cait, his desire to stay by her side proved even more powerful.

Trying to grip the handle bars with my bad hand was a real struggle, but I learned to rest it on the handle bars and steer my bike without toppling over or running into my companions. By the time we reached our destination my hand was pulsing in protest.

At the waterfront, the pier was crowded with carters and draymen loading ships, passengers boarding, and spectators and friends seeing them off. Crowds of men, already decked out in woodsy canvas pants, boots, heavy shirts, braces, and slouched hats were fumbling among their gear, tightening straps, testing ropes, re-sealing seams and boxes, and checking lists. A smaller group of women, also surrounded by gear, talked to reporters and posed for photographers. A few were dressed in the canvas pantaloons and boots they'd wear in the Yukon. Their jackets were belted tight at the waist, their long tresses trimmed close.

Almost as fascinating as the bustling activity were the ships that bobbed in the chop and bumped rhythmically against the piers. A whaling bark, *The Swallow*, its three masts fluttering with flags and tied with rolls of tightly roped canvas, rocked just behind the paddle steamer, *Marshfield*, the destination of most of the passengers milling on the wharf.

We strolled about for a half hour, absorbing the warm sun and crowd's excitement. The Denihur sisters seemed mesmerized by the women adventurers teeming on the wharf. Will finally spotted Tim Murnane standing just forward of The *Swallow's* bow, and pointed him out. Then beckoned us. We threaded our way through the confusion and equipment toward Tim.

Tim greeted us with a scowl. He pointed to my hand, then gestured at my bruised face. "What 'n tarnation? You look like someone beat on you like a red-headed step- child."

I shot a glance at Cait and Claire, then waved Tim off, telling him, "Nothing serious. I'll explain later."

He darted his eyes toward the women, then nodded, content to await my explanation. With a sudden smile he pointed to the *Marshfield* and gushed, "Jayzus, ain't she huge, though—and grand!" He didn't wait for our response. "Can you believe it? Engines with ten thousand horsepower, capable of going twenty-two knots an hour! And it carries almost twelve hundred passengers!"

Prompted by his exuberance, I studied the *Marshfield* more carefully. It sported four masts rigged with rope and canvas, and a huge central stack, already belching smoke. The loading ramp was now down and a steady stream of passengers was making its way aboard, a seemingly endless line of ants eager to get to sugar.

When I turned back to Tim, he was pointing out something on the *Marshfield's* forward deck to Sean and Cait. Motionless and silent, Claire was watching the passengers boarding the huge vessel, eyes wide, lips parted, hands clasped before her. She hadn't spoken a word to me during the whole ride.

"Thinking about what it would be like to go with them?" I asked.

"Yes," she replied, her eyes never leaving the rope of people moving slowly up the gangplank. "They're so brave. So adventurous." After a second or two, she glanced toward me. "And you? Would you like to go?"

I told her I would. "It's a brave thing they do. Cutting their ties with the past and starting fresh. That appeals to me."

Her eyebrows soared. "You feel the need to start over?"

"Yes, but whether I want to or not, I may have to." I grinned in an effort to take the edge off my comment. Aside from my love of base ball, confessing my desire to start over was as close as I'd gotten to revealing my innermost thoughts to Claire, I realized.

She looked at me, puzzlement on her face and in her eyes. "There's no turning back for those boarding the *Marshfield*," she reminded me.

Before I could answer, Sean tugged my arm. "Come on you two, we're going to get lunch and hear what Tim's learned about the ships Bradford Bent and his syndicate will have here next week to take another two thousand people to Seattle."

Claire scowled. "Why has Mr. Murnane been investigating Mr. Bent's activities?"

"He's been checking on syndicates generally," I fibbed.

Her expression told me that she wasn't satisfied with my answer, but she joined me in rolling our bicycles toward an outdoor eatery fronting the

155

wharf. We leaned our machines against a post before going inside. Virtually every post along the store fronts held up a cluster of colorful cycles.

The waiter had barely left our table with our orders when Sean started on Tim. "So, what's the dirt on Bent?" he asked, his voice tight with excitement.

Claire's jaw tightened and her face paled. But caught up in Sean's excitement, I leaned forward, eager to hear Tim's findings.

"No dirt," Tim said simply, shaking his head to emphasize the point.

"No dirt?" muttered Sean, disappointed.

"He said no dirt," Claire told him through clenched teeth.

I was as disappointed as Sean was. The more I'd thought about things, the more I'd convinced myself that betting encouraged skullduggery. That if someone was trying to keep Germany Long out of the Boston lineup it was probably to change the betting odds on the team. And if players and owners were speculating heavily in the Yukon syndicates, perhaps with money won betting against the Beaneaters, the syndicates might be the source of chicanery. When Sean told me Bent had a shadowy career in New York financial circles, I had come to see him as the engine of all the assaults and murders that surrounded wagering on the Beaneater nine. Of course his interest in Claire made me want him to be a lout, I have to admit that. Lawrence Reed's actions toward me and Long intensified my convictions that the syndicates were somehow at the bottom of everything. And now Tim tells me there's no dirt on Bent. "Well, that punches a hole in one of my theories," I muttered.

"Mr. Bent is an upright, honest gentleman," Claire stated flatly.

Tim ignored her comment. "It don't punch a hole in nuthin', b'hoy," he told me cheerfully.

Claire beat me to the punch, saying, "But you said there was no dirt on Mr. Bent."

"Aye, 'n that's what's odd, darlin'."

Sean scrunched up his face. "Huh?"

Tim hunched forward, fixed each of us in turn with his eyes. "What's odd is not that there's no dirt on Bent, but that there's no *nothing* on Bent." He smiled and arched his eyebrows as if asking each of us what we thought of that. "Not a *damn* thing," he added for emphasis. He froze, made a face. "Sorry, ladies. Not a *single* thing."

"You found out *nothing*?" I asked in disappointment, skipping over his apology.

Tim reached over, cupped his hand over my good one, and squeezed. "No, no, darlin' lad. I found out nuthin', but that's *something*. I talked to a half dozen men who'd had money dealings with our Mr. Bent. None would

156

tell me a thing. When things go well and money is made, everyone talks, lad. Everyone. When things go bad, no one does. Losing money or being played the fool is not something men like to talk about. No one would say a damn, uh, darn thing about their investments with Bent or about Bent himself, though several seemed interested to learn that the man was now in Boston."

"Aha," I grumbled, finally aware of what Tim was implying. "Aha!"

"Oh, for heaven's sake," Claire scoffed. "This is ridiculous."

"It *is* ridiculous," Cait agreed.

"Maybe it's ridiculous, maybe not," Sean said, resting a hand on Cait's arm. "I've spent a week reading through Bent's prospectuses and talking to his agents. They showed me names of ships, carrying capacities, berth facilities and amenities. And menus. I have the names of captains and crews. And shipping schedules. The *Deerfield* and the *Pillow* will be in Boston a week from today."

"Now *you're* saying he's on the up and up?" I said, frowning again in my deepening disappointment.

"Not necessarily," Sean said, holding up a finger, mimicking Tim. "I'm saying Bent's agents have answers for every question I asked. But they aren't the only individuals I questioned. And I can't find anyone, not a sailor or stevedore or captain who's heard of either the *Pillow* or the *Deerfield*."

"Have you checked ship registries?" Claire asked, leaning forward, eyes bright. "Before the depression of '93 ruined him, father was involved in the Caribbean tourist trade. He was always consulting ship registries."

Sean nodded in appreciation of her suggestion. "With the *Globe's* help, I've checked virtually every registry on the east coast. No *Pillow* or *Deerfield*."

"Lots of vessels sail into Boston with foreign registration," Cait said.

Everyone at the table seemed to absorb Cait's point and its implications. No one said anything for several minutes. It was Tim who finally broke the silence. "I'll keep digging. Maybe something will turn up."

"Nothing that will compromise Mr. Bent's character or reputation, I'm sure," protested Claire.

"Well, like Tim, I'm going to keep looking," said Sean. "I've still got a few leads worth pursuing, and I'm determined to know the scuttlebutt on these syndicates."

I leaned toward Tim and whispered, "Nothing on Molly's whereabouts?"

He shook his head. The waiter brought our food and drinks and we began to pick wordlessly at our plates. In my case, I picked awkwardly at my food, too, as I was forced to eat with an unaccustomed hand. As I did, I thought about the individuals that I knew were investing in the Yukon syndicates, Bergen and Ewing, Long and Lowe, even Deacon Bill. Surely there were others. Bergen and Ewing had made clear that they had money in Bent's venture. Friends of mine could be hurt if Bent proved to be crooked. Claire would be crushed. Not to mention thousands of hopefuls who'd put up more than three hundred dollars apiece to sail to Alaska and expected passage and succor there. But Bent wasn't the only mystery.

"If we're going to be rattling cages," I told the gathering, "I'm going to rattle Mr. Lawrence Reed's cage. And then Mr. Bent and I are going to have another talk."

"You and Mr. Bent have talked?" Claire asked, looking surprised. "About what?"

"Oh, we've just talked casually," fibbing as only I can. "I'm hoping now that he'll shed light on the Yukon and those investing in it."

Claire's look suggested that she didn't believe a word I said. "I believe that Mr. Beaman has boarded the *Marshfield*," she told the others.

They looked at her, puzzled.

I knew what she meant. Like the *Marshfield's* passengers, I was setting sail on an adventure from which there was no turning back. Amid the puzzled silence that greeted her observation, I looked into Claire's wide, dark eyes. I thought I saw there a flicker of humor, but it passed quickly and gave way to a look of, what? I wasn't sure. I stared deep into her eyes to the point of embarrassing us both, but I was unsure of what I glimpsed there.

31

Only the song of crickets and the steady clacking of cicadas broke the evening silence in the Denihurs' backyard. Sean, Cait, Claire, and I slumped in lawn chairs, sipping lemonade, conscious of the heat in our newly-reddened necks and faces. Tired from the hot ride back from the wharves, we'd slipped off our shoes. Claire sat flexing her toes.

I watched her wiggling her toes and tried to make sense of what Tim Murnane had told me when he bade us farewell at the pier: "Must be going, friends. Can't join you," he'd said.

"Join us," I urged. "You're not *that* busy."

He twirled his straw boater in his hands, glancing quickly at the Denihur sisters who were standing behind me talking with Sean.

"Got a bit of interesting news today. From the fellows down at the station," he told me, making sure that the others did not overhear.

"What's that?"

"The knife you found in the mud was the same one that killed Mul. And it was his own blade." He paused to let that sink in. "Has Dennis been in contact with you?"

After confirming the women were still out of hearing range, I told him I'd spent an hour in O'Dwyer's office.

Tim seized my arm, flicked his eyes at the now approaching women. "You and Sean meet me at McGreevey's tomorrow at noon," he whispered. "We'll talk more."

Now among us in the Denihur backyard the silence was so profound the cicadas seemed deafening. I began to think the four of us were going to spend the entire evening listening to the sounds of Boston's summer insect life. My companions seemed lost in thought, content to privately mull over the events and news of the day, grinding away at it in silence. I idly picked at the bandages on my hand, and smoothed the tape where it curled.

While fiddling with my damaged hand, I gazed at Claire's perfect profile, wandering what she was thinking. Though her brows occasionally lowered and her lips pursed, she remained unreadable to me. I could not even tell if she was conscious of my staring at her.

She eventually broke the silence, sighing and sitting up. "What a lovely day this has been," she said to me. "Perfect weather. Magnificent ships. Thousands of people off on a grand adventure." She paused dramatically and hiked her brows. "Plus, a hint of mystery. Or, rather, mysteries. And perhaps now's the time to confront those mysteries. I think you and I have some things to talk about."

Doubtless alerted by the tone of her voice, Sean pushed himself out of his chair and stood. He took Cait's hand and pulled her from her own chair, then bent and scooped up his and her shoes. He smiled at Cait. Winked at me. "You two can conduct business without us." Arm around her, he ushered Cait toward the path that ran along side the house and out through the deepening twilight into the front yard.

Claire watched them go before turning back to me. "How much does Sean know about your looking into the assault upon the ball player and Anna's death?"

"Pretty much everything."

"Has he discussed it with Cait? She's said nothing to me. And, obviously, I've said nothing to her. I told you I wouldn't."

"Don't know. But at this point, further silence seems unnecessary. If it comes up, you can explain to Cait."

"If it comes up. Sean tells us that you were a detective in Minneapolis."

Obviously Sean had kept his promise to put in a good word about me with Claire. My first urge was to respond in my usual flippant way, but it passed quickly under her direct gaze. "I worked briefly for my father's agency. I was pretty inept. And not very trustworthy, I'm afraid."

She allowed my self-deprecation to pass without comment. "It was your experience with your father's agency that convinced Mr. Soden to hire you to find out who assaulted Germany Long?"

"Yes, more or less."

"And to investigate Anna Anspach's death?"

"Soden didn't pressure me to look into Anna's death. That was my idea."

"And you've been assaulted thrice for your efforts. Do you know any more than when we last talked? You don't have any evidence that Mr. Mul had anything to do with Anna's death, do you?"

It was a fair question. One that I'd asked myself many times. "No, not really. I still think her death might be connected to the attack on Long."

"And from all that business at the wharves today, I take it you think Mr. Bent also is somehow involved?" she said, her eyes suddenly steely.

"I'm just trying to think through all possibilities," I told her, shrugging to take the edge off the implications of my words.

It didn't work. Her mouth twisted and her eyes flared as she said, "I can assure you Mr. Bent is not involved in anything nefarious or unsavory. Or with individuals who are. He's an honorable and reputable man."

"No one seems to know much about his private or professional life. Or where he came from. Is he a widower? With children?"

160

Claire's face reddened. "He's a widower. He's never mentioned children." She waggled her head as if to shake loose some unpleasant thoughts. "Mr. Bent's personal business has no bearing on this business. His marital status and the number of his children is of no concern to you."

I nodded. "True, but aspects of his personal life are relevant. Stories are circulating that his business failures in New York hurt a good many investors. And that others might get hurt here in Boston."

"Those rumors are spread by individuals envious of his success." Her mouth was a thin line now.

"Could it be that you are not entirely objective when it comes to Mr. Bent?" I tried to soften my accusation with a smile.

"Mr. Bent and I are, ah, friends, true," she blushed. "But none of the accusations I've heard about him today had any substance. Just rumors and innuendo. I detest that."

I nodded in appreciation of her concern. "That's why I would like to know more about Mr. Bent. Perhaps I could then dispel the rumors and innuendo."

"That's your only objective, is it?"

Now it was my turn to squirm.

"You're intent on smearing Mr. Bent instead of finding out what really happened to Mr. Long and Anna Anspach," she continued. "You're letting your imagination run amok."

Now I was angry. It was bad enough having the woman I was falling in love with defending some cad courting her, but now I also had to listen to her belittle me. "And perhaps you're letting your feelings for Mr. Bent blind you to his character and motivation," I retorted.

She bristled. "Meaning what, exactly?"

My anger got the best of me. Why couldn't she see the obvious? "Meaning that if Mr. Bent's business dealings *are* questionable, you are in a position to be wounded financially—and personally."

Her jaw dropped, her eyes widened. "Me? Nonsense. Don't be silly."

I cringed at her use of silly. Silly, was I? "I think there's a real likelihood that the Alaskan syndicates are somehow linked to the violence surrounding the Bostons," I told her. "There's something funny going on with those syndicates and their interest in the players. Players have more money than lots of other professions and are in a position to make more by throwing games."

I took a deep breath and plunged on, remembering what Sean had told me about Bent pressuring Claire to invest in his syndicate. "Mr. Bent has urged *you* to invest, hasn't he?"

161

"Mr. Beaman," she said, her voice rising and thinning. "*That* is none of your business. Nor are my personal feelings regarding Mr. Bent. However, I can assure you whatever Mr. Bent has suggested has been for my own best interests."

I backed off in the face of her growing anger, realizing that I was on treacherous ground. "I apologize," I said softly. "Perhaps I was a bit rash."

She slumped in her lawn chair and stared at the stars now visible in the darkening sky. Seemingly exhausted by our heated exchange, or unable to push beyond them, we sat in silence as the blackness settled around us. I don't know what preoccupied Claire's thinking, but I picked through my options, thought about my next step. I couldn't interrogate Anna or Mikey. They were dead. I couldn't question Molly, she was missing. Sweet Billy had made it clear he wouldn't be forthcoming. Long apparently had told me everything that he knew. Will said that Bent resided at The Quincy. Perhaps I should confront him there, settle this business about his syndicate and offer to me. I also knew where Lawrence Reed could be found, and I owed him a visit. I owed him a good deal more than that.

Claire anticipated me. "Earlier today you said you were going to visit Lawrence Reed. Why?" Her voice was calmer now. When I didn't answer her right away, she added, "Because he heads a syndicate?"

I wasn't in the mood to confess Reed had sicced his thugs on me and maybe had paid for the attempt on my life. "You heard him speak at the promotion. He's the brains behind the Alaska Gold Syndicate. I want to talk to him about whether Boston players are investing heavily with him. And whether he can tell me anything about Bent and *his* syndicate. Businessmen make a point of knowing who their competitors are."

She leaned forward, incredulous now, eyes glittering like black marbles. "Now you think *he's* somehow connected to poor Anna's death?"

"I don't know," I sighed.

"And can tell you something about Mr. Bent that you can't learn elsewhere?"

"They're both in the same business."

She seized the chair's arms and jerked herself into a standing position. She stood over me. "When will you see Mr. Reed?"

"First thing tomorrow."

"Take me with you. I want to hear what he has to say about Bradford. About Mr. Bent."

I waved off the suggestion. I was delighted with the prospect of spending additional time with Claire, but I wasn't about to endanger her. And to be truthful, I didn't want to chance Mr. Reed rhapsodizing about Bent's prospects and character. "No. No. You're not going with me. I've heard that Reed does not like people snooping into his business, and he's threatened individuals who have."

"I'm not afraid of Lawrence Reed or his . . . his thugs," she said. "And you know that sometimes two people can learn more than one. Who was it that got Mrs. Anspach to talk?"

Her point was valid in the Anspach case and I indicated as much with gestures.

"Nonetheless, Miss Denihur, I cannot chance endangering you by allowing Reed to know about you."

"We will be in his office. With people nearby. Safe. Besides, Mr. Reed could easily find out about you—and if he does—he'll know where you lodge. And if he learns where you lodge, he'll learn about me. My visit with you won't teach him anything that he couldn't easily discover on his own." Her expression said, what do you say to that?

Uncomfortable under this barrage of logic, and the penetration of her ebony eyes, I stood to face her, to reinforce my decision with superior height and stature. "You are *not* going, Miss Denihur. And that's *that*. These are powerful and often ruthless people. Conversation *closed*."

She edged closer to me, eyes flashing, hands on hips. "You can't tell me what to do, Will Beaman. I'm an adult, fully capable of visiting Mr. Reed on my own. And I *will* see him whether I go with you or not. You started this business about Bradford. Mr. Bent. I'm going to finish it."

A smile suddenly creased her face. "Take me with you to Mr. Reed's." she said, "In return, I'll arrange for Mr. Bent and the two of us to have a candid talk."

32

It was Claire who spotted Reed's New England Investment & Loans building, a squat, stone building on Chatham. We entered it through double glass doors adorned with gilded letters pronouncing Lawrence Reed president of the company, and found ourselves in a small, ornate lobby. An attractive, green-eyed receptionist sat behind a massive oaken desk in the middle of the lobby, apparently to direct traffic—when there was any—into the three offices behind her. A month ago I would have hustled the curvacious young thing. Before I could stop Claire, she approached the young woman. "Miss Denihur and associate to see Lawrence Reed," she informed the receptionist.

Even without even glancing at her calendar the young lady told her, "You have no appointment."

"It's an urgent matter," Claire assured her.

"Mr. Reed isn't in," she told us in a bored voice, "Would you care to make an appointment? I'm sure he could see you, say, early next week?"

I stepped around Claire, assuming my most arrogant Harvard persona. "Young lady, Miss Denihur has told you—"

I never finished. The middle door behind the receptionist flew open and Bradford Bent scuttled backward out into the lobby, angrily pursued by Lawrence Reed. "I'm not pleased, Mr. Bent, not pleased at all," seethed Reed. "If you *think* for one moment—" He looked over Bent's shoulder, saw us, and froze, his face suddenly pale.

Sensing Reed's astonishment, Bent whirled to see what immobilized and silenced him. He looked like a man who'd stepped into a chamberpot, half-furious, half-puzzled. He started to turn back to Reed, changed his mind and glared again at us, as if he could not believe what he was seeing. Then, as if suddenly making up his mind, he turned formally to Reed, put his hat on, tapped the brim with his index finger in salute. "Mr. Reed," he said stiffly.

He nodded curtly at the two of us. "Miss Denihur. Claire," he mumbled, "Mr. Beaman." He opened his mouth to say more to Claire, but obviously changed his mind. He bobbed his head, glared at Reed once more, then stalked past us and out the door.

Claire watched him depart, eyes wide and mouth a small O.

Bent's departure—and our preoccupation with it—gave Reed an opportunity to regain his composure. Pretending he did not recognize me, he looked quizzically at his receptionist. "Miss Andrews?"

She shrugged and her face reddened, whether in recognition of being caught in a lie about Reed's presence, or failure to protect Reed was not clear. "Miss Denihur and associate to see you on an urgent matter," she told Reed in a tight voice.

He exhaled audibly, apparently sensing further dissembling would be futile. He stepped to the side and motioned for us to enter. "Please. Miss Denihur, come in," Then met my eyes with a gaze that didn't waver. "You are—?"

"Mr. Will Beaman."

"Ah, Mr. Beaman." He grasped my hand, pumped it once, vigorously, then released it. He motioned toward two chairs. "Please, sit down." Moving behind his sprawling desk, he splayed his hands and, turning his attention to Claire, looked genuinely puzzled. "What can I do for you, Miss Denihur?"

On impulse, I leaned forward, slapping my hands on my knees. "Actually, I'm the one who wanted to talk to you, Mr. Reed. You *do* remember me?"

He didn't so much as blink. Here was a man who'd be a terror at the card tables. "No," he said slowly, thoughtfully. "No, I don't believe I do."

"Two nights ago, in front of Doherty's?"

"No."

Out of the corner of my eye I could see Claire's confusion. But enough of this play acting. Claire had insisted that she was an adult, capable of confronting issues head on. We would see. I knew Claire was right: Reed wouldn't do anything to us in his office and I felt confident I could focus his wrath exclusively on me. "I don't like to be threatened," I told him, "And when I *am* threatened, I like to know *why* and by *whom*."

"Those seem perfectly understandable desires, Mr. Beaman," the unflabbable Reed said without changing expression. "Really quite reasonable." The corners of his mouth twitched. He thought he was a clever fellow.

Claire was staring at me now, her eyes narrowed in question.

I ignored Reed's condescending comment and demeanor. "Well, Mr. Reed," I continued, "Why then did your henchman threaten me? And Germany Long, the other night?"

Claire's hand, gripping a handkerchief, went to her mouth.

Reed ignored her, his eyes boring into mine. He rose slowly to his full height, his face and bald pate a dark red. His eyes were as black and deep as Original Sin. He leaned forward, arms straight, balancing on rigid, extended fingers. He spoke menacingly. "Mr. Beaman. Miss, ah, Denihur. I do *not* threaten people. I am a legitimate businessman. I invest my own money and I provide fair opportunities for others to invest theirs."

165

He leaned even farther forward, his face darkening even more ominously. A vein pulsed high on his forehead. With the flat of his hand he slammed the glassy surface of his desk, the sound exploding in the room. "I do not tolerate cheating in myself or in my associates. I do not tolerate individuals implying that I cheat, or that I permit others to cheat—or that I in any way promote dishonest financial transactions. Period."

Despite his menace, I was unruffled. I've never feared any man standing face to face with him on equal terms. I knew I could handle myself if it came to that. My problem lately was that gents kept creeping up on me and battering me silly. "I didn't question your business ethics, Mr. Reed. I asked why you countenanced bullying and violence."

He leaned forward even farther, his jaw jutting. "And I gave you my answer, Mr. Beaman."

Claire pushed her chair back a few inches, as if trying to increase the distance between herself and the red-faced and bug-eyed man crouching over his desk like some giant praying mantis.

But I was just warming up, convinced that Reed was not nearly as angry as he let on. Bluster was no stranger to me. In my day I had raised it to an art form.

"And would you characterize Mr. Bent in the same words, Sir?" I asked him.

His mouth dropped open and the vein in his forward seemed to jump like a worm touching an electric wire. "Wha—?"

Claire edged forward, hands clasped tightly, and addressed him. "Mr.Bent. Would you characterize him as an honest business associate?"

Reed swiveled his head toward her, mouth agape, the worm on his forehead now dancing a merry jig. "Miss D-D-Denihur," he stuttered, "Really. I can't—"

She stood, her hands gripped tightly together, knuckles pale, her handkerchief as limp as a strangled chicken. Her voice was reed thin. "Is Mr. Bent an honest associate?"

Reed's coloring and expression left little doubt that he was seething but in part because he was not quite sure what was being asked of him. However, he was not stupid. Nor so angry or confused that he wasn't still in control of himself. He immediately picked up on our use of the word 'associate.'

"Mr. Bent is no associate of mine," he fumed, "nor does his syndicate have any connection with my business interests. None. We share only an interest in the Klondike gold strike and the possibilities it holds for private profit."

Claire wouldn't be put off. "That begs the issue, Mr.Reed. I just want to know if you think Bradford Bent is honest."

Reed lurched back into an erect position and opened his mouth to speak. But a shadow passed across his eyes and he clamped his mouth shut. He moved around the desk to stand before us. "I've told you Mr. Bent is no associate of mine. Others might be able to shed light on his business and personal ethics. Perhaps Mr. Bent himself will if you ask him." He strode toward the door. Snatching it open, he motioned us through it. "It appears we have no further business, Mr. Beaman. Miss Denihur."

Neither of us budged. "Have many Boston Beaneaters invested in your syndicate?" I asked.

Reed pulled the door open even farther and canted his head toward the doorway. "I'm not going to discuss my business with you, Mr. Beaman. Please leave."

"Have the players invested heavily in Mr. Bent's syndicate?" Claire pressed.

"Leave, or I will summon the police," Reed said, his eye twitching.

Short of physically attacking Reed—which appealed to me, but not with Claire present—I saw no real alternative but to do his bidding. Cupping Claire's arm, I urged her toward the door.

Reed watched us leave in silence, teeth clenched, jaw pulsing, the worm on his forehead still in a frenzy.

Minutes later, standing in the bright sun outside, Claire put her hand on my arm. "So, it *was* Mr. Reed who assaulted you." She did not pose it as a question.

"Mr. Reed didn't, his paid minions did."

She took my hands in hers, rubbing her thumb gently over the bandage, eyes soft and round. She nodded toward my still scarred and swollen face. "So, that's where you got your cuts and bruises."

"No, *these* scars came from someone jumping me at The Grounds." I shrugged, and laughed ruefully. "I've had more than my share of knocks in the past few weeks, haven't I?"

She shook her head slowly, puzzlement narrowing her eyes. "Well, I'm sure that Bradford had nothing to do with the attacks upon you." Her frown deepened. "What do you suppose Mr. Reed and Bradford were quarrelling about when we arrived?"

"That's the hundred dollar question, isn't it?"

"Shouldn't we try to find out?"

"Yes, and the day is young," I told her. "But I've promised to meet Tim and Sean to find out what they've uncovered. McGreevey's is no place for a lady like you. May I get you a cab?" Without waiting for her answer, I hailed a passing hansom and helped her step up into it. "Perhaps we could continue this conversation later this afternoon?" I asked hopefully, looking up at her. "And perhaps you can arrange that talk with Mr. Bent for me you promised."

"Oh, we're *both* going to talk to Mr. Bent," she said.

I was still holding her hand as the hansom began to move. "Later, then?"

"Yes, absolutely. I'll contact Mr. Bent," she said, and then added with an edge, "and I want to hear more about Michael Muldine." She settled back in the soft leather seat, then turned back toward me. "*And* his sister."

33

Fifteen minutes after seeing Claire off, I found Sean waiting for me outside McGreevey's. He was sketching blue- and red-clad firemen bustling through a mock exercise, getting accustomed to a spanking-new pump engine. Even with the presence of the new fangled contraption and the frenetic antics of the fire fighters, the noontime crowd in front of McGreevey's was thin. Only a few lads hauling growlers and "pushing the can" for pennies were scurrying about, darting through and around the busy firemen.

Sean completed his sketch, gave me a wide grin and a nod, and we pushed through the doors into the darkened pub. There were fewer patrons than usual inside McGreevey's as well. Less than a dozen customers nursed drinks at the bar and picked at the free lunch plates. We joined Tim at his table. From the almost empty glass in front of him and the number of wet circles on the table around his drink, I figured he'd been there a while. We'd hardly pulled off our hats, wiped our brows, and settled in before a waiter approached us and took our orders.

Once the waiter was gone, Sean leaned forward, hands clasped before him like a pious clergyman, and asked, "Okay now, boyos, what's our next step?"

Tim motioned for him to be patient, then leaned out and signaled to someone behind me. "McGreevey! Hey, Michael McGreevey!" he shouted.

Twisting, I saw a small but solidly built man disengage from two patrons and move toward us. He sported a dark mustache that drooped dramatically. He walked with the tight movement of a bantam rooster, arms straight at his sides.

"First, lads, we get some answers from my old friend, McGreevey," Tim said, speaking too quietly for the still-approaching publican to hear. "Let me do the talking."

He gestured for McGreevey to slide in beside him, but the publican waved him off good-naturedly and took up post at the end of our table. He shook hands all around, exhibiting a large hand covered on the back by coarse black hair. "Thank you for your patronage," he said, smiling at us. Then, turning to Tim, he added, "Still able to pleasure the little lady, Timmy, you old goat?" He laughed loudly at his own scatalogical wit.

Tim looked up at McGreevey, feigned sadness in his eyes. "'Tis a pity, but no, Michael. I'm too busy pleasing *your* little lady."

McGreevey roared his appreciation of Tim's masculine wit. "An' she tells me you're no better at it than a grave-digger with a trowel," he bellowed.

The men's booming laughter cascaded through the room. Customers paused in their conversations and gawked at our table.

It took a few more minutes of stale insults between McGreevey and Tim before Tim lost interest and began to look around. "Molly about?" he inquired.

McGreevey wiped a laughter tear from his eye and shook his head. "Nah. Hasn't been for three days now."

"You can her?" Sean asked. He wasn't one to follow orders, even Tim's.

"Nah, I didn't *can* her," McGreevey replied, looking like he'd just eaten bad fish. "She just stopped coming in. Happens all the time with the help."

"You don't know where she is?" I asked. If Sean could ask questions, so could I.

McGreevey shrugged non-committally. "Uh uh. She'll come in at some point 'n want her pay."

Tim wasn't about to turn the interrogation completely over to us. "We'd sure like to find her," he told McGreevey.

"You 'n half the town," McGreevey muttered.

"Meaning what?" I asked, trying to hide the sudden anxiety I felt.

"Meanin' that the police have been plaguing me regarding her whereabouts. Seems Lieutenant O'Dwyer shows up ever' hour on the hour." He glanced over his shoulder as if to check on whether O'Dwyer had appeared again. "Not to mention all the others," he groused.

His observations about the police didn't surprise me, but those regarding others did. "Players?" I asked, as casually as I could.

McGreevey shrugged. "Some players, yeah."

"Who?" asked Tim.

"Marty Bergen and Germany Long both asked about her," McGreevey said, shrugging impatiently. "Two nights ago Billy Ewing came in inquirin' about 'er. There's been others."

"What'd you tell them?" Tim asked.

McGreevey glowered at Tim as if he couldn't believe what he'd just heard. "Just what I told you," he snorted.

"You said half the town. Who else?" I asked.

"Her father."

McGreevey couldn't have stunned us more if he'd dug a stick of dynamite from his jacket pocket, lit its fuse, and set it in the middle of our table. There was absolute silence as the three of us stared stupidly at McGreevey.

"Her father," I repeated dully.

McGreevey looked quizzically at Tim. "What, I speak Ethiopian? I said her father."

"What's his name" Sean asked, his face pinched in puzzlement.

"Hell, I don't know. Mr. Muldine?" McGreevey said, spreading his large arms in a gesture of bafflement.

"What's he look like?" Sean wanted to know.

Again McGreevey spread his arms. "I don't know . . . . Big fellow. Handsome. Mustache. Nice clothes. I have to admit his spiffy garb surprised me, considering the way Molly lives."

Sean flipped open his sketch pad and began to draw, his pencil flying across the page. I knew instantly that he was sketching Bradford Bent from memory. He thrust his sketch at McGreevey. "Look something like this?"

McGreevey squinted. "Yeah. Something like that. Pretty damned close to that."

I groaned and massaged my forehead with the tips of my fingers. This business was turning into a farce, with more twists and turns than a well-digger's drill. When I peeked through my fingers at Sean he was holding the sketch so Tim could see who he'd drawn. Unwilling yet to accept what the two of us were thinking, I pressed McGreevey. "How do you know the man was Molly's father?"

"He told me he was, man," he growled, looking at me as if I had two heads. "And I'd seen him with Mikey and Molly before. Why shouldn't I believe him? What the hell's this all about?"

Tim made calming gestures with his hands. "We've been worried about Molly," he said, "she suddenly disappearing and all, and what with her brother's death."

Now it was McGreevey's turn to calm us. He made patting motions with his hands. "Molly kin take care of herself. She's a North End brat and you learn to survive quickly there. Don't worry none about Molly. When the time is right, Molly'll show up—or she'll move along an' survive somewhere else. Molly's as slick as they come."

None of us could think of much to say to that. We sat there fiddling with our glasses, staring at the brew sloshing in them.

McGreevey, observing our sudden muteness, and apparently having nothing more to add himself, slapped Tim on the shoulder. "If Molly comes in, I'll let you know. 'Nough said."

We nodded dully as McGreevey wandered off to play the thin crowd.

171

"He's probably right about Molly," Sean sighed, rubbing his face with both hands.

For the next few minutes we sipped absent-mindedly at our drinks. Sean and Tim picked at their food without enthusiasm. No longer hungry either, I merely pushed the food around on my plate.

Tim finally let his breath out loudly and asked what each of us had been asking ourself. "Could it be, darlin's?"

"It would explain a lot of things," I said.

"Shouldn't we check it out?" Sean asked.

"Don't worry," I assured him. "Claire is arranging a meeting with Bent for me. I'll flat out ask him. I'm going to get to the bottom of this, quicker 'n you can say Phineas T. Barnum."

"If there's a story in this, it's going in *The Globe*," Tim said. He jabbed at me with the utensil to punctuate his point.

"Just you remember that *I'm* not the story here," I said, mimicking him with my own fork.

His smile broadened and he sat back, suddenly sitting so that he was leaning back slightly, his arms straight in front of him, his hands pushing against the edge of the table.

"Ah, so that's what's been galling you all these days, is it? Afraid I'll dig something up about you an' spread it over the pages of *The Globe*!" He nodded to confirm his own judgment.

"Look," I protested, "I don't want my past made available to my bosses *or* readers of *The Globe*."

"You've a criminal past, darlin'?" Tim asked, shooting me a funny look.

Sean snorted and slapped the flat of his hand on the table, startling several patrons at the bar. "Nah, Tim, nuthin' like that." He shook his head emphatically. "Nuthin' like that a tall."

"My past smacks more of immaturity and irresponsibility than of criminality," I assured him. "Still— " I left the sentence unfinished.

"Look, Tim," Sean said, leaning over and seizing Murnane's sleeve. "Will's not the issue here. There's bigger fish to fry."

Tim quieted, sipped his beer, and stared at us, his eyes darting from one to the other. He finally nodded, as if suddenly convinced of something. "Okay, b'hoy, let's hear your version of this fish fry."

For twenty minutes I spun out my suspicions to them. I started at the beginning, relating my suspicions that the assaults upon Long and me were connected to Anna's death. That there was a link between Long's absences from the Beaneater lineup and gambling. That there was also a connection, however tenuous, between betting on Beaneater games and the Alaskan syndicates with their promises of riches. I told them that Mikey Mul was perhaps a tie between the two schemes, and maybe Molly. And now there was the possibility that Molly, Mikey, and Bradford Bent were in it together somehow. I confessed I had no idea how many players were involved in one or both of the activities—or how many owners, either. I told them about Reed's and Bent's heated exchange in the lobby of Reed's building. I confided to them that the more I thought about it, the more I was sure that Molly held the key to what was going on. Either she was missing because she was a murderess in hiding, because she was a witness to a murder and feared for her life, or because she—

"Okay, okay," Tim said, obviously having heard enough. "The question is what do we do *now*."

"I've been thinking about that very question," I confessed. "For all my sniffing around the edges of the thing, I've never really taken the initiative. Never taken a bold step."

Sean pounced on that. "Exactly, Will. You can draft only so long in a race. At some point a biker has got to make his move, grab the lead, make others react to him." He beamed at me. "Like in baseball, too. To whip the Orioles, teams have to match their ginger, hit them before they get hit. That's what we've got to do here."

"And *how* do we do this?" Tim asked, massaging his temples with his fingers.

It came to me in a flash. "Molly," I told them. "Molly'll do it."

173

34

For the next hour we talked strategy. I knew I hadn't killed Mikey, whatever Lieutenant O'Dwyer might think. My ploy revolved around the assumption that Molly was not responsible for the assaults on Long and me, or for the deaths of Anna and Mikey. However, she must know who did. That is, if she were still alive—and I was betting she was. Her disappearance on the same day of her brother's death convinced me she'd seen the killer, or was aware of who was in her brother's room at the time of his death. Moreover, I was persuaded whoever was responsible for the death of Mikey Mul, *knew* Molly knew. Of course, there remained the possibility that while Molly had not perpetrated the assaults and murders, she was an associate of those who had. My best hunch was that Molly was hiding from those culpable, not that she was their confederate.

Tim and Sean agreed. Molly did not impress them as capable of killing her own brother, or of conspiring to kill him. And like me, they figured if the person who killed Mikey also killed Molly we'd have found them both. Where her father fit in—Bradford Bent, if he was in fact Mikey's and Molly's father—escaped us.

Tim, deep in thought, chewed on his lip before finally observing, "The problem, of course, is we have no idea where Molly currently is, or how to find her."

Sean bobbed his head in agreement, but I shrugged them off. "That shouldn't prevent us from using her. We can use her—or, rather, her proxy—as our lure to identify the culprit—or culprits. It isn't the most imaginative or convoluted scheme I'd ever come up with. My father can testify to that, as can any number of my women friends in Minneapolis. However, there are times that simplicity is its own virtue—and this is a simple plan."

"We can't go beyond using Molly as a proxy and decoy," warned Sean, "we ain't policemen, now. We got no authority. We can maybe smoke out the culprits, then let the constabulary take it from there."

"I can persuade Lieutenant O'Dwyer to join us in an unofficial capacity," Tim assured us. "O'Dwyer and I are long-time friends and I know he's champing at the bit to solve the Mul murder and to clear up Anna's death." He winked and pointed at me. "Even if that means associating with someone he still considers a suspect."

I laughed. "He'll find out soon enough I'm innocent."

Sean scooted forward. "Well, boyo, what's your idea? So far you've been stingy with details."

"I suggest we send notes, ostensibly written by Molly, to every suspect, however improbable, telling them she knows of their criminal acts and will go to the police if they don't meet with her and pay handsomely for her silence."

"We could telephone them," Sean said.

"Telephone calls are out," I argued. "Some suspects have no telephones. Ones who do could easily trace the calls through the operator switchboards, or refuse to accept them from someone such as Molly. There's the real possibility, too, that someone would recognize it wasn't Molly's voice."

"What about one of those new-fangled typewriters?" Sean asked. "There's one in Anna's former office, I saw it the night of her death. You could get to it, Will."

"It'd take us too long to peck out the damn messages," Tim groused, adding an obscene sound. "None of us can type. Besides, Sean, no one who knows Molly would expect a type-written note from her."

Sean slumped in surrender. "Okay. Notes, then."

"The notes'll be ignored by those who have no knowledge of Mikey's murder or who have no reason to fear what Molly knows. Or by those who have no idea who Molly is," I told them. "Only the guilty will want to meet Molly to negotiate her silence, or to otherwise shut her up. And we'll be waiting for him—or them."

"All very smooth," Tim said, slapping the table. "Unless, of course, Molly knows absolutely nothing and is no threat to anyone. There's the outside chance that, like so many young women at the mercy of low-paying jobs, she has simply moved on to greener pastures—as Michael McGreevey thinks. And that her move has only coincided by happenstance with her brother's death. There's also the possibility that she'll return as abruptly as she's disappeared and bollix our plans."

"Why'd Molly move away with her father?" Sean asked, the creases in his forehead deepening.

"We don't know if she has," protested Tim, "And we don't know for sure that McGreevey's description was that of Bradford Bent."

"Hell, he identified my sketch of Bent," Sean said, "an' said it was Molly's da'."

"True," said Tim as he stood up. "Look, I've got to go. These questions should all be answered shortly." When Tim departed for *The Globe*, Sean went with him but with the idea that he would meet me later at the boardinghouse to share our scheme with the Denihurs who we hoped would provide the female handwriting we needed.

I jumped a streetcar for the short ride to The South End Grounds. Though there was no game today, I still needed to write up bills for advertisements. An hour later I was so engrossed in preparing the billings that I didn't hear Arthur Soden enter. I was unaware of his presence until he spoke.

"We need to talk, young man," he said. "It's long past due."

I spun in my chair, its swivel squeaking loudly. "Mr. Soden!"

He scooped up a chair and carried it across the room with him. He placed it in front of me and sat down. "Completing your billings?"

"I sold some late ads," I told him.

He pulled out a dead cheroot and examined it carefully before putting it in his mouth. He dug into his vest pocket and extracted a match that he also scrutinized, as if it was the first one he'd ever seen. "You've worked hard. I concede that. You've put together several promotions that have spun the turnstiles pretty good. You've also kept most of our old advertisers and brought in new ones. There's no denying that. You've also not shied away from work around the office. That's to your credit, son."

He struck the match on the bottom of his shoe and held the flare to his cheroot, drawing on his stogie hard enough to cave in his pale cheeks. His gold-wired glasses flickered brightly from the reflection of the burning match. He exhaled blue smoke toward the ceiling and watched it disperse.

I knew there was a 'but' coming. I'd been around him too long not to recognize his habit of doling out a few miserly positives before pounding away at the negatives. I decided to let him lay it out on his own terms—and in his own time. And he took his time, crossing his legs with exaggerated slowness, meticulously straightening the crease in his trousers, and sending another curl of blue smoke toward the ceiling. "Can you tell me who assaulted Germany? Or why?" he asked.

I could have shared my suspicions with him. I could have explained what had transpired an hour before at McGreevey's and filled him in on the scheme that Sean, Tim, and I had cobbled together. I didn't want to do that. Not yet. Not until we'd sprung the trap and knew more. "No," I admitted, "I don't know who attacked Long. Or why."

"You talked to the Anspachs. Any idea whether Anna killed herself?"

I confessed I wasn't sure whether she had or not.

"Have our players been betting heavily on games?"

I shrugged my shoulders, helplessly. "If they have, I've no proof of it."

"Despite O'Dwyer's sniffing around, I know you didn't kill Mikey Mul. Has Mul's death anything to do with our club?"

I felt like a schoolboy who'd skipped his lessons and now faced a stern and disappointed schoolmaster. "I don't know, sir. But thank you for your confidence in my innocence."

His annoyance registered on his face and he skipped over my comment. "You've made no progress on these issues? None at all?"

"I've found out nothing that would stand up in a court of law. No, sir."

He sucked at his cheroot, its ash a bright orange. He uncrossed his legs and scooted his chair toward me, eyes ice cold behind his glasses. "I try to be honest with young lads like yourself, Mr. Beaman. You've proven helpful around the office. True enough. However, not so helpful in my opinion to warrant you becoming a permanent part of our staff. I believe if our team wins more consistently attendance will increase without promotions. I also now believe that the trouble with Germany was an isolated incident. It poses no long-range threat to our organization. I'm convinced that while you have tried to fulfill your responsibilities, your salary is more burden than benefit to us. In sum, Mr. Beaman, I'm prepared to recommend that you be terminated at the end of your sixty days." He sent another blue ribbon of smoke wafting toward the ceiling. "I thought it only fair to tell you to your face." He tilted his head toward me. "It's bottom line, son. Business. Nothing more."

To his credit, he looked me in the eye and told me straight out that I was to be fired. And he didn't lie to me about being sorry about my leaving. As an added bonus, he directed his plume of cigar smoke away from my face while imparting word of my forthcoming dismissal. When you deal with Arthur H. Soden, you're always thankful for small favors.

Well, there it was, then. I sat there long after Soden had left, numb. I had maybe ten days left. An hour ago I'd been exhilarated about our plan to trap the culprits responsible for the shenanigans plaguing the Bostons, and for putting many a knot on my head. Now I was mired in the depression of forthcoming unemployment. Like many a ball player pumped up after hitting a scorcher barely foul, I felt like I whiffed feebly on a wicked slow ball.

35

Two hours later I sat at the kitchen table with Claire, Cait, and Sean, trying to hide my gloom. I didn't tell them of my conversation with Soden or the likelihood that I would be moving out shortly. Nor did I confess to them how close I'd come to skipping our present meeting and, instead, going to a grogshop to drown my sorrows. I agreed to continue with our scheme only after a long and heated argument with myself.

"I've explained what's going on to Cait," Claire told me. "And Sean's told us about your idea for a note."

"Molly is Mikey Mul's sister?" Cait asked.

She was much more than that, of course. To me, and to others. But I saw no profit in bringing all that up at the moment. "Yes," I said. "She is. Or was."

For the next half hour the sisters practiced writing a message I dictated. As Claire crumpled a failed attempt, Cait held up her last effort for the rest of us to see. "Mine's convincing," she enthused. "It's more, ah, crude."

We studied Cait's note in silence. Then several by Claire. Cait was right. Her handwriting was more childlike than Claire's. Claire's penmanship seemed too precise for that of a working girl. None of us had ever seen Molly's handwriting, but she'd mentioned to me quitting school when she was very young. Sean shot me a look, making clear he agreed Cait should be our forger.

Cait wrote nine identical notes, signing Molly's name to each. The notes said that if the recipient did not meet to talk about her brother's murder, she would turn certain unspecified evidence over to Lieutenant O'Dwyer and name Mikey's associates.

"Who are the notes going to?" Cait asked.

"Friend and foe alike," I told her. "Conant, Soden, Billings, Lawrence Reed, Marty Bergen, Billy Ewing, Germany Long, and John Haggerty, to everyone who was even remotely associated with Mikey Mul." I looked at Claire and held her gaze before adding, "And one's going to Bradford Bent."

"Wait until we talk to him tonight," she pleaded, her face grim. "If he doesn't satisfy you that he had nothing to do with all this business, you can send him a note."

Having not yet seen or heard concrete proof that Bradford Bent was Molly's father, and having not mentioned to the Denihur sisters that McGreevey had insisted that Bent was, I moved cautiously. I understood that if Bent *were* Molly's father, there would be no purpose in sending him a note. On the other hand—. I jabbed an index finger at the blank paper in front of Cait. "Write one for Bent," I told her, then turned to Claire. "We'll write one for your Mr. Bent. We can always withhold it if our meeting with him tonight goes well."

"Stop calling him *my* Mr. Bent," She huffed. "Go ahead Send him a note. You'll soon find out what. He's had nothing to do with any of this."

"He's not *my* Mr. Bent either," muttered Cait, looking at her sister and shuddering. "I don't know what you see in him. It's obvious that he's more interested in this house and your money than he is in you."

Claire's face flushed. "Cait, for heaven's sake—"

"By all that's Holy, ladies, enough," Sean said, waving his hands wildly, a cowboy trying to halt a stampede of horses. "Please, now. We've got work to do."

His words sufficed, and we returned to our labors. After Cait finished the notes and addressed them, we decided to send them by urchins who we'd pay a penny a missive. Sean, who knew the streets better than the rest of us, suggested that we offer them ice cream or maybe one of the new tootsie roll candies as a bonus if they refused to tell recipients the source of the notes.

The plan was to wait for our mystery man—or men—near the new ventilator stack in the public gardens off Boylston. The ventilator provided air to the newly constructed subway that ran under Boyleston, beneath Park Street and on to the Union Station at the end of Washington. The expansive public gardens surrounding it would provide a number of advantages to isolate the perpetrator and to permit us to observe him from a distance. We hoped people milling around the subway entrance and exit would cover our surveillance. We wanted no physical confrontation. Surprise and bluff were to be our weapons. Lieutenant O'Dwyer would be our enforcer.

Claire gathered the notes and placed them in a neat pile, tapping them on the table to align them. "Cait has written the notes," she said imperially. "I shall pose as Molly."

"Oh, no," squealed Cait. "Please, let me. I can do it." She clasped her hands before her, eyes bright. "This is so exciting."

"Nonsense, Cait," Claire said sternly, "it is too dangerous for you. I'll do it." She twisted to face me, her black eyes shining with mischief. "You'll have to tell me about Molly, of course. The more I know about her—and her habits—the better able I'll be to pose as her."

I thought I heard Sean swallow. Or, perhaps it was my own nervous gulp I heard. Whatever, it seemed disturbingly loud and I was surprised the others showed no signs of hearing it. The women were still seated at the table, their dark, bright eyes riveted on me, as if I held the winning lottery ticket and was about to present it to one of them. I put a hand on a shoulder

179

of each of them and took a deep breath. "Neither one of you is going to pose as Molly."

Sean nodded his head vigorously in agreement, eager to speed down the road I'd chosen. "Absolutely not!" he said. "It's much too dangerous for either of you." He moved toward Cait and put his hand on her shoulder where I had just removed mine. "I can't let you put yourself in jeopardy. I won't."

"These people have killed before and won't hesitate to try again," I added to close the argument.

Cait screwed her face in disappointment. "Well, who then?" she pouted.

Sean and I looked at each other. We hadn't gotten that far in our discussion at McGreevey's. Hadn't even thought about it, actually. But, obviously, we needed someone to pose as Molly in the gardens. Our plan would be useless without a hare for our hounds.

It came to me in a flash. This little production of ours might turn out to be fun after all. I watched Sean's eyes narrow in concentation as I slowly rose to assume my full height. I towered over him by a good half a foot, shrugging and grinning.

He'd have to have the intelligence of an earthworm not to know what I was thinking. He rolled his eyes in resignation. "Me," he croaked. "I'll be Molly."

36

It was still early evening when Claire and I left for dinner with Bradford Bent. Bent had pressed me for an acceptance of his job offer by the weekend and, considering Soden's sober news earlier this afternoon, Bent's proposal was more inviting than ever. Yet I didn't know whether to accept Bent's offer or not. After all, the possibillity of losing my position with the Bostons was one thing, leaving Boston and Claire was another. Complicating matters further, of course, was McGreevey's insistance that Bradford was Molly's father. And my own growing suspicions that Bent was at the bottom of the assaults and killings recently. Was Bent nothing of what he seemed? Was his job offer as bogus as his business? I hoped tonight's dinner would shed light on all these questions.

We took a hack to the restaurant. The driver was an elderly man, black as the devil's breeches, with snow white hair and beard. He hummed tunes unfamiliar to me as he rhythmically flicked the reins against the back of his high-stepping bay. For the most part, we rode in silence through the growing dusk. Claire was more pensive than I'd ever seen her.

Our destination was the Quincy Hotel on Brattle, one of the oldest granite buildings in Boston, now newly remodeled and frequented by many visiting base ball clubs. And home to Bradford Bent. Streets along our route were chewed up by construction and partially blocked by scaffolding for the new elevated. The elevated had been proposed as a solution to the city's mounting traffic congestion. At the moment, however, it was a contributor to it. Twice we were forced into circuitous detours. My mind was elsewhere and I paid little heed to our glacial progress.

Not so, Claire. She leaned forward and touched the driver's shoulder. "Please hurry," she said. She turned to me, worry pinching her face. "We're already late, I'm afraid."

"Mr. Bent will wait for us," I assured her.

She didn't respond, peering around the driver to observe our progress, as if by seeing our route more clearly she could eliminate further obstructions and delays. It was obvious she was eager to see Bent. The more that reality soaked in, the more I brooded. For the first time, I acknowledged to myself that I might learn more about Claire's feelings for the rich and powerful Mr. Bent this evening than I wanted to know. Or could accept.

We reached the Quincy Hotel nearly twenty-five minutes late. Claire was out of the cab and to the door before I could pay and thank the driver. She was so eager—or nervous—she dispensed with the convention of waiting for me or the driver to help her from the carriage. I caught up with her just as the doorman swung open the big glass door and bowed to her.

"I'm sorry," she apologized to me. "I should have waited for you. I don't know what's wrong with me tonight."

"Apology accepted." I put my hand in the small of her back and urged her through the door and toward the restaurant. The lobby was bustling with well-dressed men, splendidly-coiffured women, and starched-shirted black porters. We edged our way through the long foyer and into the restaurant. A half dozen people were queued up in front of the maitre d' and we took our place behind them.

"I'm sure he's worried," Claire fidgeted.

"Mr. Bent? Oh, I suspect he's very aware of the delays posed by city transportation."

"Perhaps he's not here yet himself," she said, straining to peer into the dining room.

"He's here."

"Maybe not."

She seemed worried, but something in her voice told me it wasn't exclusively for Bent's welfare. I looked at her with renewed interest. "Why wouldn't he be here?"

She shook her head, but just barely, saying, "It's nothing. I've been nervous all day for some reason." She again looked past the maitre d'. "He'll be here," she said unconvincingly.

Several minutes later, we stood before the maitre d'. I informed him that we were expected at Bent's table. He frowned. Then, eyes brightening in recognition, he pulled from his inner pocket a note and handed it to me.

I unfolded and read the typewritten note. 'My regrets,' it said. 'I will be unavoidably delayed, but will join you shortly. Have a glass of wine and accept my most profuse apology.'

I handed the note to Claire who stood frowning beside me. As she read it, the maitre d' remained frozen, his back so straight it seemed to bow inward, his hands clasped piously in front of him. When she'd finished and nodded vaguely, he led us through the crowded and noisy room to an empty table near a fireplace bright with flame. With exaggerated courtesy, he seated Claire, now stony-faced and pale. The wine was already at the table and the maitre d' lifted it from the bucket of ice and cupped it into a toweled hand. "Would this be satisfactory?" he asked me. "Mr. Bent himself chose it."

Twenty minutes later, our goblets nearly empty, there still was no Bradford Bent. Our conversation had run as empty as our wineglasses. I'd tried to keep the conversation light, focusing on Cait and Sean. Claire remained pale and distracted.

She bit her lip and looked at the entrance of the restaurant for the two-dozenth time. "Odd," she said dully.

"Odd?"

"Mr. Bent not being here."

"He's been delayed. He said he'd be here," I replied, taking a sip of what remained of my wine. I picked up the bottle and held it up to her. "More?"

She shook her head irritably. "Something's been wrong for . . .some time. He's seemed . . . restless. I've had a strange feeling about this dinner all day."

"A strange feeling?"

"That it might end in disaster."

"Disaster?" I was beginning to sound like an echo.

"It was just a feeling of dread," she said while studying her wineglass. "I can't explain it."

I saluted her with my goblet. "Nonsense. Everything's going to be fine." But it wasn't—and I knew it. Her beautiful white neck, pale cheeks and sad eyes broke my heart. It came to me as I observed her perfect mouth, softened by sadness, this was the woman I'd always been looking for, without knowing it. And Bent's absence was my opportunity to take the man down a peg. Being a gentleman is one thing, being gallant to the point of losing the woman you love is another. It was time for candor. "Did you know Mr. Bent has offered me a position with his syndicate?" I asked her.

Her body stiffened and her eyes widened. "No," she replied in a small voice.

"In New York."

Her brow furrowed. "New York? Why 'n earth New York?"

"Apparently the market there hasn't responded as vigorously to opportunities in the Yukon as Boston's has. He wants me to perk up interest in the syndicate there."

"You mean Philadelphia."

"No. New York."

"But it's Philadelphia he's worried about."

"Philadelphia?" The echo again.

"Mr. Bent is shifting his operations to Philadelphia. He's leaving shortly. He asked me—" She paused and again glanced toward the doorway. Though she didn't finish her sentence, I had a good idea what Bradford had asked her. She lapsed into silence, her face clouded.

Twenty minutes later the maitre d' approached our table. Still no Bent. "Would you care to order now?" he asked, eyebrows arched severely.

She stood and looked at me, her mouth grim. "I think not. Will you take me home?"

I wasn't prepared to leave yet. By staying, I hoped Claire would see what a cad and bounder Bent was. I wanted to bait him about his overture to me, and the inconsistency in what he'd told me about it and what he'd related to Claire. Because of this, I found myself defending him. "Mr. Bent is a busy man," I told her. "He has lots of responsibilities. I'm sure he has a legitimate reason for being late. Let's give him a few minutes more." I reached over and cupped her hand. "A few minutes longer, please. We owe him that."

She remained standing. "I would like to go. His rooms are here at the Quincy. I can't believe he cannot be on time for an appointment in the same building. Please take me home."

Eager to have our confrontation with Bent, I struggled over how best to keep Claire at the restaurant a bit longer. I motioned for the waiter to leave us. "Did Mr. Bent ever mention that he had children?" I blurted.

She floated to her seat as if the strength in her legs had disappeared in an instant. "Children?" she asked, puzzlement narrowing her brows.

"A grown son and daughter?"

"No." Her voice was small and her face fish-belly white. "*Does* he have children?"

"I heard talk of it. What about Mikey Mul—or Michael Muldine—did Bent ever discuss him or his death with you?"

"No." She let the word trail off.

"Did he change after Mikey was killed? Seem more depressed, for instance?"

She was up on her feet again, tucking her purse under her arm, her face ashen.

"Please. I want to go."

I couldn't force her to stay. I led her out of the dining room and into the lobby. As we passed the front desk, she stopped me with a touch of her hand. "I want to leave Mr. Bent a note. Please. Wait here." She spoke in almost a whisper.

She requested pen and paper from the night clerk. As she did so, I turned to see the maitre d' leaning close to our waiter, listening intently to the man's whispered message. I beckoned the maitre d', and moved to meet him half way.

"Yes?" He arched his brows in anticipation.

"When we arrived, you gave us a note from Mr. Bent. Did Mr. Bent personally give it to you?"

"Indeed," he said, shooting me his best professional smile. "He also requested the table by the fireplace and ordered the wine be placed there for you." He looked suddenly worried. "Is anything amiss, sir?"

"What does Mr. Bent look like?"

The maitre d' looked like I'd just offered him a nickel gratuity. "Medium height. Slender. Clean shaven?" he said, making it half statement, half question.

I felt like Alice in Wonderland, surprised, disoriented, and a bit frightened. The man who'd provided the note and table certainly wasn't Bradford Bent. I mumbled my thanks and wandered over to the reception desk. By then Claire had finished her message and was handing the note to the clerk. "For Mr. Bent," she told him.

His eyes narrowed. "Mr. Bent? Ma'am?" His eyes darted to me, confused.

"He has rooms here," she explained.

He spun toward the array of individual boxes behind him. Most had keys or papers in them. Even before he turned around to face us again he reached for the buckrum register to his left and pulled it in front of him. He scanned it quickly, expertly flipping a few pages back and forth with long delicate fingers. "I'm afraid there is no Mr. Bent registered, Ma'am."

She seemed to shrink beside me. "He's had rooms here for several weeks," she protested, her voice thin.

Again the clerk flipped through the pages, scanning them with brows knitted. He then looked at each page more methodically, running his finger up and down each page.

"No, ma'am. There's been no Mr. Bent registered here in the past three weeks."

We rode home in silence. There was much that needed saying, but neither one of us was up to it. I asked lamely if she wanted to stop somewhere to eat, but she declined with a slight shake of her head.

At the boardinghouse, she invited me into the kitchen where she cut a large slice of apple pie and handed it to me. "I'm sorry about dinner. I hope this will suffice."

"I'm sorry, too," I told her as I moved toward the stairs to my room, holding the warm plate of pie. I stopped. "Do you want to talk about this evening?"

"Perhaps tomorrow."

I barely heard her. She looked like a beautiful doll, two large ebony eyes in a small pale face. It broke my heart to see her so sad. I wanted to embrace and comfort her. Instead, I nodded stupidly, mumbled that I was sorry the evening had turned out badly for her, and moved up the stairs.

I was happy Claire had seen what a liar and bounder Bradford Bent was. At the same time I now also knew him to be a damn scoundrel. His collapsed reputation dashed more than Claire's dreams. My hopes for future highly-remunerated employment had disappeared as well.

37

Wednesday was a blustery day. Low, gray clouds skimmed the city, threatening to darken. Talk around the breakfast table was minimal even for a group whose communication generally consisted of a series of grunts and groans. Boarders kept their eyes on their plates, wolfed down their food, and hurried off to punch their time clocks. Sean was nowhere in sight, and Cait didn't know where he was.

I ate quickly and, after a visit to my room and the W.C., descended the stairs and stepped out the back door into the cool, damp backyard. I was going to stop by The Grounds before heading to the public park.

Claire was standing alone, next to a large trellis, fingering a pale blue flower, one of many cascading down the lattis work. Her back was to the door and she did not see me. Or, apparently, hear me either. She wore a light sweater and with her free arm she hugged herself, hunching against the cool air.

I stopped to observe her. She continued to finger the flowers, tracing them, drawing her nails slowly along their edges. Still, it was clear that neither her eyes nor mind followed her fingers' movements. She was deep in thought and her whole demeanor suggested sadness. I stood there wondering whether I should interrupt, perhaps offer solace. Frankly, however, I didn't know what to say to her this morning any more than I had the previous night. I decided to leave her be.

"Mr. Beaman. Will." She said it quietly, tentatively.

"I thought you might want to be alone," I told her. "I didn't mean to be rude, ignore you."

"Are you in a hurry?" she asked.

I approached her. "No. Not really. Why?"

She took my arm and indicated the gate, saying, "Walk with me?"

I put my hand on hers. It was cool to the touch. "Of course. Going to be warm enough?"

She continued to hug herself with her left arm, leaning in close to me. "I'll be fine."

We walked through the gate and strolled arm-in-arm through the neighborhood under the huge, arching trees lining Magnolia. The combination of darkened skies and overarching trees kept the morning pewter gray. We walked without speaking, occasionally acknowledging carriages that clopped past us. Children were playing indoors on this bleak morning. We had the residential area virtually to ourselves, save for a random milk wagon or rag man.

It was Claire who finally broke the silence between us. "I've been such a fool," she said, so quiet I almost didn't hear her.

"No you haven't."

"Yes, and blind, too."

I thought she was going to cry. "Mr. Bent?" I asked gently.

She nodded.

"You had no way of knowing who or what he was," I told her. "We still don't know for sure that he's done anything unethical or illegal, although he's lied by omission and commission."

"He certainly has," she said, still in a whisper. "I knew nothing about a son or daughter.Or, apparently, a good many other things."

I stopped and turned to her. "You love him?"

Her eyes puddled. "I don't know," she sighed. "He was so sure of himself, so generous, so enthusiastic about his—our—future together."

That hurt. I'd known she was attracted to Bent, knew that she was taken by his wealth and success. I never suspected her feelings for him were truly serious. I rolled my shoulders in sympathy. "You're not the only one Mr. Bent has taken in. I came within a whisker of falling for his phoney offer."

She didn't react to my comment. She cocked her head and looked up at me, her eyes clearing. "I didn't love him. Not really. I saw in him the security and stability that Cait and I have struggled for since papa died." She smiled ruefully. "He's a lot like papa. Confident. Full of wild visions. Schemes, really. Cait saw that more clearly than I did."

"Your father had a bit of the blarney in him?"

"That's putting the best face on it," she said, her shoulders sagging. "He was quite a scoundrel actually. His eyes were always bigger than his purse."

"He left you a beautiful home."

"He left me a mortgage and piles of debt. Poor Cait wants to marry her Sean, but feels she can't leave me to work alone." She shrugged. "I thought Bradford could free us."

It would have been a wonderful moment to step in, as in the melodramas playing at the Tremont Theater, to save the fair maiden. To offer her love, wealth, security, success. I could offer her but one of those. Thin soup, indeed. "You'll find happiness, Claire," I told her lamely.

She smiled. "Mmmm."

"I hope so, anyway. More than anything."

She tilted her head and eyed me for a long moment. Then nodded in appreciation of my sentiments.

"We should turn back. We have much to do today, and Cait will wonder where I've gone," she said.

At the boardinghouse I paused at the gate and opened it for her.

"We should know more about Mr. Bent soon. He may step into our trap." I consulted my watch. "You and Cait will be at the park by ten?"

She smiled wanly. "We'll be there."

I brushed her fingers with mine and turned to leave.

"Will?"

"Yes?"

Her cheeks flushed. "Will, I—"

"Yes?"

"I've come to . . . lean on you."

I moved close to her.

She touched my lower lip with a slender finger and whispered, "We . . . can talk later. This afternoon."

She hurried toward the kitchen and Cait.

38

Our plan to flush out the murderer was in place by ten o'clock. Fortunately for Sean, who had agreed to pose as Molly rather than have either Denihur assume the risk, the unpromising weather allowed him to don rainwear and a large bonnet which obscured his features and muscular body. He could pass as a plump woman prepared for wind and rain—at least from a distance. As planned, he took his place near the ventilator stack in the public gardens by the Underground.

Tim Murnane and Dennis O'Dwyer took up positions forty yards away, in front of a newsstand on Boylston. Before drifting off to his position, O'Dwyer had approached me and, with exaggerated concern, brushed an imaginary object off my shoulder. "I can also watch you from where I'll be," he told me, a hint of a smile at the corners of his mouth. "Some ploys work better than others." He again swiped at the imaginary object on my coat and gave me one last cynical sneer to make it clear that while he was prepared to see where our little scheme might lead, he'd not eliminated me as a suspect in Mikey Mul's death.

Under constant pressure from Cait and Claire, we'd agreed to let them be part of our ruse. In rain hats tied by colorful scarves, they cycled unobtrusively in the park with other bicyclists, in sight of the ventilator stack.

Still stewing over O'Dwyer's lingering suspicions of me, I positioned myself next to the recently-opened subway station on Park Street, hoping to lose myself in the light subway traffic while easily spotting anyone approaching Sean.

The notes we'd written for Molly told recipients to meet her at 11:00 a.m. We'd chosen that time to correspond to the slowest times at the subway system. The fewer the people, the better to spy our target.

By 10:50, the clouds had lowered and a light drizzle began to fall. The park was deserted except for a few cyclists, and clusters of people who moved under trees and against buildings to shield themselves against the rain. The sloping walkways to the station entrance and from the station's exit were empty.

The rain increased as the minutes ticked by. Strollers along Boylston, Tremont, Park and West pulled up collars, buttoned coats, whipped out umbrellas, and cursed the weather. The crowds seeking shelter under the trees swelled. Eleven o'clock came and went. The drizzle turned to a torrent and the low-lying clouds rumbled ominously. I began to fret about what

O'Dwyer was thinking. The man probably thought that I'd staged today's drama to deflect suspicion from me and maybe even confederates of mine.

By 11:20, I was soaking wet and discouraged. Obviously, our stratagem had failed. Poor Sean remained huddled under an umbrella near the ventilator, the wind whipping it to and fro. More kite than umbrella, it provided little protection. Claire and Cait had ceased their cycling and joined Tim and O'Dwyer under a tailorshop's awning.

I would be lying if I didn't admit I was relieved when O'Dwyer stepped out into the rain to wave me off, despite the possibility that he would still think I was somehow culpable. Clearly he thought it was time to fold our tents, a conclusion that I'd reached ten minutes before. Sean, who probably would have given anything for a tent, had his back to O'Dwyer. Knowing that Sean couldn't see O'Dwyer's signal to come in out of the rain, I strode across the wet grass to tell him.

People huddling under trees gave up and scuttled toward the protection of the subway. Individuals jumped out of open cabs and omnibuses and joined the race toward the Underground. So did pedestrians. Lightning streaked across the sky. The ensuing thunderclap sounded like a cannon shot.

Because I was still watching O'Dwyer who was without umbrella and being drenched as he signaled me, I did not notice the slim gent who had crossed Boylston at West and strode toward Sean. When I did spot him, I noticed his coat collar was up and his fedora was pulled low over his eyes. He hunched his shoulders so that from where I stood his hat seemed to rest on his body.

O'Dwyer must have noticed him at the same moment. He froze and said something to Tim and the Denihurs behind him. At that distance I couldn't hear what he said. Jeez, I could barely see him what with the rain cascading down in heavy gray sheets. A second bolt of lightning flashed across the sky.

Apparently the lightning made up Sean's mind to jettison our plan. Because he'd kept his eyes on the nearby treeline as the source of danger, he remained unaware of our activity, or that of the approaching man. Nonetheless, immediately after another lightning bolt, he moved around the ventilator and started toward me. That brought him in full view of the man approaching him, now no more than forty feet away. Sean recoiled in surprise.

The man nearing Sean, his back to me, also froze, then leaned forward from the waist to peer more intently at the rain-drenched 'woman' before him. His hand shot out of his coat pocket, clenching a knife. Hunching slightly, knees bent, he moved deliberately toward Sean.

191

Seemingly in one motion, Sean stooped, gathered up the hem of his rain coat and full skirt, and yelling like Aunt Nellie in the washtub when the preacher came in, darted behind the small building housing the ventilator. The man sped after him, slipping and sliding on the wet grass and cursing loudly.

I bolted for the ventilator shaft. Tim and O'Dwyer did the same, though they were a good fifty yards farther away than I was, dark-gray silhouettes against a lighter gray backdrop. Even over the sound of my feet pounding on the sodden grass and my own ragged breath, I could hear Sean's bellowing somewhere behind the ventilator.

I skidded around the ventilator housing, swearing wildly, to find Sean thrashing on the ground, completely entangled in his sopping longcoat and full skirt. His bonnet was tugged down so that it obscured everything but his mouth that was pouring forth a stream of obscenities that would have made Old Beezlebub himself blush. Dropping to a knee in the mud-slickened grass, I rasped, "You all right?"

He flopped over on his stomach and struggled to pull himself to his knees. He was stretching his wet overclothing to view the rents the man had put in them. "Sunnuvabitch!"

The profanity told me he wasn't badly injured. I shook his shoulder roughly and leaned in toward him. "Who was it?"

Still on his knees, tugging frantically at his sopping coat and skirt, he angrily waved me on. "Not sure. His collar and hat hid his face. Get that sunnuvabitch and find out! Go!"

I stood and scanned the park. Tim and O'Dwyer, no longer approaching us, were angling toward the subway from where I'd come. Glancing in that direction, I spotted the man racing toward the crowd surging down into the Underground's entrance, out of the storm. He'd circled the ventilator shaft while I was on the other side. I scrambled toward him, trying to find traction on the slippery grass. Even with the treacherous surface, my younger body and longer legs got me to the Underground before Tim and O'Dwyer, neither of whom, it was obvious, had run any distance for years.

Getting to the Underground's gates before them did me little good. The man had already entered by the time I got there and I found myself blocked by additional people pouring off the streets and from the park. Using my size and strength I pushed and jostled through the crowd.

My progress ended abruptly when someone with a steel-like hand seized my shoulder and jerked me to a stop. "What's your rush, bub?"

I found myself staring into the grizzled face of John Haggerty.

39

"What're *you* doing here?" I asked him.

"I got this damned odd note from Molly," Haggerty said, scowling. "Came to see what the hell was going on." He canted his head. "Didju get one too?"

I had to make a decision fast. The man who assaulted Sean was rapidly putting distance between himself and me. I couldn't afford to stand jawing with Haggerty. He looked so confused that I couldn't believe he was involved, and he was much bigger than the man I was pursuing. I decided to trust him. "A bloke tried to knife Sean," I told him, "and I've got to catch him." I pointed to the crowd in front of us. "He's up there somewhere."

He shoved me in the direction I'd pointed. "I'll follow you."

We succeeded in bullying our way to the gate where we were stopped by a colored attendant. I furiously fished in my pockets for the requisite coin, but without luck.

The attendant stood his ground. "No ticket, no entrance, suh," he insisted.

John Haggerty rummaged in his pockets, pulling the pockets inside out and swearing loudly. The people wedged in behind us told us in polite and not so polite ways to pay the attendant or move out of the way.

It was Haggerty who broke the deadlock. Reaching in between his vest and shirt, he extracted something that he shoved in the face of the black attendant. "They're yours," he growled. He shook them in the man's face. "Yours."

"Thank *you*, suh," the man grinned and plucked the objects from Haggerty's hand. He opened the gate to permit us through. "Have a pleasant trip, suhs."

We plunged through the gate, managing to hold up a lady whom we nearly knocked off her feet. Before us hundreds of people scrambled to gain seats in the cars. A heavily-laden car was already moving out. I craned to see the man, but amidst the crowd of gray coats and hats—the man's attire—it was like looking for a particular turd in a three-hole privy. Gritting my teeth, I plowed through the crowd, Haggerty at my elbow.

"What'n God's name did you give the man to get us through the gate?" I shouted at Haggerty.

He was pushing and elbowing his way through the mass, as I was. "Two tickets to tomorrow's game!"

"Lucky the man was a fan," I laughed.

Haggerty literally picked up a dapper man in a bowler hat and set him aside so we could continue. "Either that or he knew he could sell 'em.," he said, standing on his tiptoes and craning to see above the crowd. "Who's this we're looking for?"

"An excellent question," I huffed as I shouldered my way past a large woman holding a bawling, cherubic child. "I'll know him when I see him."

As we bulldozed our way through the mass of commuters, I was conscious of how pathetically our plan had turned out. By selecting the site we did, we'd offered our prey an easy escape. Our concentration on the man who approached Sean may also have permitted associates of his to go undetected. I hoped Haggerty wasn't one of them. And, anyway, other than Sean's testimony that a man had approached him with a knife, what did we have? Maybe Sean could provide coppers with a sketch, but would a jury take that seriously? My own deposition that an unidentifiable man threatened Sean with a weapon, considering my distance from the attack and the angle from which I saw it, would not long stand up under cross-examination—even if I did eventually run the bastard down. What a bunch of chuckleheads we were!

I still wanted to get my hands on the bastard. But we'd now jostled our way past two crowded cars without spotting him. Beyond them, two more cars were being inundated by the rainy-day crowd. Across three sets of tracks and a small concrete wall were incoming cars.

Haggerty saw the situation at the same instant. "If the guy skips across those tracks and that low wall, he'll be able to lose himself among the exiting passengers," he huffed.

Sweet Agnes! That's exactly what'd he done! Even as I absorbed Haggerty's words, I caught a fleeting glimpse of the man just as he anxiously turned and peered back while pushing through the exit. For a brief second his was the only face in a sea of heads facing our way.

Billy Ewing!

"It's Billy Ewing," I shouted at Haggerty, pointing as Billy plunged deeper into the crowd. I tugged his arm. "Come on!"

He twisted toward me, his eyes wide with surprise.

"We're chasing *Billy*?"

There was no time to explain, but the look on Haggerty's face told me he was no associate of Billy's. Again, I pulled at him. "Come *on*."

Knowing Sweet Billy's identity did not solve our immediate dilemma. Separated from him by about one hundred feet, several barriers, and perhaps five hundred damp, sullen people, I cursed our predicament. We had about as much chance to overtake him as Custer had against Sitting Bull.

Nonetheless, my anger propelled me on. It was anger borne of knowing Billy was behind all the violence, and realizing our chance of catching him was virtually nil. I led Haggerty between two cars, hopped into the track area, and danced over the rails, careful not to touch anything hot. We scrambled over the small wall, clambered over the tracks between cars, and pulled ourselves up on the platform. We then raced for the exit gate, bumping into and careening off startled pedestrians. Haggerty shouted apologies as we careened among the pedestrians, huffing so loudly I can hear him above the din.

We plunged up the walkway to the street, sweating and puffing. Haggerty stopped, bent forward, hands on his knees, gasping, "Oh, Lordy, lordy."

I looked around. No Billy Ewing.

"He's over there! In the public gardens!"

It was Claire. She'd peddled down Boylston, following on street level as we pursued Ewing beneath the pavement.

"Sean okay?" I shouted.

She pointed excitedly toward the public garden. "He's there, chasing the man!"

And, sure enough, he was—Sean, on Cait's bike, raincoat and skirt flapping in the breeze, bonnet hanging precariously behind his head. He was peddling furiously after Ewing who was hoofing it. As with Claire, Sean pursued Ewing on street level, guessing that the man he chased would surface at the exit. He was off and flying—like Lilly's drawers—a cyclist in his element.

What was I going to do? Be a spectator?

Sensing my frustration, Claire shouted, "Take my bicycle. I'll wait for Mr. Murnane and Detective O'Dwyer."

Still bent over, sweating and wheezing, Haggerty glanced up and flapped his hand.

"Go. I'll catch up."

I didn't argue. Seizing Claire's bicycle and taking a running start, I leaped upon it and headed into the public gardens, knowing I had scant chance of catching Sean. Still, I peddled with great determination. Fortunately for my tortured lungs, I didn't have to catch Sean. I was only half way around the third turn in the bike path, already gulping for breath, when I saw them. Sean had easily run Billy down, and both were now afoot, warily circling each other. Ewing was again brandishing his knife.

Skidding clumsily to a halt next to Sean's cycle and dismounting, my momentum carried me stumbling toward the two of them. "Give it up, Billy," I wheezed.

"Stuff you," Ewing snarled, never taking his eyes off Sean.

"Put the knife down, Billy," I called.

"Like hell I will." He lunged at Sean who danced back, out of harm's way. For a stocky fellow Sean was light on his feet.

I moved closer, behind Billy, so that Sean was on one side, me on the other. "Drop the knife, Billy, the police are on their way."

"Like hell," he growled and turned partially toward me. "An' besides, I ain't done nothing."

"Then why're you running, Billy? And threatening us?" asked Sean, still circling in a low crouch and feinting as if to charge.

Billy continued to dance in place, swinging the knife back and forth between Sean and me. His eyes were wild, flicking back and forth from one of us to the other. "I saw people chasing me. I, ah, did what anyone, ah, would do."

He addressed this last comment to me. As he did, Sean, like a mongoose with a snake, feinted toward him, yelling, "Hey!"

Billy pivoted back toward Sean, thrusting his knife at him but shouting at me.

"Stay back or I'll slice you good."

"Not this time, Billy," I told him. "I'm facing you. You've done your last harm to me."

At that instant a carriage carrying Cait, Claire, Tim and O'Dwyer rounded the trees shielding us from the streets and Underground and screeched to a halt. Haggerty was riding at the back, clinging to the whipstand like a family servant. Haggerty and O'Dwyer were on the ground running before the carriage was completely stopped.

"Here now, what's going on," O'Dwyer shouted.

"Will, Sean," cried Claire, "don't get so close to him!"

"Billy, you bastard!" Haggerty roared, and charged.

At the sight of Haggerty tearing toward us, Billy's eyes bulged. He shouted something unintelligible and came at me in a rush, trying desperately to break out of the circle. Claire and Cait screamed. The knife flashed past my nose as Billy swiped at me, his momentum taking him in front of me and to my right.

Good athlete he was, he sensed he'd lunged too hard. Instinctive, like a fighter, he went up on the balls of his feet and spun to square off with me again. In that brief moment he faced me, arms wide, knife in his right hand.

I moved forward in a quick sliding step and knocked Billy cold. My poke caught him square on the button. His legs buckled in slow motion and his knife seemed to float to the muddied grass at his feet. He didn't make a sound, unconscious before he sagged to the ground.

"Jayzus!" exclaimed Sean, "That was some punch. John L. hisself would be proud of that one."

Haggerty, still breathing rapidly, stared down at Billy, hands on his hips. "Sure'n it's a rare sight to see you standing and unblemished after a tussle," he told me.

Grinning, I shrugged and glanced quickly at Claire who stared back at me with round eyes and mouth agape. "It's the only worthwhile thing I learned at Harvard. I was pretty good, actually. Intermural champion, in fact." I rubbed the knuckles of my right hand, now hot and smarting. "This was the first time I've been able to face the scoundrels attacking me! I owed him one—or two."

Tim joined O'Dwyer and Haggerty looking down at Billy. He lay in a heap, the rain splashing noisily on the pavement around his crumpled form and bouncing off his face. O'Dwyer shot me a glance and shook his head in wonderment. "It seems every time I run into you, Mr. Beaman, someone's lying flat out, mouth open and eyes vacant."

"Better that craven hoodlum than Mr. Beaman," Claire told him. She couldn't have erased the pain in my knuckles faster if she'd kissed them.

Yesterday's storm was now pounding Halifax. Sunshine bathed Boston and though the Grounds were sodden, Haggerty's tender care had rendered the field playable. The whole bunch of us—Claire and Cait, Sean, Haggerty, Lieutenant O'Dwyer and I—were seated in the pavilion, guests of Conant and Soden. Tim, who had abandoned his perch in the press box, was there, too.

And so was my father, muscular and formidable looking even at sixty. He'd arrived early this morning after receiving a telegram from Conant. He was his usual taciturn and gruff self, but his eyes were alive with pride. I introduced him to many of the players before the game. Captain Duffy let him hit a few grounders during infield practice and Germany loaned me his glove so that I could join in. I fielded flawlessly, prompting Germany and Lowe to kid Selee he should sign me. My father drapped his arm across my shoulders as we left the diamond.

The fun on the field capped a fine morning. I had awakened fresh and rested. My dreams had been short and comforting. None took place on a ball field. In one, my mother sat in a park, her chin on clasped hands. She watched as my father pushed me on a swing. As I soared under my father's push, she tossed her head in girlish delight, black curls catching the rays of the sun. Other dreams involved Claire. Propriety prevents me from providing details, but suffice it to say, I awakened with none of the usual listlessness and sense of guilt and failure.

It was the second inning before Sean and the Denihurs arrived. By that time, Boston was thrashing Cincinnati, 5-0, before a large, jubilant crowd. Boston now led the league by two games and its supporters sensed a pennant.

Claire cupped my hand in hers and ran a finger across my reddened knuckles, back and forth, as if to transfer my pain to her. I reluctantly shook off the mesmerizing motion of her hand and turned to O'Dwyer. "So what did you learn from Billy? Did he admit killing Anna and Mikey?"

"Sweet Billy was a bit sullen in his cell this morning," O'Dwyer said, pulling off his hat and scratching at his thinning hair. "Insists he's as innocent as a choirboy. Guilty only of failing to report an accidental death. Says he's sorry about that. And of mistakenly menacing you and Sean. Apologizes for that, too."

"*Whose* accidental death?" I asked.

"Mikey Mul's. Billy says they quarreled and Mikey threatened him. In the struggle, Mikey was stabbed."

"But what about the attacks on Germany Long and Will, and Anna's death?" sputtered Sean.

O'Dwyer shrugged and replaced his hat, tipping it low over his eyes. "Billy claims he had nothing to do with them. Says Mikey Mul did, when he became frantic to win by betting against the Beaneaters. He disabled Long to guarantee Boston would lose."

"What was the point of putting that damned rat on Long?" Haggerty asked.

"Just to confuse people," I suggested. My father nodded as if that made sense to him, too.

O'Dwyer confirmed our assessment. "That's Billy's story."

"What about Anna?" Claire asked.

O'Dwyer shook his head in bewilderment. "Billy insists Mikey was pressuring her to embezzle larger sums, but whether she panicked and killed herself or whether Mikey killed her, he has no idea. Thinks she probably killed herself."

"And Molly?" Tim asked, seemingly stunned by what he was hearing.

Thank goodness for Tim. It was the question I was wrestling with but was reluctant to bring it up with Claire present.

"All Billy knew was Mikey had convinced his sister to get close to Will here to learn what she could about the team so Mikey could win more betting," O'Dwyer told us. "She also knew Billy had gone to Mikey's rooms the night Mikey died. He wanted to find her to explain about Mikey's accidental stabbing. He has no idea where she's gone. At least, that's the story he's sticking to."

It may have been my imagination but I thought Claire moved closer to me when O'Dwyer told us Molly had been working in her brother's interest when she romanced me. Certainly, I became more aware of her thigh pressed against mine. "And the knife attack on me?" I asked.

O'Dwyer smiled ruefully. "Ah, Sweet Billy knows nuthin' of that. Nary a thing," He laughed at his own phrasing. "We're going to give him room and board while he thinks harder about that one."

Claire had been listening to Lieutenant O'Dwyer, nibbling on her lower lip, eyes squinting in concentration. "So much for Billy Ewing's version of things," she said. "What about the role of the syndicates? Mr. Bent and Mr. Reed?"

O'Dwyer looked like he'd bit into a wormy apple. "Well, first things first. In point of fact, Billy's stories hold up pretty well. Our investigations confirm much of what he's told us. His speculation about Mikey and Anna is consistent with our evidence. Except, of course, for his obvious lying about the attack upon Will under the pavillion and the last episode in the park.

He'll change his tune on those stories once he's spent a few days in the clinker."

O'Dwyer shot a glance at Claire. "Now, you ask about the syndicates. According to Billy— "

I didn't let him finish. "I think I've figured out that much. Billy was paid by Bradford Bent to encourage players to invest in the Klondike Mining Syndicate. Billy had faith in Bent and put money into his syndicate and Mr. Reed's, too. Aware of his father's scam, Mikey put all his gambling money—and that which Anna embezzled for him—into Reed's organization. I'm not sure about Marty Bergen. He may have been working for Bent and with Billy, but I doubt it. I imagine, like a lot of players, Marty was just looking for a fast buck. Nothing illegal there."

My father puckered his mouth and nodded his head to indicate my conclusions made sense to him. We'd talked about the whole business at breakfast that morning, two detectives huddled over a wonderful puzzle.

O'Dwyer also bobbed his head. "Billy insists Marty was just an investor."

"What does Bent say about all this?" I asked.

Tim couldn't wait for O'Dwyer to tell me. "Oh, our friend Bent has disappeared. Again," he said. "Probably with Molly, heading for another city and another scam. The world's full of opportunities," he added facetiously.

O'Dwyer snorted. "They'll show up. We've already had reports they're in Providence. Billy claims he didn't know Bent was Mikey's father until Mikey's death. He did know that Bent was working to make Will scarce around here."

I broke in again. "It's clear now that Bent and Mikey encouraged Molly to find out as much about the team's operations from me as she could. Between what Billy knew about the team on the field, and what they could learn from me about player personnel and roster moves, they thought they could clean up. When Bent learned I was asking questions about his syndicate, he had me roughed up a couple of times, probably by Billy. Later, when he discovered I was spending more and more time with Claire, he tried to get me out of the city."

O'Dwyer confirmed that with a nod. "Billy says Bent lost interest in his syndicate after Mikey's death, and eventually skedaddled with Molly."

Claire sighed. "Have you questioned Lawrence Reed about assaulting Will and Mr. Long?"

O'Dwyer canted his head and smiled at her. "Oh, he's been a mite coy on that issue, Miss. Admits he's made a point of "straightening out" people who've publicly misrepresented syndicates. Denies any strong-arm stuff. We've checked him out. He's a legitimate businessman. Unlike Bent's,

Reed's syndicate is on the up and up. We're less sure about his business methods, however."

Silent to this point, Deacon Bill Conant leaned forward, clasped his hands between his knees, and twisted toward O'Dwyer. "So, you're telling us Long was assaulted to weaken the club so Billy and Mikey could bet against it, then use their winnings to invest in the syndicates, though Mikey knew that Bent's was a scam? And that Mikey assaulted Will because he was asking too many questions? And Anna embezzled money from us to invest and to give to Mikey Mul because . . . ?" He made a gesture as if scattering ashes to the wind. "She loved him?"

I answered for O'Dwyer. "She loved him."

"And when Mikey bulldozed Anna to embezzle more, she killed herself?" Conant continued. "Then Mikey and Billy quarreled over Billy's tactics and Mikey was accidently stabbed by his own knife?" He seemed unable to digest it all.

O'Dwyer slapped the top of his thighs with the flats of his hands. "Well, sir, that's Billy's story and it's pretty much what we believe happened."

Conant shook his head in dismay. "And he denies any attempt to murder Will? Or most recently, Sean?"

"You got it," said O'Dwyer. "Says he thought they'd gone mad, chasing him and yelling at him. Just tried to defend himself."

"It's horseshit, is what it is," snorted Haggerty. He winced and ducked as if a bullet had whizzed by him. "Oops. Sorry ladies, I forgot me self."

My father spoke up for the first time. "Crimes are messy things. They're seldom clear cut, and often inexplicable."

Arthur Soden had been sitting quietly, listening to the exchanges, frowning. Now he spoke up for the first time. "Thank you, Lieutenant. I trust we can rely upon you to minimize references to the ball club in your public statements?"

O'Dwyer bobbed his head. "I owe a great deal to Will and his friends here. They smoked Billy and Bent out."

To my relief, Conant agreed. "Oh, I think Will has found a longtime job with the Beaneaters. Will's the kind of young man we want in our organization, right Arthur?"

My father reached over and clamped my thigh with his huge hand to show his pleasure.

But Art Soden wasn't yet ready to let go of his previous concern—or to concede me continued employment. He glared at Tim. "You'll show some restraint in your reporting of Billy's role in all this? And his connection with the team? It could hurt us financially."

"I'll think about it, Art," Tim sneered.

"And you, Sean?" Soden persisted.

Sean made a face and surreptitiously winked at me. "Tim's the boss."

Soden glowered at each in turn. "I'm trusting you two to do the right thing by us," he told them in a threatening tone. "It could cost us a good deal. People will stay away from our games."

Clearly disturbed by the rapidly changing tone of the conversation prompted by Soden's implied threats and preoccupation with profits, Conant changed the subject. "We need to celebrate," he said and clapped his hands. "We've caught ourselves a rascal—and possible murderer—we've dismissed him and his poisonous influence from the team, and"—he waved at the field—"the team's winning steadily now in front of good crowds. Please, everyone—Tim, Sean, Will, Claire, Cait, John, Lieutenant O'Dwyer, Mr. Beaman—join me and Arthur for dinner at The Liberty Tree following the game. Among other things, we can celebrate Will's—"

At that instant, Hugh Duffy laced a ball high over Dummy Hoy's head in centerfield and the crowd roared. Cranks around us screamed deliriously and stamped their feet as Duffy rounded second and streaked for third. I didn't hear the end of Conant's remarks.

"Suffering ghosts!" Soden snarled at Haggerty, "Duffy would have scored if it weren't for all that sawdust you shoveled between the bases."

"If it weren't for all that sawdust," Haggerty growled, "Duffy woulda drowned his goddamned self between home and first! Oops, sorry ladies."

Duffy stood on third, hands on hips, breathing heavily from his effort. The crowd quieted as Chick Stahl stepped to the plate.

I leaned expectantly toward Conant. "You were talking about a celebration. Celebrate my *what*, sir?"

He clapped a large hand on my knee. "Your promotion and raise, young man."

Well. Well. Well. A promotion *and* a raise. I grinned at Claire and my father.

Beaming, Claire leaned against me and squeezed my hands. Sean and Cait hugged, their heads pressed together. Tim saluted me with his cigar, O'Dwyer following suit. John Haggerty arched his eyebrows and formed an okay sign with his thumb and finger. My father slammed on the top of my thigh with the flat of his hand again. Only Arthur Soden looked stunned, paralyzed.

Conant gazed at his partner and waggled his head, half in humor, half in dismay. "Arthur's treat," he said.

HISTORICAL NOTE:

The historical record tells us that the Boston Beaneaters, owned by Arthur
Soden, William Conant, and J.B. Billings, and managed by Frank Selee, won
the National League pennant in 1897. Germany Long, Marty Bergen, Kid
Nichols, Jimmy Collins, Chick Stahl and others played major roles. The
team's successes can be followed in the *Boston Globe* columns of T.H.
Murnane, who not only reported on the players and games, but on
groundskeeper John Haggerty. Michael T. ("Nuff Ced") McGreevey's Third
Base pub was a popular meeting spot for fans of the team, including The
Royal Rooters. So, too, was Tommy McCarthy's pub and bowling alley, and
J. J. Cosgrove's Base Ball Exchange. Boston buzzed with excitement in 1897
over the discovery of gold in the Yukon and witnessed the formation of a
number of investment schemes to capitalize on that bonanza. Bostonians of
1897 were justly proud of the city's new La Touraine Hotel and the subway
which opened that year. In great numbers they also visited the new Charles
River Park track which, because it was illuminated by electric lights,
permitted night bike races. Crowd favorites were racers Jimmy Michael,
Major Taylor, and Eddie McDuffee, Stenographer Alice Barrett, who died
from a self-inflicted gunshot near an open safe one stormy Boston night in
1897, was initially thought to have been struck by lightning.

Parallel Lines and the Hockey Universe by Grant Tracey, 198 pp., $12.95. The 21 stories in *Parallel Lines* are set against a backdrop of parallel universes—sports and families—linked by the life of Matt Traicheff. His parents, second-generation immigrants, are splitting apart because of marital discord, but through sports—hockey, football, and public speaking—each member of the family seeks some type of transcendence. Matt's work as a sports reporter sets up stories focusing on the Waterloo Black Hawks, a losing Junior A hockey team struggling for wins in the highly competitive United States Hockey League, while the Traicheffs try to remain a family. Cover art by Gary Kelley. ISBN: 1-929763-13-1.

Lost People by Paul Perry, 180 pp., $14.95. As a follow-up to his acclaimed *Street People*, Paul Perry returns with another short story collection about life's downtrodden. Perry's portrayals of sympathetic characters is dead on, and he creates a remarkable cast of people caught up in everyday struggles for survival. The stories work by themselves, but are more powerful as a whole. Abraham Maslow identified Food, Clothing, and Shelter in his Hierarchy of Needs. Yet, these people, as we all do, need far more than that. Like all of us, they need love and affection, and safety, and a sense of self and self worth.

In this book, Mexicans try to cross the border, people live in buses, in parks, prisons, half-way houses, under bridges, even cardboard boxes. A profound sense permeates these stories that the author is grateful and so should we all be for the gift of life, for roofs over our heads, for the ability of good and ordinary people to care for others. In a secular way, these tales are a metaphor for good works. There's a lot of befriending to be found inside. The endings remain hopeful, contemplative, introspective, and courageous, like many of the wonderful characters. ISBN: 1-929763-15-8

Best Bet in Beantown by G.S. Rowe, 210 pp., $17.95. The year is 1897. The place: Boston, Mass. Star short stop Herman Long has just been beaten and left for dead, alone and in the locker room of the Boston Beaneaters National League base ball team. But, who-dunnit and why? It's up to ne'er-do-well Will Beaman, who stumbles across Long while trying to secure a front office position with the ball club, to solve the case. Filled with romance, red herrings, exciting game reportage, heart-pounding chases, and shady characters, *Best Bet in Beantown* dives deeply into the sordid world of 19th century base ball. ISBN: 1-929763-14-X. Cover art by Todd Mueller.

Send check or money order. Add $2.00 shipping per book. Priority Mail $4.00 per book. Foreign orders extra. Also available on website for credit card purchase.